NO TURNING BACK

Brandon stuck out the two last fingers of his left hand and reached for the door latch. He went suddenly cold as he realized that he didn't know if it opened in or out, and forced himself to relax and visualize Hawken's entry into the shack.

Before he reached again for the latch, a spate of Cole Brandon thoughts boiled up, demanding attention: This is unlawful, plain murder; you could get in touch with the police, have them capture these men; you won't survive it. . . .

The thoughts whirled through his mind like blown leaves in the fall and were gone. This next moment was what he had been moving toward since the moment he killed Gren Keneally's henchman Casmire and knew that the account would have to be completely settled. He had made himself into someone, something, that had to do this, and there was no turning back.

And there was no such person as Jess Marvell.

He crooked the two left-hand fingers on the latch, felt the coldness of its metal, and slowly lifted.

Also by D. R. Bensen

Deathwind (Tracker #6)
Rawhide Moon (Tracker #5)
The Renegade (Tracker #4)
Death in the Hills (Tracker #3)
Fool's Gold (Tracker #2)
Mask of the Tracker (Tracker #1)

Published by POCKET BOOKS

THE TRACKER #7

› Final Mask ‹

D.R. BENSEN

POCKET BOOKS

New York   London   Toronto   Sydney   Tokyo   Singapore

This book is a work of fiction. Names, characters, places, and incidents either are products of the author's imagination or are used fictitiously. Any resemblance to actual events or locales or persons, living or dead, is entirely coincidental.

An *Original* Publication of POCKET BOOKS

POCKET BOOKS, a division of Simon & Schuster Inc.
1230 Avenue of the Americas, New York, NY 10020

ISBN: 0-671-86906-X

First Pocket Books printing December 1993

10 9 8 7 6 5 4 3 2 1

POCKET and colophon are registered trademarks of Simon & Schuster Inc.

Cover art by Bill Dodge

Printed in the U.S.A.

Final Mask

1

Face seamed and dirty as the buckskin shirt and breeches he wore, the lank-haired man leaned on his rifle and stared ahead, as if scanning a distant ridge for game on which to test his marksmanship.

He ignored the two men who shared the shelter of the open-fronted log shed with him and were busy keeping a pot simmering over a smoky open fire, the pot perhaps containing the edible portions of the late tenants of the skins that lay on the earthen floor of the shed or were pegged to its rear wall.

He also ignored Cole Brandon, who was inspecting the shed and its occupants from a distance of perhaps ten feet. Brandon considered that the standing man looked disreputable enough to be the genuine article, the wilderness hunter he seemed to be; but the others, clad in Hudson's Bay–style wool shirts and canvas breeches that seemed to be having their first wearing, were less convincing. They also, though not looking directly at Brandon, seemed to be aware of his presence, as well as that of the dozen or so others who were studying them.

1

"I wannabe a hunter, Ma!" a fat-faced small boy near Brandon said.

"You wanted to be an engineer when we saw the locomotives, and you wanted to be a fireman when we saw the engines and pumpers," his mother said. She was tightly encased in a wool jacket and skirt and wearing a hat that clung to her head like a compress without providing a brim to keep the mid-June sun from her face, which was glistening with perspiration and reddened, whether with incipient sunburn or vexation at her child Brandon could not tell. "If we go to the Chinese Department, I expect you'll wanta be a Chinee."

"I wannabe a *hunter!*" the boy whined. The buckskinned man shifted his gaze from the distance to the boy and seemed to be considering how his pelt would look pegged on the back wall of the cabin next to those of the black bears and the white polecat, which Brandon had heard mentioned as a remarkable rarity.

"If you're a hunter," the mother said, making, Brandon thought, the elementary mistake of arguing with a being incapable of reason, "you'll hafta live in the woods and wear dirty clothes and never take a bath and never see nice people, just Indians and such trash. And eat dogs, like as not."

The boy fell silent, contemplating the delightful vista his mother had presented.

"If you go to school an' grow up as you should, you'll have a nice job in a nice office and wear nice clothes like this gentleman here," the mother said, pointing at Brandon.

Brandon acknowledged the compliment by touching the brim of his hat with a forefinger, at the same time moving off as if he had exhausted his interest in the Hunters' Camp, an Authentic Portrayal of Wilderness Life, as the guidebook put it; he had no intention of remaining to figure in what was probably a chronic bicker between mother and son.

"He's a fool," the boy said dismissively. "*He* ain't no hunter."

Right once, wrong once, kid, Brandon said silently.

He had only been to the East Coast once before, and had forgotten how humid it was in the summer. Even his native St. Louis, dampened by exhalations from the Mississippi and the Missouri, was drier than the Turkish bath Philadelphia was providing free of charge for the legions of visitors to the Centennial Exposition. On the other hand, he thought, ten thousand or so people packed into Fairmount Park might go a long way toward creating their own steam bath with their body heat. He remembered the astonishing heat from the stampeding cattle that had sent their razor-sharp horns slashing by him last year; it had been like being next to a steam boiler. The purported hunters stirring their pot over the fire were showing remarkable devotion to their duty of showing the rigors of life in the Far West, but he supposed that they were following the rule Edmund Chambers, the old touring actor, had set out for him: The important thing is to believe you *are* whatever character you're portraying, and the audience will accept you as that character.

Holding to that rule, Brandon had over the last couple of years convinced himself somewhat, and others as much as had been needed, that he was, in turn, a cattle buyer, a wandering hardcase, an itinerant gambler, a newspaper reporter, a trail cook, and a windmill salesman. At all times, though, a hunter . . . and maybe, as the kid had said, a fool.

Right now he was one of the legion of fairgoers who were poaching themselves in Sunday-best clothes and circulating among and through the fantastic, ornate buildings that had sprung up in the park over the last year, gaping at the exhibits from all over the world and mostly feeling that the hundred-year-old (less a few weeks) U.S.A. had curiosities and prodigies to match or outclass the rest of the planet. Still a hunter, all the same, but doing a good enough job of playing the role of tourist to find himself relishing it a little. The more convincing a tourist he was, the more likely he was to find the game he hunted.

Like the whine of a mosquito, an exchange between the mother and son at the hunters' camp drifted to him:

"If you was a hunter, and slep' out on the ground, snakes'd come and bite you in the nighttime and you'd never wake up."

"He ain't snake-kilt."

"Dead right, son," a hoarse voice said. Brandon stopped and turned to look at the buckskinned hunter, who was now leaning down to address the plump boy. "Many's a snake has crawlt towards me with pizened fang ready to sink inter me, but there ain't none as done it. And they ain't about to whiles as I sleep, for we men of the wild can outsmart 'em. Lemme show ya."

He leaned his rifle against the cabin wall and shambled over to two trees that stood about nine feet apart; Brandon saw what looked like a tangle of ropes draped between them four feet or so above the ground. The man spread this out, revealing it to be a hammock, and clambered into it. "You kin hear the snakes a-hissing and a-snarling below," he said, "but they cain't get up at you once you're safe in this."

Brandon considered that this might work for snakes or even homicidal rabbits, but that a grizzly would look on the hammock as a convenient wrapping for its late-night snack.

The buckskinned man set his hat over his face and gave a powerfully convincing demonstration of someone passing a night untroubled by fear of snakes. The mother and son looked at him for a while, then drifted away.

Brandon looked up at the bridge that spanned the ravine eighty or so feet above where he stood, then pulled from his pocket and unfolded the map he had bought at the same time as the guidebook. He saw that there was a restaurant not too far off, up the far slope of the ravine and next to the Portuguese pavilion. It might be shorter to scramble up the near slope and cross over on the bridge, but it would also put him on the unshaded, crowded paths and roadways that he had learned to dislike in the short time he had been at the Exposition. The long way would take him through the wooded ravine and be a good deal cooler and more comfortable.

I've gone across prairies and deserts and mountains in storm and heat, Brandon thought, and not paid much heed to whether I was comfortable or not, but once I'm back in a city, why, it's on my mind steadily. Might be a good idea not to live in a city when this is over. . . . He shook his head. Not the time to be looking ahead, but he had been doing it a lot lately. Looking past the present moment put him in danger of missing something he might have to do now, to carry out his purpose . . . or to stay alive.

Even this comparative wilderness had its share of crowds, and a man approached Brandon on the narrow path among the trees. Brandon stepped aside, noticing something familiar in the man's face under its shallow dome of a hat and catching a look of half-recognition as he passed. A hundred feet farther on, Brandon went cold as the familiarity solidified: Jenkins or Meyer or some such, a court clerk in St. Louis he'd seen dozens of times when he tried cases. And just now maybe Meyer or Jenkins (Slavin, that was it) was deciding he'd passed by Cole Brandon, Esq., last seen in St. Louis two years ago and gone nobody really knew where.

Well, so what? Nobody in St. Louis was looking for Cole Brandon, so far as he knew, and the body in the old Indian mound on the farm out north of the city seemed to be undiscovered, so what was there to worry about in a possible recognition, even if Slavin (almost certainly Watson) thought it worth talking about back home?

Brandon had not thought about it, but given the fact that several million people were expected to funnel through Fairmount Park during the half-year of the Exposition, it was not surprising that he would run across people he knew or who knew him. In fact, he was there solely in order to run across someone he knew—although he had never seen him—but who did not know him.

And there was someone at the Exposition whom he did know, and who knew him very well, and when he considered the time ripe . . . all right, when he found the nerve for it . . . he would go and see her. Just a matter of turning up

Belmont Avenue at the Sons of Temperance drinking fountain, and there you were at the Women's Pavilion, including among many examples of women-owned enterprises a scaled-down version of a Marvel Hall, one of the chain of eating places serving railroad travelers across the West, presided over by its inventor and proprietor, Jess Marvell. Brandon still had to consult the map to know where the Main Building was, let alone Photography Hall or the Department of Public Comfort, but had known where Jess Marvell was to be found six seconds after he had opened the map.

Ahead on the path he saw a semi-collision as a man in a shabby jacket and battered hat jostled in passing a prosperous-looking man, who stepped aside with an affronted glare. Another man in a tight frock coat took a sharp look at the encounter, then jumped and seized the jostler.

"Hold on here!" he said. "You took that man's wallet when you bumped him, don't deny it!"

His quarry wriggled in his grasp. "I don't need ter d'ny not'in', Cap, for I ain't got it! No wallet that's mine, let alone one that ain't!"

The frock-coated man shook him as if to detach the wallet from its hiding place.

The man the shabby one had jostled slapped his back pocket hastily, then called out, "Sir, sir! No need, I still have my wallet!"

A voice next to Brandon's ear murmured, "And one, and two, and three . . . right." Brandon saw a short, unobtrusive figure glide past the prosperous-looking man from the rear, with a quick, delicate movement of hand and arm, then silently pass down the path and among the trees.

"Callison, isn't it?" the voice said. Brandon turned and saw a face last seen a year and more ago and close to two thousand miles away. "Savvy Sanger," he said. "You Fagining a pickpocket ring now?"

The jaunty Sanger, elongated and elegant in a checked suit that did not seem to be cooking him like most of the fairgoers' clothes, said, "Good Lord, no! My trade, Brother Callison, is one of seduction; I tell the marks the tale, and they freely offer me their all. Pickpocketing, even the triple cannon, is a crude and unintellectual enterprise, but it has its simple appeal when done well, and when I saw the opening stages, I felt constrained to guess when the culmination would transpire, and got it to within a second."

By now the two who had put on the brief drama had gone their separate ways, and the unknowing loser of the wallet was making his way down the path. Brandon got about half an inch toward wondering why Savvy Sanger hadn't called out and foiled the pocket-picking, then realized that Sanger never had and never would display a scintilla of responsibility to society and its laws. He also reflected that he himself had made no move to warn the victim. You've been out West long enough to get out of the habit of pushing into other folks' business, even if it's for their own good, Counselor, he told himself.

And of course, he continued the thought, Sanger wouldn't intervene, any more than a lion would deign to take a paw in a jackal's affairs. Savvy Sanger had been legendary when Brandon ran across him out in Arizona Territory, year before last or whenever it had been—Brandon had been living for some time now in a realm in which the calendar had lost most of its relevance—a confidence man whose swindles had an epic quality. In the mining town of Kampen, he had surpassed himself, going beyond his usual practice of fleecing individuals possessed of enough capital to make the effort worthwhile to flimflamming the town into making him its mayor and de facto dictator. Sanger had been the only man to notice that Beaufort Callison was playing the role of a roving gambler rather than actually being one, but had not made an issue of it, especially after discovering that Callison had some tenuous connection with one Tsai Wang of San Francisco. Nobody who knew the name of Tsai Wang cared to give unnecessary offense to anyone who might be connected to the tong lord. This was especially true of Savvy Sanger, whose abrupt exit from San Francisco was caused by his awareness of having earned Tsai Wang's displeasure. Sanger, he recollected, had also been rumored to have swindled a good sum out of one Goren Kraft, the alias Gren Kenneally used for his season by the Bay.

"Here to see if the jays fancy their chances going up against a real live cardshark, Callison?" Savvy Sanger said sardonically. "I've been out here a couple of times, and I'd better tell you that this ain't no county fair, with discreet poker or what going on in a tent off to one side. This is a corseted and buttonhooked operation, high-minded and edifying as all hell, and not a saloon within the precincts. Though there's samples given out in the brewery building, and some of the wine merchants showing here have a free hand with the samples, so a man needn't parch out like a cowpat bleaching in the sun."

"An interesting idea, worthy of study," Brandon said. "And no, I'm not here on gambling business."

"No more you were in Kampen," Savvy Sanger said. "Not that I knew what it was you were really there for, and am pretty sure I don't want to know, so I won't ask you if you're here for the same thing, 'cause if you are, I still wouldn't know what it was, so why bother asking? Join me for a drink, Callison, and I'll put you wise about the wonders of this century plant of an exposition."

Brandon was amused to find, as he sampled some pungent German beer he had to admit surpassed Dolph Busch's product back in St. Louis, that Savvy Sanger could not resist practicing his art even on an unpromising candidate like the supposed Callison, with a fabulous tale of a preposterous device, on a par with the money-manufacturing machine beloved of confidence tricksters.

"And after that a little hand comes out of the machine and writes down what you just heard, so you have a permanent record of it?" Brandon asked. "I expect you've got a special arrangement with this Bell man so's you can

8

sell me shares for just whatever cash I happen to be carrying with me, is that it?"

"If I had any shares in what Bell's got, I wouldn't be selling them," Savvy Sanger said. "I would sit back and listen to the sound of greenbacks sifting into my account. But let me tell you, Callison, there'll be telephones in 'most every town in a few years, and then from town to town, and I'm already studying out ways how to use that. That machine is going to give fellows in my line of work muscles in places we didn't know we had 'em. Won't have to go out in the streets and saloons after the marks, but corner them amid the comforts of home, where they're happy and unsuspicious." He sipped at his beer and gazed in awe at some distant prospect he seemed to behold beyond the bright green trees and the hard blue sky. "Why, imagine it, man! The tale told on the telephone, the mark telephoning his bank to authorize the transaction, the money sent to another bank by telegraph transfer . . . the whole operation concluded without contact of hand or eye, a testimonial to the wonders of the Age of Electricity! And a lot less problem about being described to the cops afterward."

Brandon wondered why Savvy Sanger persisted in his ludicrous fiction, even when it was clear that it was not finding credence. Maybe it was another example of the Edmund Chambers doctrine: If Sanger made himself believe in a machine that carried voices instead of clicks over a telegraph wire, then he might be able to make that conviction contagious, and empty some poor sucker's pockets.

"Hey," Sanger said softly, setting his glass down. "Where's my wits gone to? I just said if I had shares, I'd be a rich man. Well, I've got a roll, and Professor Bell's going to need investors, sure enough. No reason Savvy Sanger shouldn't be in the herd, and there's probably enough fellows like you so that there won't be a stampede to press cash upon him just yet. Believe I'll get on over to the Main Building and see if he's still there showing it off, and if he ain't, find out how to get hold of him. . . . I got to thank you,

Callison, for jarring my brains so's I could see where the real opportunity is in this. Come along with me if you want, and see how the part of Croesus fits you."

Brandon admired the art with which Sanger had concealed the hook, misdirecting attention until the last instant, then casually offering the chance to get in on a good thing—doubtless by meeting a confederate of Sanger's impersonating this Bell man, if there was in fact any such person, and handing over all available cash in return for convincing-looking documents granting him a share in a telegraphic talking machine. He shook his head. "All my capital's tied up in perpetual motion engines right now," he said. "Interest you in a swap, share for share?"

Sanger stood and looked at him. "They say you can't cheat an honest man," he said, "and it may be so, though it's fun to try to. But it's for sure true, it's hard to do a favor for a man who knows he knows what he knows and don't have the least notion of what he don't know. You know, Callison, a sucker'll bite on anything, and that's often the end of him; but the fish that keeps his mouth closed all the time, why, no, he don't get hooked . . . but he'll starve to death in time. So long." He touched his hat brim and moved off toward the distant mass of the Main Building.

Brandon looked after him with a wry smile. Sanger was a real artist, conveying that note of regretful reproach with such conviction. He fingered the ancient metal disk in his trousers pocket as he considered what to do next. The Exposition was his hunting ground, but there was no indication what part of it might be more productive than any other. Would his quarry, if indeed he were still here, be studying the prize swine and cattle, inspecting the giant Krupp cannon, coveting the silverwork from Russia, ogling the marble naked ladies in the Memorial Hall art exhibit? No way of telling. The only thing to do was keep quartering the ground, alert for a sighting. And after that, the stalk: Fairmount Park, jammed with about an army division of fairgoers, was no place for the kill.

His fingers traced the irregular ridge on one side of the disk in his pocket, the image of a snake with its tail in its mouth, eating itself or perhaps, as Chief Atichke out in New Mexico had said, giving birth to itself. On the other side of the disk was the image of a wolf, which Brandon had come to see as his personal totem, the animal that lives to hunt. At times in the past, the metal circle had seemed warm under his touch, or even electrically charged (like Savvy Sanger's mythical telephone), and such times had usually been close to an encounter with one or another of those he hunted. He had never been convinced that what he sensed was genuine, but in any case, the disk, cool and inert, had no message, real or fancied, for him.

The state of Brandon's feet made him feel a certain sympathy for the boiled sausages, swollen till their skins split, he had seen offered for sale at some of the food stands. Town shoes weren't meant for hours of walking on gravel heated close to the temperature of charcoal. He wondered if the Shoe and Leather Building, off to his right, might have some loose-fitting size 14 slippers they could sell him, but decided not to try it. He was almost at the railroad passenger concourse, where he could pick up a fast train back into town and his hotel, and he had probably done what he could for the day. His feet gave him every excuse for not walking halfway across the Exposition's grounds to the Women's Pavilion, and whether he would do that tomorrow . . . tomorrow would tell.

The next train was not for half an hour, he found, and, rather than sit with his legs outstretched and see if his feet would burst like two boils, he decided to stroll through the Mineral Annex to the Main Building. If there were jewels, reasonable enough in a mineral display, they might attract his quarry.

A uniformed man pushed a comfortable-appearing woman by in a wickerwork rolling chair. Brandon envied her, but, seeing that only women and extremely frail old men were using the chairs, decided that an able-bodied man indulging in such luxury would be sneered at—and, worse, taken notice of. No great harm if such as Savvy Sanger recognized him, or the St. Louis court clerk, Slavin (or perhaps Gerry), had a glimpse of the former junior partner of Lunsford, Ahrens & Brandon in passing; but it would be a poor idea to be steadily noticeable.

Brandon found the first exhibit in the Mineral Annex somewhat baffling, since there were few or no mineral products apparent. Fancifully colored kites and elegant basketwork aplenty, and straw hats and mats, and tobacco and tea. There were some teapots and cups to establish a feeble mineral presence. Brandon wondered if in China the term "mineral" was treated more loosely than in the dogmatically minded world outside the Empire; more likely, he thought, the exhibit was made up of whatever wouldn't fit into the main show at the Chinese Department in the Main Building. Against the wall were some immobile figures of men and women in elaborate dress: a man in a long tabardlike coat with a stiff lacquered hat; a woman with a kind of bead veil and brocaded trousers; a sullen-looking man with a hat like a shallow dish; and others stationed down the wall. One of them seemed to have been misplaced and set on the floor facing the others: a stoutly built man with a round hat and a long, simple linen coat, with a seamed face and wispy white beard and mustache.

Brandon knew it was not a dummy, but it was still a shock to see the hand at the side rise up and send the inches-long curved nails sliding through the beard. It was considerably more of a shock when the face slowly turned to him and said, "Mr. Brandon. It is well you are here. He whom you pursue has been among this great throng and may return to it, and in any case there will be threads that you may seize and follow to where he is. And then this one's purposes and your own will be accomplished."

It was years since Brandon had gaped at anything, and he did not do so now, but if a spirit image of him had been manifested in the dusty corridor of the Mineral Annex, it would have been gaping. The speaker was that haunter of Savvy Sanger's nightmares, the San Francisco tong leader, dealer in opium, women, and any other high-markup merchandise that might come to hand, Tsai Wang . . .

The only man in the world who wanted Gren Kenneally dead as much as Cole Brandon did.

2

Just about the time of the Union's semicentenary, in the 1820s, an enraged citizenry descended on Natchez-under-the-Hill, Mississippi, with fire and generously used it, tired of the depredations of its population of river pirates, murderers, gamblers, and other undesirables. This freed Natchez of its canker of criminality, though spreading the infection all over the frontier, if in a less concentrated form. Peter Kenneally and his brother Quint were part of the involuntary exodus, and exchanged the rich life of river-based crime for the security of a fastness in Arkansas's Ozarks. The brothers and their cousins and in a while their sons became a formidable dynasty of lawlessness, operating over several states and territories, prospering as the growing trans-Mississippi settlements provided more and more towns, farms, and businesses to prey on.

Quint Kenneally's son Gren seemed like an ideal family member, a good rider, adept killer, and skilled thief. During the War he rode with Quantrill's guerrillas, and distinguished himself with his enthusiasm for atrocities, some of them more than even the brutal Quantrill was comfortable with. In the years after the War, Gren adhered to the family

14

tradition by staying in crime, but gave his relatives more and more unease by his wanton viciousness. Then, one fall morning, he led about ten men in stopping and robbing the Chicago, Rock Island & Pacific southbound train some distance north of St. Louis.

It was one of the first train robberies, and set the pattern for the Jameses and others; it also was needlessly brutal, with the engineer and express clerks gunned down. What gave it its place in the newspapers and the history books was the pursuit and the culmination of that pursuit.

The escaping gang was spotted and closely followed by a hastily assembled posse. They took refuge in a stone farmhouse, Mound Farm, and held the inhabitants, three women, one man, and a boy, hostage, after killing a farm worker as they shot their way in. When darkness came, the holed-up outlaws opened fire on the posse's approximate position, discouraging a stealthy approach; then fire puffed up from the farm buildings, and when the besiegers ran up, they found the hostages shot dead and the outlaws gone under cover of the fire.

Attorney Cole Brandon, hastily summoned from the city as soon as the news of the siege came to the authorities, arrived in time to see the bodies of his wife Elise, her father and aunt, the cook and the stableboy, being carried from the still-burning house.

The numbness that pervaded Brandon was a little lifted when one member of the gang was captured by private detectives he hired and brought to trial. To his horror and rage, the man, one Casmire, was acquitted through perjured testimony and the cynical cleverness of a brother lawyer, both purchased by the seemingly limitless Kenneally bankroll.

Cole Brandon sank into a kind of living death, from which even the plainly stated interest of his wife's sister Krista, now inheritor of the Ostermann family business, could not rouse him. It took a chance encounter with Ned Norland, a refreshingly disgraceful trapper, hunter, guide, trader, and all-round reprobate, to do that; and it was

Norland who initiated him into the lore of hunting and tracking, and stood by him in the encounter in the ruins of Mound Farm that left Casmire dead. The midnight burial in the ancient Indian mound that gave the farm its name turned up the curiously fashioned disk, which Norland advised Brandon to keep—it would be "bad medicine" to ignore something so obviously meant for him to find.

From Casmire Brandon had learned that Gren Kenneally had kept most of the CRI&P loot with him, promising to share it out in a cow town along the rail line in Kansas. It was not much of a clue, but for Brandon there was now no object in life except to find and kill Gren Kenneally and all those who had ridden with him. He was not moved by rage any more, but it was an absolute with him that those men should not be alive if the universe was to make any sense at all.

In the town of Inskip, he found a strong indication that one Jack Kestrel, foreman of a ranch in Texas, could be the man he sought; he also met Jess Marvell, then manager of the local hotel, and her eager assistant, Rush Dailey, both of them looking to horizons beyond Inskip. Mistaking Brandon for a detective on a case, they offered to gather information from the flood of travelers passing through town, and Brandon took them up on it, receiving their reports at general delivery windows wherever he traveled across the West.

Jack Kestrel turned out to be a detective himself, working on an unrelated matter, but their encounter, with Brandon masquerading as a wandering gunslinger, resulted in the death of one of Gren Kenneally's men. A report from Jess Marvell sent Brandon on to San Francisco, where he found that Gren had been there, and that he had left hastily, taking with him certain possessions that the tong lord Tsai Wang valued highly. Tsai Wang had little difficulty in penetrating Brandon's current disguise, and wished him well in his pursuit, also considering that Gren Kenneally's death was needed in order to balance the constituents of heaven and earth. Eerily, from time to time more or less information would be got to Brandon, indicating that Tsai Wang had methods of keeping track of where he was and who he was passing as.

As a gambler in Arizona and a newspaperman in Colorado, he accounted for two more of Gren Kenneally's men, though circumstance removed the actual killing from his grasp. In Colorado, he acquired yet another ally or set of allies, even odder than Tsai Wang: the Kenneallys.

As a pillar of the community explained it to him, successful criminal activity breeds success in other areas. Ill-gotten gains will do as well as honest earnings to invest or to finance new ventures. Forty-some years after the flight from Natchez, there were as many respectable Kenneallys and Kenneally connections as there were outright lawbreakers. The legal and illegal Kenneallys maintained a comfortable if distant relationship, often lending each other the kinds of aid and support their situations fitted them for. One thing on which they had lately come to firm agreement on was that Gren Kenneally was a liability. Americans have a tolerance for criminals as well as businessmen and politicians, but Gren's monstrousness—the Mound Farm massacre chiefly, but there were other excesses less well known but at least as revolting—went beyond the limits of that tolerance. Kenneally thieves and extortionists would soon be receiving extra attention and penalties because of their connection to Gren; and the hidden Kenneallys, most of whom had abandoned the family name, might survive being linked to a criminal dynasty of long standing, but never to Gren.

With this explanation, the community pillar handed over to Brandon the most complete list that could be compiled of Gren Kenneally's surviving associates: names or aliases where known, last known whereabouts, any information that might help identify them.

Three names had been crossed off the list since then, leaving three, plus Gren—seven in all gone, four still to go. The lifetime Brandon had lived since leaving St. Louis and the identity of Cole Brandon seemed timeless, infused with purpose rather than duration, but from time to time disturbed by an encounter with Jess Marvell. When he was with her, when they talked in the way that came so naturally to them, as if they had known each other since everlasting, his mission could seem a kind of mania, something that had nothing to do with real life, with the kind of life Jess Marvell lived, that someone would live with Jess Marvell . . . Brandon would find himself thinking about what he would do when this obligation was done with, thinking as if he had a future, and that, he knew, was dangerous. What he had to do could only be done if he lived and acted as each moment called for; looking ahead could mean missing what an instant presented, could mean failing, could mean dying. His own death was not that important to him, so long as it did not come soon enough to prevent the four deaths he was still bound to oversee.

It might be best not to see Jess Marvell at all this time, though she was certainly here. On the other hand, it was word she had sent by Ned Norland's hand, all the way to where Brandon was in Nebraska, that Gren Kenneally had been seen at the Exposition, that brought Brandon to Philadelphia.

And since Jess Marvell was not supposed to know of Brandon's interest in Gren Kenneally—he had concealed it, considering that encouraging her to gather information on Gren or any Kenneally would expose her and Rush Dailey to considerable danger—it seemed that she knew more of his business than he had ever told her or ever would. And she also should have had no way of knowing where he was to be found. He sensed Tsai Wang's hand in that, though any connection between Jess Marvell and Tsai Wang seemed improbable.

Now he looked at the bland face of the tong leader and knew that it would be pointless to ask him. Any answer he gave would be courteous, convoluted, and completely uninformative. Brandon realized that he would have to talk to Jess Marvell to sort out anything at all, and felt relief at not having to mull the decision over further. And there was something beyond relief that he preferred not to look at closely, an excitement that had no place in his life just now.

Only a few seconds had passed since Tsai Wang spoke, but Brandon had to reach to recall what he had said: ". . . this one's purposes and your own will be accomplished."

He nodded. "Yours, sir, and some of mine. But there are others, men I am concerned with and you are not. I expect my purpose will take longer to accomplish than yours, if I am successful here."

Tsai Wang stroked his beard with a combing gesture. "Perhaps not. Gren Kenneally is not here to enjoy the wonders of this display of goods and machines, of that you may be sure. He has his debts to pay, aside from those for which you and I hold him accountable, and it may be that he has chosen this place to settle those accounts he chooses to acknowledge."

Brandon considered this. So far Gren Kenneally had avoided sharing out the proceeds from the CRI&P robbery, whose final act had made him and the others with him fugitives shunned even by the underworld, and the last of those fugitives Brandon had met and dealt with had said something to suggest that the delayed reckoning might be about to take place. That was one indication that the three survivors of those who had been with Gren Kenneally at the robbery and at Mound Farm might be turning up in Philadelphia. Another, even stronger, was Tsai Wang's comment. He was not a man to speculate idly, and his "it may be" made it close to certain that he had definite information, and also made it clear that he had no intention of going into further detail.

"Then I'll keep looking around here till I run across him," Brandon said. "I've seen a picture of him, and he doesn't know I exist, so I've got the advantage there."

"You have many advantages, Mr. Brandon," Tsai Wang said. "This person's feeble aid is but one of them. It will be well for you to use them all."

He bowed almost infinitesimally, then turned and walked away, vanishing quickly in the crowd.

Brandon made his way toward the station, considering what "advantages" Tsai Wang might have been talking of, and taking not much more than half a minute to arrive at one: Jess Marvell.

Possibly Tsai Wang hadn't meant her at all; but now that her name had surfaced in Brandon's mind, he knew that he would have to see her, if only for the explanation of the link he had inferred between her and the tong chief. And, he reflected, if he took stock of anything in his life resembling "advantages," somehow Jess Marvell would have to be prominent among them—not for any specific reason, just for being Jess Marvell.

Across the wide avenue Brandon saw a giant copper hand holding a torch to the sky with a swirl of gilded metal presumably representing a flame pointing upward. The ornamental rim of the torch displayed flickers of motion, which Brandon made out as the upper bodies of visitors who had climbed the hollow arm and were peering down at the fairgrounds. The general impression given was that the Exposition had partly uncovered a metal version of the Cardiff Giant, long concealed in the depths of the earth, and that the scurrying insects of the surface were busily exploring it. Brandon recalled reading that this was part of a statue that the French were for some reason giving the United States, that would stand in New York Harbor, like a modern Colossus guarding the city and threatening any misbehaving shipping with arson.

The torch slid by him as the horse car rolled along Belmont Avenue. Brandon curled his toes with pleasure; his feet still ached from yesterday's endless walking on pavement, grass, and floorboards, but the mere state of sitting while the horses did the work was gratifying.

He wondered why he had persisted in spending the whole day afoot, and decided that it was both the thought that he might at any moment come face-to-face with Gren Kenneally and the fever that strikes expositiongoers, even those there for nonexposition reasons, the conviction that

20

some prodigious curiosity will be missed unless one traverses every square foot of the place. Well, the horses would take him past more chances to spot Gren Kenneally in a shorter time, and in any case, this morning he had a destination and might as well be taken to it directly.

On the right he saw the imposing structure of the Women's Pavilion, not unlike the Brewer's Hall in basic appearance, with its central cupola topped with a domed, eaved roof supported on slender pillars and topped with a tall flagstaff. It gave the building the air of wearing a rather dashing hat that had been influenced by a Prussian spiked helmet.

He got down from the horse car and entered the pillared, arched doorway of the wing facing the avenue. Like most of the Exposition buildings, it reminded the visitor of a big-city railroad station vastly expanded in size and then crammed with objects from a giants' lost-and-found office. There were many men in the throng of visitors, but it seemed dominated by women; perhaps it was not their number so much as the confidence they seemed to draw from being in a building in which not one of the array of exhibits involved a man. In the central rotunda he saw a briskly puffing and clattering steam engine, tended by a woman, supplying the motive power for a press busily turning out newspapers.

Art created by women, inventions perfected by women, businesses run by women . . . He worked his way past the exhibits, then saw a white-painted clapboard building front with wide plate-glass windows and a neatly gilt-lettered MARVEL HALL above the doorway. Inside, green-and-white-clad young women moved briskly among half a dozen tables, serving diners a late lunch. A placard outside the front door explained the Marvel Hall concept, restaurants geared to the railroad age, set up to serve good food fast, a meal set out and eaten during the short stop the timetable allowed. The key was advance planning: The conductor took orders from passengers and wired them ahead, so that each diner's meal was ready when he arrived.

The creation of Miss Jess Marvell, aided by her capable partner, Mr. Rush Dailey [Brandon was glad, but not surprised, to see that Jess Marvell's fairness and loyalty kept her from claiming all credit for herself or for women], Marvel Halls are now a recognized feature of the Far West, with several new establishments planned for the coming year.

Now here I am chasing Gren Kenneally and the rest all over the country, and half of them dead now and the others when I can get at them, and when it's done they're dead and maybe me, too . . . and the one thing left to show for the whole business is a bunch of railroad restaurants, for likely she'd never have got them started without the money she got from me.

Brandon pushed through the door and one of the waitresses—Marvel Girls, that was what she'd named them —came over to him and said, "There'll be a table free in a moment, if you'd care to—"

Coming from someplace he had not seen, Jess Marvell said, "I'll see to the gentleman, Flora. He's not here for lunch." She nodded to Brandon and turned and walked away. He followed her through the double doors that led to the small kitchen, followed her through its bustle and clatter and roiling confusion of appetizing smells (unlike any restaurant he knew of, and, he suspected, unlike most Marvel Halls, there were no male cooks or kitchen help) and into a quiet room with a desk and two chairs at the rear of her exhibition space.

3

Jess Marvell dropped into the chair behind the desk and Brandon took the one facing it. This was, what, only the fourth time he had been with her—the few days in Kansas when they had met, a couple of meetings and a near-fatal train ride in Colorado, not much more than an hour in Kansas again last fall—but it was as if they had known each other for a long, long time and could begin speaking like people taking up a conversation interrupted only that morning.

"So you knew I was here and were expecting me?" Brandon said.

Jess Marvell shook her head. "No, I didn't know you were here. But I was expecting you, in a while if not today."

"Ned Norland got your reports to me, out in Nebraska," Brandon said. "Also word that he'd seen . . ."

"Gren Kenneally," Jess Marvell said. "Mr. Brooks . . ." She used the name she had known him by two times out of the three they had met. "Rush Dailey and I have been collecting information for you for a good while now, without all that much to go on at the start, just that you were a detective, after some train robbers wanted for murder in Missouri. Nothing said about who they were or when and where the robbery was, or whether you were working for the railroad or the Pinkertons or who. Well, it was your money, and we needed it to get started, so that was all right. And we didn't go prying into your business. But, Mr. Brooks, Rush and I, we've got brains enough to make sense out of things, and we couldn't help learning after a while that there wasn't but one train robbery with killings into it in Missouri about that time, and it was known that Gren Kenneally did it. So it had to be Kenneally and those with him that you were looking for."

"Did you know that when we ran into each other in Colorado?" Brandon asked.

"No," Jess Marvell said. "Last year in Kansas, yes. But there didn't seem any reason to talk about it then. There were other things."

There were, indeed. In the manager's quarters in the Chesley, Kansas, Marvel Hall, Jess Marvell had pretty plainly offered him the choice between a night with her right then or the chance of something a good deal longer-lasting when Brandon (or Brooks) finished what he was doing. For the first time Brandon had an actual sense of a post-Kenneally future, and realized that, as he had sensed strongly in their earlier encounters, Jess Marvell's presence would make that future something remarkable; and he said, "Some day I will be free of it, you can count on that."

Jess Marvell's reply, back then, was a simple "I will." Evidently she was still counting on it; and, Brandon realized, so was he. It was horrible, but inevitable, that the way to her was paved with four corpses, men now alive who would have to die for Brandon to be free. Free, he saw, not from the need for vengeance but from Elise. Her life, and the others', had been taken wrongly, and they would not rest, not leave him, while the men who had killed them still drew breath. Maybe it would have been different if chance had not thrown Casmire in his way and forced Brandon to kill him. He had been on the point of putting it all behind him because there didn't seem to be anything else he could do, but Casmire's killing changed that, started something that had to be seen through.

And now it was something more than halfway through, maybe a lot more than that. If Tsai Wang's hint that all of Gren Kenneally's men who yet lived might be gathering here had any substance behind it, the next few days—even the next few hours, come to that—could see an end to it, with Jess Marvell on the other side.

The thought of Tsai Wang brought up something else, how Jess Marvell had known where to send Ned Norland after him—indeed, how she knew Ned Norland. Those two things suggested strongly that she knew far more about him than he thought, far more than he had ever meant her to know. "Ned Norland told me you and he decided it was best he deliver your reports to me in person, out in Nebraska."

"Once he'd actually seen Gren Kenneally here, yes," Jess Marvell said. After a moment she seemed to understand the question behind Brandon's statement. "He looked me up, of course; there was plenty of mention made of the Marvel Hall exhibit in the papers; Rush Dailey saw to that. He was over in the United States building, working on the dinosaur display, since he'd guided the expedition that dug up the bones, and he came here." She waited a moment and saw that Brandon had still not made the obvious deduction. "Unlike Rush and me, you told Mr. Norland everything about your doings whenever you got together, including at least something about me, though not everything, I expect."

"Not everything, no," Brandon said. He recalled regaling Norland with the story of his amateur information service, down in Bascomb in Texas, when Norland passed through with a mule train, and there had been little else to say about Jess Marvell then, except the disturbing effect she had on him almost from the first time they met. And, of course, his unsettling encounter with Tsai Wang in San Francisco—especially unsettling for the brief time Tsai Wang appeared to take him for a friend of Gren Kenneally and so a reasonable surrogate for the vengeance to be visited upon

Kenneally—he had passed on to Norland that time they shared some unexpectedly good beer in Santa Fe.

"And Mr. Norland said that if anyone knew where you were, it would be Mr. Tsai Wang of San Francisco, though he didn't say why. And I already knew that most of the places I had the restaurants' linens laundered at had some connection to Tsai Wang, who I understand lends money to get laundries started, so he's some kind of philanthropist, I expect. So I sent word through a laundry here, and sure enough, in a day or so there was the name of a town in Nebraska on a paper pinned to some tablecloths that came back. And I sent the reports on there, and then Mr. Norland saw Gren Kenneally, and we decided it'd be best if he took that news to you personally, and so he did. Whatever you were wondering, that's what there is to it."

Brandon considered this. Jess Marvell's matter-of-fact account made the whole business seem far less mysterious than it had been starting to appear to him. He had had a sense of Ned Norland, Jess Marvell, and Tsai Wang as shadowy figures looming over him and studying him as he capered puppetlike, jerked by invisible strings they held. That might still hold for Tsai Wang, who had a vast legion of Chinese workers and entrepreneurs available to observe and report on whatever might interest the "righteous man under Heaven" in his red-and-gold palace in Chinatown, but now it appeared that what Ned Norland and Jess Marvell knew followed logically from what he had told Ned Norland.

Subtract that mystery, and he was left with the far greater one of what he felt for Jess Marvell, and she for him. In Colorado and in Kansas there had been moments when it seemed that two individuals who inhabited them had spoken deeply and truthfully to each other as if the bodies and identities they dwelled in were merely inconvenient masks.

"Now you know what I know about you," Jess Marvell said. "And what I don't know is why you are hunting Gren Kenneally and the others, or what your real name is. Mr. Norland didn't tell me, and I don't care to know, anyhow. All that is part of this time, and it's the time after that's important to me, and I'm close to certain it is to you. When that time comes, I'll know what I need to know. You already know what you need to know about me."

She spoke flatly, almost wearily, and, in her neatly starched shirtwaist and pleated skirt, looked like a young girl dressed beyond her years, sober and, with her usual alertness and animation subdued, distinctly plain. Brandon's insides seemed to turn over like the giant flywheel on the huge engine in the Hall of Machinery as a flood of yearning and compassion suffused him. The inner surfaces of his arms ached, as if great force were being exerted on them to keep them from their natural state, embracing Jess Marvell.

To do that, to stuff Elise and the others finally into their graves, to let Gren Kenneally and his men find their fates on their own, to accept at once the immense gift offered, that would be the course of wisdom, of sanity. But wisdom and sanity had to do with the past and just possibly the future; in the present, the years-long moment through which he moved, there was only the matter of what had to be done and working out the best way to do it.

"I know you as well as I can now," Brandon said. "I'll know you better someday—we'll . . ." He spread, then clenched, the fingers of his right hand, the gesture of frustration replacing the conclusion he could not find words for. "Soon. It could be soon."

Jess Marvell's face was tight and her eyes narrowed. He could hear her saying, and with every right in the world, "It had better be!" but her face softened and she looked at him with clear eyes that seemed to see and accept everything he was and had done and could ever do; and the flywheel inside gave another half revolution that left him unsteady on his feet.

She stood up behind the desk and held out her hand. "I'll be seeing you then, when you're done with it."

"Oh, yes," Brandon said. "You know that." He took her hand in both of his and held it for a moment. The fingers, a shade warmer than his, lay quietly in his grasp, and he could

27

sense the softness of skin, the springy tendons, the gentle flaring of bone at the knuckles; the hand, so much smaller than his, seemed vast enough to explore and study for a long time. They had had moments of talk before, moments when both of them silently acknowledged what had grown between them, but this brief, flat exchange of words and the touch of hands were a ceremony of binding.

He let the hand go, took a deep breath, nodded to Jess Marvell, turned and left the office, finding his way to the main hall of the pavilion through the kitchen and dining room.

In his mind thoughts and feelings tumbled and whirled like the gears, pulleys, pistons, and governors set into motion by the rotating flywheel, the sum of these motions amounting to a chaotic excitement and anticipation. Into the buzzing confusion of emotions he felt the invasion of a chill of fear. So far, he had not much cared at any moment if he lived or died, except that early dying would leave his work unfinished.

But now, for the first time since he had begun that work, he had something to lose. And the last time that had been true, he had lost everything . . . to Gren Kenneally.

Brandon bit off the end of the cigar he had just bought at the stand, spat it out, and lit it. He eyed the bizarre structure of the elevated railway and the odd cars that sped passengers a few hundred feet to one terminus and then back to the other. They got a longer ride than those who took one of the elevators that hauled fairgoers to the top of untrustworthy-looking towers, but not as much of a view of the grounds. Brandon considered that there was no need to venture into the air, horizontally or vertically; there was enough to see just walking around or, like those who resorted to the rolling chairs, being pushed around. One of these now veered from its course down the avenue and was brought to a halt in front of him by its blue-uniformed attendant.

"Mr. Brandon."

Brandon looked at the linen-coated figure, topped by a curly brimmed domed hat, lounging comfortably in the rolling chair his ample figure fitted in snugly, and with some difficulty, recognized Tsai Wang. Out of his usual rich garb, the tong chief could have been a wispy-bearded old farmer, permanently tanned, with the Asian look to his eyes concealed by round-lensed wire-framed spectacles. Brandon supposed the drab clothes were an incognito, designed to keep Tsai Wang from becoming the object of gawkers his standard costume would have attracted, and wondered if the glasses shared that function.

Tsai Wang divined Brandon's unspoken question about the glasses and reached up to touch them. "I can read three thousand characters in the writing of the civilized world with no aid, as well as the primitive forms of your alphabet in books and newspapers, but the abominable print of this"—he held up the open guidebook that lay in his lap— "defeats me, and I must for the moment resort to devices designed for the elderly."

Brandon supposed that even a man who looked as if he had been mummified a dynasty or so back would prefer to think that "elderly" referred to dodderers at least a little older. "Anybody could use some help with those," Brandon said. The wares of the guidebook boys demonstrated a dedication to economy both in paper, by setting the text in agate type (with some passages in pearl) and crowding a remarkable number of words on each page, and in the stereotype plates, by forming them of some material (from the results, possibly bread) other than metal.

"It is my fixed intention to see every exhibit while I am here," Tsai Wang said. "I will thus be able to confirm my conviction of the superiority of my own nation in all important aspects. Do not look on this as a quaint piece of Chinese arrogance, for I believe that your fellow countrymen visiting here will do precisely what I have said, as indeed will your visitors. Persons from Prussia, or Russia, or even, to take the point to an extreme length, Norway, will see the wonders of the world and the display put on by their own country, and be persuaded that the whole Exposition demonstrates that the United States, Prussia, Russia, or, yes, Norway if you will, is preeminent among the nations of the world. This is why, as you may have noticed, such international expositions meant to promote friendship among the nations of the world are often quickly followed by brutal wars between nations which exhibited at them."

"I expect I'll get to see most of them while I'm on my rounds," Brandon said.

"You may wish to see what is said to represent a camp of hunters of wild beasts in the valley just below us," Tsai Wang said.

"I already have," Brandon said, remembering his encounter with Savvy Sanger, and a little amused that he was chatting lightly with the monster that haunted the con man's nightmares.

"Another visit could be propitious," Tsai Wang said. "One of those who present themselves before the public in it has sometimes diverted himself in an establishment whose owner is, so to speak, one of my ears and eyes. What he has said is obscure and confusing, which is only to be expected . . ." True enough, whether what the dive offered was opium or girls, Brandon thought; neither indulgence was likely to produce good expository conversation. Saloon talk would have been more productive, but Tsai Wang's connections in that world were almost nonexistent. "But there was talk of a bloody robbery and a reference to imminent prosperity."

"Suggestive, but not much to go on," Brandon said.

Tsai Wang fixed Brandon with a stare that the glasses magnified. "It is said that a detailed map is of no use to the fool but that the sagacious man can read a nine-volumed saga in an unaccustomed shadow and a bent reed. The one who resorts to the premises of my informant for some few pipes of *yen shee gow* is clad in the skins he may have removed from animals he has killed, but has since neglected to clean."

"You're right," Brandon said. "I'll look him over."

"Do so," said Tsai Wang. "Do you know where the nearest popcorn stand is? This excellent stuff was until now unknown to me, and I find it sustains me admirably in my explorations."

"Just down at the next avenue," Brandon said, pointing in the direction Tsai Wang's chair was headed.

"Thank you," Tsai Wang said. "I shall provide myself with an adequate supply, well buttered, and proceed to observe the scarf dance at the Turkish coffee house. From what I have heard of it, I believe that, with some modifications to suit the tastes of the local clientele, it would be an excellent addition to the entertainments provided in some of the establishments in San Francisco in whose amenities I have a voice."

"Good luck with it," Brandon said, and took a path leading down into the valley, for a moment grappling with the picture of the ancient tong chief, derby-hatted and gobbling popcorn from a paper sack while watching the undulations of a Near Eastern lady built along the lines of some of the heftier statues in the art gallery. Brandon had seen the dance and considered that if the costuming were simplified down to the scarf, dispensing with the brocaded jacket and baggy trousers, it might well appeal to the kind of men who patronized the kind of places Tsai Wang would have a hand in. He had a brief vision of Jess Marvell so costumed and dancing, which first did—and then didn't—clash with the intensely emotional, even spiritual, attraction to her he had experienced not half an hour earlier. Whatever he felt for her, and she for him, there was as much body in it as soul.

He paused when he had the Hunters' Camp in view, and saw the buckskin-clad man leaning on his rifle, seeming to model himself on engravings of Natty Bumppo in the collected works of J. F. Cooper. Was he actually one of those who had ridden with Gren Kenneally and been denied the profits of their shared crime, at least until now? Or just a fairgrounds performer with a weakness for opium and a habit of babbling meaningless boasts when drifting out of his drugged dream?

Brandon saw the buckskinned man lift a leather drinking

pouch that hung from a cord over his shoulder and take a draft of whatever it contained. Even at this distance he could see the drinker's body twitch in a way that suggested it was not water or cold tea. Opium wasn't his only indulgence, then; good.

Brandon thought a moment and had his plan. There was one thing he could do to further it, just retrieving a valise from the checkroom at the Department of Public Comfort, until just before closing time, a couple of hours from now. He debated how to use the time, and considered climbing up inside the French statue's arm, then considered that it seemed unpleasantly like imitating a grave-worm; a look over in the United States building at the petrified monster bones that Ned Norland's clients had dug up should be more interesting. There was one, Tyrant or something, that was said to be the most efficient killing creature the world had ever seen. Maybe Brandon could learn something from some moments of silent communion with the old murderer.

4

Brandon seemed to be looking into the eyes of the buckskin-clad man, getting a clear view of the bloodshot whites and the web of wrinkles around the eye sockets. The man's lips moved, but Brandon could not hear what he was saying, though a brief half-open–pursed–quarter-open sequence of lip motions coupled with a shake of the head could very well have been "No, sir." Or "Too hot."

Brandon had no idea what the man addressing Buckskin was saying; he could only see a broad, brown-clad back of body and head, and one ear protruding from under a broad-brimmed hat. He could of course hear nothing, as the two men were over a hundred feet away.

He lowered the field glasses, the most powerful that the hunting outfitters' store on Market Street had been able to supply. Probably there were superior instruments on display in one or another of the exhibits, but they would not be for sale. He had bought the glasses as soon as he arrived in Philadelphia, and brought them with him each day, leaving them in the Public Comfort building's checkroom packed in a small valise along with the loaded .38 revolver he had carried almost since the beginning of his hunt. The glasses were rather larger than a tourist wanting to get a closer look at a distant attraction would be likely to carry, and he had not wanted to draw attention by carrying them around the fairgrounds—or, for that matter, to be burdened with their weight in the damp June heat. With the crowds thinning at the day's end, the glasses would be less likely to be especially noticed, and he suspected he would be needing them in a while.

Brandon had debated carrying the .38 on his search through the Exposition, but decided that it was not necessary, and, as he had seen in Savvy Sanger's company, pickpockets infested Fairmount Park, and very likely some would be expert enough to relieve him of his weapon unnoticed. He had provided against a sudden dire need with the other component of his arsenal, a single-shot .30 pistol carried well out of the reach of pickpockets, in a spring-actuated mechanism in his sleeve, capable of delivering the weapon into the palm of his hand with a slight squeeze of arm against side.

Both guns had been the property of one Dan Doyle, a gambler Brandon had known briefly, mainly during the last thirty or so hours of Doyle's life. Brandon had been impressed by Doyle's ability to quell complaints or threats solely by the confident menace imparted by the weapons—a tactic that failed only once, when Doyle mistakenly assumed that an aggrieved party would *not* shoot him in the back—and bought them cheaply from the sheriff who appointed himself the executor of Doyle's estate. Brandon had trained himself to some expertise with the .38—with the single-shot, it was a matter of pointing your hand at the most vulnerable area at a close enough range so that a miss was unlikely—and had come to appreciate the hair-trigger double action that made it easy to cock and fire with one trigger pull.

Brandon stooped and dropped the glasses into the valise and snapped the catch. He lifted the valise and took a deep breath, mentally rearranging his stance and attitude to those of an impressionable tourist who would be honored to offer a genuine Far West hunter drinks at the nearest saloon as soon as the Exposition closed, which it was minutes from doing, in return for being regaled with absolutely true, or at least plausible, tales of life on the frontier. A little slackness in the jaw and a glassiness in the gaze would bolster the role, he decided.

Half an hour later, in a saloon called the Black Pig, Brandon was keeping his consumption of whiskey down in order to keep the glassy stare from becoming genuine. His companion, Tom Hawken, had a hearty thirst for it, but fortunately did not insist on his patron keeping pace with him.

"You have come to the rightest source they is for accounts of the strange doings in the Rockies and the desert and the prairies," Hawken said, having gathered that Brandon, an Ohio farmer, had never been west of Dayton, and preparing himself to take in as much of the Black Pig's booze as the Buckeye Stater would pay for.

Brandon listened to Hawken's narrative, some of which he recognized as distortions of events he knew of, and others he suspected of being regurgitated dime-novel stuff. Nothing in it provided a clue to whether Hawken—a name that sounded as if it had been stolen from a dime novel itself, only a mumble away from "tomahawk"—was one of the three men remaining on the list the "respectable" Kenneallys had given him:

Nine-Finger Nate—Hawken grasped glass and bottle with a full complement of fingers;

Jed Vogeler—said to be from western Pennsylvania originally, no other information, but Hawken's accent was so stagily western that any geographical indicators in his speech were buried;

Dick Roe—the first time Brandon had ever come across the law's name for an unknown, John Doe's sidekick, actually being used by anyone.

Brandon decided it was time to start guiding Hawken's talk toward something more forthcoming.

"Now, in the sheltered lands of Ohio, a man don't come acrost varmints like grizzlies and mountain lions," Hawken said. "But out amongst them mountains, such is as common as weevils, and you got to be ready to take 'em on with knife or gun or yer two bare hands."

"No lions in Ohio, no," Brandon said. "But we got our varmints, too, monsters that'll kill us just as sure, if some slower."

"What's that?" said Hawken.

"Railroads," Brandon said. "They raise rates on produce till we can't hardly make a living off farming, and they'll have us all in the poorhouse before long. Us in the Grange—"

"You a Granger?" Hawken asked. "You'll be staying out in them barracks they built for their folks over by Elm Station, I guess, which that ain't above a mile or so from where I'm at."

"Uh, yeah," Brandon said, having no idea where Elm Station was. His only acquaintance with the fast-spreading farmers' organization, the National Grange, came from a brief recent stay in Nebraska, where he had learned something of the group's complaints; he supposed that they would be similar in Ohio, and that if they weren't, Hawken was unlikely to know. The main thing was that Grangers hated the railroads, and that was the line to follow now.

"The railroads and the men that run 'em, men like John B. Parker, they're worse than rattlesnakes and grizzlies rolled into one," Brandon said. A few weeks back, he had kept a party of farmers, most of them Grangers, from roughing up, or possibly lynching, John B. Parker, usually called "the Killer Elephant of Wall Street" in the papers, and could draw on the bitterness they had expressed in the way he spat out the name now.

"What I hear, that Parker don't mess around, sees what he wants and goes after it," Hawken said. "Kind of man it's uncomfortable to work for, but pure pizen to work against."

"About so," Brandon said, wondering if Hawken was thinking that what he had said applied equally well to Gren

36

Kenneally. "But Parker's only a man, it's like the railroads has come to be critters in their own right, lying acrost the land like giant snakes, gobbling up everything. I'm a law-abiding man, but I got to say that it cheers my heart when I hear about somebody doing something to railroads."

"Doing what?" Hawken asked.

"Doing like Jesse and Frank James," Brandon said. "Stop the snake and make it give up some of what it's et and spread it round to the poor folks."

"Jesse and Frank James is pismires," Hawken said. "A few hundred, a thousand or so here and there, that don't hurt the railroads to speak of. A real big robbery, and some dead, that's the kind of thing they feel the sting of. Sixty thousand at a go, say, that's something they don't like to lose."

"Well, they wouldn't," Brandon said. The hairs on the back of his neck were bristling. To someone who had experienced Gren Kenneally as a leader, the James brothers might well seem as puny as ants. He realized that he had never heard a figure for proceeds of the CRI&P robbery, and guessed that the company would not be inclined to advertise that that kind of money could be had from them. Even with eleven or a dozen men to the gang, each would walk away with the equivalent of several years' wages for a skilled workman, more than that for a cowhand. Provided, of course, that the loot was ever shared out . . . "That'd be a lot of money to spread amongst the poor, the way they say the James boys do."

"Be a lot of money to spread amongst anybody," Hawken said gloomily. "Sometimes the spreading ain't as wide as it might be." He darted a sudden glance at Brandon, then gulped at his glass. *"Trains* ain't my business," he said truculently. "Bears and catamounts and Injuns, them's what I know about, thass what's meat and drink to Tom Hawk-eye."

"Hawken," Brandon said.

"Whatever."

Brandon fingered the old Indian medallion in his pocket.

It seemed to tingle on his fingertips; if it were sentient, it might have been feeling like the back of Brandon's neck.

Hawken was not staggering when he and Brandon parted outside the Black Pig, but he was unfocused enough not to express any surprise that Brandon did not seem to be going with him to the train station at the edge of the Exposition grounds, even though they supposedly were headed for the same destination.

Brandon let him get well ahead, then followed. At the station, he saw the train that Hawken tumbled into, and boarded it two cars back. Elm Station, that was the name.

"Elm Station," he said to the conductor who came through just when the train began to shudder like an ague-plagued python as the locomotive's driving wheels began to turn over.

"A Granger?" the conductor said. "I'll have to see your card."

"No card," Brandon said. "I'm not a Granger."

"With the Granger card it's a ten-cent fare," the conductor said, "half a dollar without. You better find your card, for you can't ride for a dime unless you show it."

Brandon fished coins from his pocket. "Here's four bits. Like I said, I'm not a Granger."

"If you was a Granger, you could ride for ten cents, fifteen for a round trip," the conductor said. "If you was to *tell* me you was a Granger, I could maybe let you ride for the dime. But you could be an inspector trying to trap me, and I would lose my job over trying to save some fellow I didn't know forty cents, and nothing in it for me anyhow."

"I'm not an inspector," Brandon said wearily. "Tell you what, you let me ride for the dime, and you can keep the rest of the half dollar as a present, okay?"

The conductor took the money, punched a hole in a blue strip of paper, and handed it to Brandon. "Trip slip for a ten-cent fare, Granger rates," he said with a wink. "Don't let on I let you ride cheap, huh? I could get in trouble."

Brandon did not see how the conductor could get through an hour of everyday life without serious trouble if this transaction represented how he dealt with things.

It was about twenty minutes after sunset when the conductor stuck his head in the car and bawled, "Alum Haitian," which Brandon and the outdoor-looking men who shared the car with him recognized as an announcement that they had arrived at Elm Station. As he left the car he noticed that the floor was strewn with blue trip slips, and inferred that his fellow passengers were Grangers, as they looked, or had had the benefit of the conductor's special offer. He doubted that the conductor issued many, if any, fifty-cent trip slips.

Most of the passengers headed toward a collection of long, two-story buildings some distance off; the specially built Granger lodgings, Brandon supposed. He hung back on the platform until he saw a dung-colored figure meandering on a tangent to the course the majority were taking. Hawken was walking roughly west, into the last light of the sun, which meant that if he did turn and look behind him, a follower would be indistinct against the eastern sky, now darkening with more than night as a curtain of black cloud lifted from the horizon. A chill breeze brushed Brandon with dankness, and a flicker in the east told of a storm which would not be distant for very long.

Brandon trailed Hawken for about a mile and a half, through lightly wooded country which after a while gave way to broken, rocky terrain, and then an abrupt hill, which seemed to have undergone massive surgery, with one side and most of its base scooped out. In the dimming light Brandon could not see it in detail, but it was clearly a quarry of some kind. It did not seem to have been recently worked, and the sheds and shacks spread around it had a look of desertion that went beyond the fact that, except for one, they were unlit.

The largest building, which Brandon estimated at about

twenty feet square, with a peaked roof, showed a flickering light in two windows, and Hawken made for it.

Brandon stopped and took the field glasses from the valise. The windowpanes snapped into view, and he thought he could make out the shape of a kerosene lantern behind one of them, and some blurs of movement that had to be the occupant or occupants. One of the windows was blocked by Hawken's moving silhouette, and then an irregular oblong of brightness appeared as the door opened to admit him, and vanished as it shut.

Brandon lowered the glasses and looked at what he could make out of the ground between him and the shack. There was no reason to suppose that Hawken would be the last arrival at this place, and it would not do to be caught in the open by a newcomer; but he had to be a good deal closer in if he were to see anything conclusive. In spite of the feeling Brandon had about Hawken, almost amounting to a conviction that he was one of Gren Kenneally's men, he could equally well be a low-level Exposition employee, living on the cheap with a few cronies, or meeting some friends here for a poker game; and now was the time to make sure of just what the situation was.

Brandon could make out a shallow ditch that ran partway toward the lit shack, and a shed fairly near each end. In New Mexico, in a brief stint with a Texas Ranger–like force, he had learned a good deal about stealthy approaches, and believed he could use what cover there was to good advantage. The farther shed would be a good place to observe the shack from.

He slipped the .38 into one jacket pocket and the field glasses into the other, crouched, and began moving silently toward the lit building.

At the first shed he paused and closed his eyes for a full half minute, then opened them and found that his vision was sharpened, even in the gloom of the nearing storm. He could see some motion in the lighted windows, but not clearly enough to make out what it was. No point in using the glasses just now, he decided; he was going closer in, no matter what, and they would be more useful then.

Brandon looked around, staying quite still, for three minutes, and saw no motion, not even an evening-rambling skunk or possum, except for the grasses stirring in the rising wind. He moved along the ditch, bent over enough to protrude only slightly over its rim, moving slowly and smoothly, so that his shape, even if spotted, would not appear as that of a walking man.

The second shed, when he reached it, proved to have its open side angled obliquely toward the lit building, so that he could peer past the wall but be mainly concealed from a look from that direction. He took out the field glasses and pointed them toward the bright rectangles of the windows, about twenty feet away.

The scene the lenses brought to him was clear but slightly distorted and flattened. He could see a table covered with a worn, patterned oilcloth, with glasses set out on it. The lantern was hanging from the ceiling, though the top of the window frame cut off his view of how it was attached. One man's back was a featureless mass, facing the window and receiving no light. He saw a hand at the end of a buckskin-wrapped arm reach for a full glass, and presumed that Hawken was making himself at home. A man facing the window, sharply illuminated by the lantern, grasped a bottle to pour a drink. Brandon turned the glasses to the next man, then abruptly back.

Unlike Hawken in the bar, this man held the bottle with his thumb and three fingers. If his other hand was unmaimed, his present complement of fingers was nine. Any number of agents could lose a man a finger, from almost any kind of machinery to fireworks to a horse's (or a barroom antagonist's) teeth, so that any number of men would be shy a digit or so, but Brandon had the conviction that his glasses were focused on Nine-Finger Nate.

In a moment the question became moot. Nate, if it was him, looked to his left, then moved out of Brandon's field of view to his right. The space vacated was filled with a burly figure in a stained but once luxurious shirt, very likely silk, Brandon guessed. The hawk nose and deep-set glaring eyes were as Brandon had heard them described, and once seen them photographed.

He was surprised at how steadily he held the glasses as he looked directly into Gren Kenneally's eyes.

5

The wind was strong enough now to create a constant level of varied sound: rustling of leaves, creaking of tree branches set to rubbing each other, variously pitched rushing noises as wind flowed over the clapboards and shingles of the shack and whirled around its corners and projections, and the encompassing sigh of the whole air mass pushing ahead of the storm. Brandon did not fear that his footsteps would be heard as he ran lightly from the shed up to the lit building.

He pressed himself against the wall next to the window. He breathed deeply, trying to force his heart to beat less rapidly, and his blood to stop rushing so noisily through his veins; he could hear the talk of those in the room only indistinctly, as if he were trying to understand a conversation while standing next to a waterfall. The smell of a rank cigar, perhaps more than one, came to him and stung his eyes.

After a moment the noise abated, or he became accustomed to it; he could hear and understand some of what the men inside were saying.

". . . and now Nate's here, it looks like he's the last there'll be. I've been here for a month, and the word's been out that long, and them that's going to get it has got it, and if they ain't here, it's because they can't be here or 'cause they ain't interested in getting what's coming to 'em."

The voice was grating but deep, like a steam organ with rust in the pedals and distortions in the pipes. It seemed to vibrate in Brandon's gut as it scratched on his eardrums. Gren Kenneally, no question: No group that size had room for two men whose voices held that amplitude of malign power.

"Jack Ryan can't, for sure," someone said. "Kilt shooting it out with some train robbers out in Colorado."

"Jack shoulda knowed not to mess with train robbers," Gren Kenneally said. "Was him did the CRI&P engineer, cool as a clam." Brandon remembered Jack Ryan's death, fighting at his side; he had not appreciated the irony at the time, since it was only later that he read the name on the list Gren Kenneally's disowning relatives had provided him.

"Seen in the papers a year or what back that a man called Tatum was found dead in a mine shaft or such out in Arizony," a voice that sounded like Hawken's said. "I reckleck your cousin Oscar useter go by that name, Gren."

"And Peter got chewed up in a steamer's paddle in the Gulf," Gren Kenneally said. "Seems like a lot of the boys has run out their string of luck. And if Kid Philly, Neb, Curly, and Casmire ain't also joined the silent majority and no notice taken, they ain't found their way here in time for the share-out, which is 'most unlucky as being dead, to my way of thinking." He hawked and spat, and then there was a scratching noise, a juicy inhaling sound, and the pungent odor of a sulphur match and another whiff of the bad cigar.

It struck Brandon as curious that the only deaths they seemed to know of were those of the gang he had not killed himself. The demises of his own four victims had escaped attention . . . which meant that so had he.

Gren Kenneally's next words confirmed the thought. "So many gone, and others missing, in not much time; I got to say that'd make me suspicious, but it looks like no more 'n a run of bad luck. Nobody killed Peter but his own foolishness, and Ryan was dumb enough to take on fellows in his own trade that turned out to be better at it, and what Oscar was doing in any kind of mine, I can't figure, as he was always dead scared of being shut in any place. So, whilst it makes sense somebody'd be hunting us, there's nothing to show there is, or that Peter, Oscar, and Jack was anything but unlucky."

After a moment, someone said, "Gren? You ever get a feeling . . . like some of them folks we did at that farm that time, like they cain't lie easy? Sometimes in a dark night, it's seemed to me I seen a face, 'specially the young woman, looking at me."

"What I remember of her, you'd have a better night if you seen more of her than her face," Gren Kenneally chuckled. Brandon was astonished not to feel an explosion of grief and rage at the gang leader's words, then realized that since he had looked into Kenneally's eyes through the glasses, a new entity seemed to have invaded him, infusing every muscle, nerve, and vein with its presence, a creature whose one purpose was to kill, an engine of death without passion or fear of emotion, only calculation.

He had a vision of the four faces inside turned to his as he burst into the shack, his face, the face they had never seen, the last sight they saw before they died . . . and he saw the danger in that vision. It didn't matter what they saw, only that they died. And if something went wrong, and some or all of them didn't die, then the face of Cole Brandon was something they shouldn't see.

He pulled a handkerchief from his pocket and tied it around his face, anchored by the bridge of his nose. It did not impede his breathing, and the sense of its concealing folds seemed right; faceless death was what he felt like, not a man with features and an identity.

He listened closely to the talk inside, and slid back and forth along the building wall, estimating the location of each speaker as best he could. A hunting wolf might have moved so, muzzle swiveling from side to side as its keen nose hunted the scent of a creature destined to have its throat torn out. A distant rumble of thunder drummed through him and he smelled the odor of dampened earth.

"Dead's dead," Gren Kenneally said. "That's why you kill folks, so's they won't be a trouble to you. Mainest reason, anyhow—I got to say, when it's for diversion, it sets you up in a way booze or snow don't. When you got to kill in the way of business, it's a nice extry that you enjoy the job, which I don't expect ribbon clerks and book salesmen can say."

There was silence as Kenneally's fellow killers absorbed this. Brandon sensed that the creature within him, though not concerned with pleasure, would understand Gren Kenneally better than Cole Brandon could. So would the nightmare giant murdering kangaroo monster whose bones Brandon had viewed that afternoon, waiting for the moment to approach Hawken. If old Tyrant Lizard, fleshed out and slavering, were standing there in the night, the business would be over in seconds: the huge thighs flexing for a leap that would send its multiton body smashing the shack flat, the dwarfish arms scrabbling in the ruin for screaming tidbits, the saberlike teeth mincing them like the massive machines he had seen in Chicago that turned pig haunches and other parts into sausage meat.

The being dwelling in Brandon was not that powerful, but no less unquestioning in its intent, sifting information and arriving at the best way to kill, and to survive long enough to complete the killing.

"What I ain't been seeing in the night," Hawken said after a moment, "is visions of my share of what we got from the train tucked away safe or out a-making money for me, or even happy recklections of what I wasted it on. It's been a long time, Gren, and I'm happy we're about to share out finally, but I'd admire to know why it is we had to wait. I know we had to scatter after we burnt out that farm, but a bunch of us went out to Kansas half a year later when you grapevined it that that was the time and place, and nothing to show for it. We got ourselves on every Wanted list around for the CRI&P job, and been staying outer sight ever since, and it ain't paid off, so I figure we're owed some explaining."

From what Brandon knew of Gren Kenneally, it seemed as if there was a good chance that Kenneally would do part of Brandon's job right then; Kenneally was not the kind of man you reproached without having made your will. But the gang chief seemed in an uncharacteristically mild mood, saying, "You got a talking point there, Jed." Hawken was Vogeler, then, Brandon realized. Probably he would not be able to match voices to Nine-Finger Nate and Richard Roe before the business was done, which he found obscurely troubling, but unimportant.

"It weren't any thought of holding out on you boys," Gren Kenneally said, "and you know better than to give head space to any such notion, I'm sure." The grating note was back more strongly in his voice, and the other men in the room mumbled a chorus of reassurance.

"I got a sniff that the Pinkertons and the Nationwides was onto the rendezvous in Dysart," Gren Kenneally said. "'Twas just at the last minute. I was on the damn train through Kansas, with all the stuff with me, when I was tipped to it. No time to warn anybody, so I stayed on the train and got through to Frisco."

"I was at Dysart, and I seen Curly, and Neb, and Jack Ryan, most of the others," a man said, "and no detectives snooping around."

"And you was there, too," Hawken/Vogeler said, apparently to the third man, "and so was I. And no Pinkertons and no Gren."

"Well, the Pinkertons and the Nationwides, they didn't get to be knowed as longheaded detectives by standing around with badges saying 'Detective' on their coats, now did they?" Gren Kenneally said. "And it could be I was told wrong, too, there is always that chance. But I wasn't about to take chances with the take, or with you boys' lives, come to that, so I done what I thought best. And it's been a long wait, but if we'd shared out all round in Dysart, you'd have had a 'leventh share each, and now it's a fourth."

"A fourth of what?" a man said. "You still got it all, Gren? Kinda hard keeping it all together when you're livin' on the run."

"Lost every dollar of it," Gren said cheerfully. "Lost some at the tables in Frisco, then I got into business with a Chinaman and he did me down and had me shanghaied onto a whaler bound for the South Seas."

Brandon recognized the grain of truth at the center of this baroque pearl of fable: Gren Kenneally had indeed had some dealings with Tsai Wang, but the doing-down had been at the hands of Savvy Sanger, and, rather than having had him removed as an inconvenience, Tsai Wang had sought Kenneally diligently until the appearance in Brandon of someone with an even stronger motive to find and kill him.

Gren Kenneally stilled the medley of protest and anger with what could have been a small-caliber pistol shot, but which Brandon guessed to be the impact of the flat of his hand on the table. "Hear me out, you turd-heads! Accourse I wouldn't have brung you together here if all's I had to show you was an empty poke. There's everything we took from the train here, and more, and sit back and have a drink whiles as I tell you."

Brandon tensed at the clink of the bottle on the rim of a glass. This could be the time for it, with most of them paying attention to pouring the drinks, pull the door open and—

"Gotta make room for more," Hawken/Vogeler said, his voice shifting position; Brandon heard the click of a lifted latch.

"Well, don't do it against the wall like someone done before," a man said. "Go away some, up past the shed out back. Rain'll be here soon, but it won't wash it away good enough if you piss on the shack."

Brandon relaxed. With one man out of the room, even the

48

slim chance of success would vanish. Wait for the next chance, then. He also, he found, wanted to hear what kind of story Gren Kenneally proposed to try on the survivors of his gang. It would almost certainly be lies, since it had started that way, but there could be some clue to the truth in it. In some way it would be unsatisfactory to kill Gren Kenneally before he had some kind of understanding of him. That, he realized, was Cole Brandon thinking; the hunting creature that pervaded him twitched impatiently at such trivial considerations.

"Like I said, I was shanghaied," Gren Kenneally said. "Mortifying, I will tell you, me, Gren Kenneally, a deckhand on a whaler, and tasting the rope's end if I stepped out of line."

"Not like you to let such pass, Gren," a man said.

"Nor I didn't, Nate," Gren Kenneally said. As a latch-click and footsteps announced Vogeler's reentry, Kenneally continued, "I palled up with a harpooner from the Sandwich Islands and a few other fellows that didn't care to spend two years at sea hunting big fish—"

"Not fish," the man who had to be Roe said. "Whales is animals, like pigs and cows. I seen an exhibit at the Exposition that showed that."

"A fucking animal that fucking swims in the fucking water is a fucking fish," Gren Kenneally said softly. "Do we agree on that, Dick, or do you care to disputate it to the bitter end?"

"Fish, that's it for certain, Gren, fish from tail to tooth, no question, Gren. Whales is fish."

"And the captain and the mates was animals. Anyhow they squealed and bled like animals when my pals and I went for them with harpoon and knives and a couple guns. And we sent 'em over the side, along with the boys in the crew that didn't see it our way, and we had ourselfs a nice ship that didn't want nothing but some scrubbing stains off the planks. Now, we was southering then, somewheres off Honduras, and we made for land, thinking to sell off the ship and have ourselfs a good time in the tropics. But we got wrecked in some little new country called Santa Coralia, where there was a civil war going on."

"Like the one we had?" Nate said.

"Naw," Gren Kenneally said. "No slaves or secession, just who gets to run the place and squeeze the farmers. So I threw in with the fellows that was trying to take over, and talked up what I done with Quantrill and showed them some of what I could do, and they made me a general."

"And you helped 'em win and they loaded you down with doubloons and jewels?" Vogeler said. They all seemed to be grouped around the table now.

"Not quite," Gren Kenneally said. "The staff and the fellows that wanted to be *presidente* and other big cheeses was having a palaver before a big battle, and I was off to one side with the artillery, and loaded a battery of six-pounders with chain and grape and swiveled 'em to aim point-blank at the nabobs and touched the guns off and blew 'em all to hash. They had two chests of gold handy to pay the troops with after the battle, and me and the boys that was in on the scheme with me, we scooped up the chests and took out before as anyone got their minds together and thought to stop us. I got one chest, the rest took the other one, and we split whenas we got acrost the border. I won't go into what it took to get that chest back here, where I can split it with you boys, but you can take it that it was considerable."

Gren Kenneally's audience turned this over with respectful silence, as if they could hardly believe it, and no wonder, Brandon thought. Spout that from the witness stand, and the judge would be sending for a couple of men with a straitjacket; but outlaws seemed to be less critical.

"Is it as much as the take from the train, Gren?" Roe said.

"Twicet as, almost," Gren Kenneally said. "Over a hundred thousand in coin and bullion"—about four hundred pounds, plus the weight of the chest, Brandon calculated; an improbable load for a fugitive to bring through Central America and Mexico—"so there's twenty-five thousand for each of us, boys!"

There was another silence as Vogeler, Roe, and Nine-Fingered Nate each contemplated the impact of half a century of a cowhand's wages on his life. Brandon's cold companion saw that the men inside would never be less alert.

He squeezed his arm against his side, delivering the single-shot pistol into his palm, and shifted it to his left hand. He took the .38 revolver in his right hand and squeezed the trigger until he felt the hammer begin to lift, and maintained the pressure at that point. That risked premature firing, but he had the sense that his body was responding to the needs of the moment with the precision of a machine and that his finger would not exert that next fraction of an ounce of pressure until he willed it. He recalled something Anson Carter, the old Texas Ranger, had told him out in New Mexico, and turned his right hand slightly, so that the gun lay almost on its side. "The pistol kicks upwards, so if you're sweeping a room, make that work for you," Carter told him. "Start on the right and the recoil'll bring it 'round to bear close to the next target."

Brandon stuck out the two last fingers of his left hand and reached for the door latch. He went suddenly cold as he realized that he didn't know if it opened in or out, and forced himself to relax and visualize Hawken's entry into the shack. Yes . . . he'd stepped to the right a bit when someone inside opened the door to admit him; so it opened outward. Good, no chance of pushing it open and giving sudden concealment to someone who might be standing next to it.

Before he reached again for the latch, a spate of Cole Brandon thoughts boiled up, demanding attention: This is unlawful, plain murder; you could get in touch with the police, have them capture these men; you won't survive it. . . .

The thoughts whirled through his mind like blown leaves in the fall and were gone. This next moment was what he had been moving toward since the moment he killed Casmire and knew that the account would have to be completely settled. He had made himself into someone, something, that had to do this, and there was no turning back.

And there was no such person as Jess Marvell.

He crooked the two left-hand fingers on the latch, felt the coldness of its metal, and slowly lifted.

6

In other times of high demand and mortal peril, Brandon had had the sense of time slowing down, as if his gearing had been shifted from engaging a large cog to a small one. So it was now: He pushed the door open as fast as he should, without hurry, and without hurry squeezed off the first shot at the shoulders of a man who sat facing away from him.

Smoke blossomed in front of the revolver, masking the effect of the shot; the kick of the recoil moved the muzzle to aim almost at Hawken, whose eyes had just started to widen in surprise. Brandon's left hand found a target in a man just rising from a chair at the far side of the table and he squeezed off the .30 at the same instant as he fired the revolver's second load at Hawken, though his slowed but acute senses registered the sounds as fractionally separate.

Gren Kenneally was facing him directly, right arm with a gun in the hand already clear of the table, though not yet up and aimed; he must have moved with phenomenal quickness at the first motion at the door. He seemed to rise suddenly toward the ceiling as Brandon found himself falling forward, propelled by the skidding of his left foot on something that slid under his foot—his mind, to no particular purpose, matched feel and smell and recollection and tagged it as a discarded, beslobbered cigar butt. Brandon caught himself before hitting the floor, not slowing his rate of fire but conscious that his aim was off.

As the sixth shot jolted the revolver in his hand, he let the recoil add its impetus to the sprawling sideways spring he made that took him out of the doorway, even as a slug gave its high-pitched shout of passage not much over his head. Gren's shot, and it would have taken him in the body if he had not skidded. Brandon reached the near shed, then dove into the ditch, raising his head just enough to see over the edge. It was, he calculated, a good bit less than ten seconds since he had flung the door open; he would have emptied the revolver in under three. He flipped the cylinder open and slid another half dozen cartridges into it.

From the shack came a steady screaming, indicating that one of his shots had found a significant mark; shouts of alarm and rage seemed to be coming from only two sources, so that one other man was uninterested in expressing himself, or incapable of doing so. Brandon fired two shots at the shack, sprang up and ran twenty feet to his left, crouched and fired another shot, ran back ten feet and fired twice again, sought the ditch, slammed five more cartridges into the cylinder, fired three times, all the while giving vent to a series of mumbling, incoherent outcries. It was the best he could do to suggest to the two or so able-bodied men left inside that they were facing several attackers and would do well not to show themselves.

The window dimmed and darkened. Brandon snapped off another shot, then ran and sent two more in from the side. For the moment he had the advantage. He could see the shack dimly, even though it was now nearly full dark, and could pick off anyone who came out the front, or the side windows. They could escape through the back, but he hoped that they would, for a while at least, fear that the attacking force had the place surrounded. With their eyes accustomed to the lantern light, it would be a while before they could see outside clearly enough to spot Brandon as he moved, and come to realize that their assailants were either very cleverly hidden, or amounted only to one. A few wet drops hit his face, and then, persistent but light, the rain set in.

He wondered if the screamer, now giving a mechanical rhythmic cry like that of an annoyed donkey, was Gren Kenneally. If the shot squeezed off as the pistol and its wielder were falling forward had connected, it would be somewhere between the fourth shirt button and six inches below the belt, which would make anyone but perhaps a Chiricahua Apache hee-haw in agony.

Brandon was astonished to see a flicker of light in the cabin; lighting the lantern again would lose them any chance of spotting him in the night. Then he saw that it was not the lantern; the light strengthened, and he could see it through the cracks in the clapboard siding. As a tongue of flame licked through the roof, he saw what they were up to. They would have slipped out the back and fired the shack as a diversion, just as they had at Mound Farm . . . no, not diversion this time, illumination. He saw his shadow dancing to one side in the growing glow, and ducked into the shelter of the shed. Out there, behind the fire, they could look past its edges and see whoever was anywhere in front of the shack.

Fire wrapped the shack, and the screaming inside became sharper and louder. Remembering Mound Farm, Brandon felt neither vengeful nor pitying. The man inside would not suffer much longer, and he had seen hundreds of sunrises that Elise Ostermann Brandon, Berthold Ostermann, Gertrud Ostermann, Annie Wysock the cook, Billy Heggins the stableboy, and Tom Burke the hired man had not; the world, and Cole Brandon, owed him nothing.

Brandon peered at the fire. Beyond the outline of the flames was an indistinct area in which he could see nothing, and detail was visible only after ten or so feet away. The two or more survivors could be looking for him, masked by the flames, and he would never know.

He felt a tug at his feet and heard a kind of coughing

sound, as if the earth had belched, then it was as if the sun had risen up from the center of the earth behind the shack.

He threw himself facedown into the ditch, which shook as if trying to expel him, and clasped both hands over the back of his head, covering his ears.

Furnace-hot air sledged over him, driving him into the protesting earth; his hands vibrated like drumheads, transmitting the raving flood of sound that hammered him, but keeping his eardrums from bursting.

When the blast subsided, he rolled over, sprang to his feet and ran to the farther shed, ducked into its shadow, and looked around its edge. The fireball dwindled almost to nothing in seconds as he watched, leaving a giant irregular circle about fifty feet across, profusely decorated with flaming fragments, flaring and hissing as the rain hit them, but not going out. Brandon cursed and leveled his revolver at the site of the shack, then lowered it and dropped it into his pocket. There was nothing left to do.

The place looked like a quarry, so it made sense there'd have been blasting powder stored there, say in the shed behind the shack. Either the Kenneally men hadn't known about it or hadn't figured the fire would be hot enough to set it off, or had panicked, which suggested that Gren wasn't one of those who'd had the idea of setting the fire.

It would be a damned good thing to know for sure that they were all dead, though. Brandon started to walk toward the smoldering ruins, then slowed and stopped as the heat increased as he approached. Not much left to burn, but burn it would till it was done, since the rain didn't seem to be affecting it, and the fire department and other authorities would be here long before it was cool enough to look at, would already be on the way from Elm Station or Philadelphia or wherever. Brandon could not think of anything he wanted to say to any authority whatsoever about this. He picked up his valise, from next to the farther shed, dropped the pistols into it, walked toward the wooded hills at the far side of the quarry area. It wouldn't do to meet the fire wagons or the police or the newspapers and be invited to explain what he was doing near an event that was likely to push the Exposition off the front pages of the Philadelphia papers.

Brandon walked through the night, automatically avoiding rocks, trees, and gullies, not thinking much about anything, just letting thoughts come to him and drift away. Faces of men dead in Missouri, in Texas, in Arizona, in Colorado, in Nebraska, and now in Pennsylvania. Some he had killed, others had found their own deaths, but he had wanted all of them dead.

And now they were. Now the hunting creature that wore Cole Brandon's body and face had no quarry and no reason to exist. Calvin Blake, Carter Bane, Charles Brooks, and the rest . . . now only inert masks to be stored in an attic of the mind, or maybe just smashed and thrown away and forgotten.

Cole Brandon could come back to life now. Brandon wondered if there was a recognizable Cole Brandon to be reborn. The amiable young lawyer had nothing to do with the man who had ridden over the West and experienced everything it had to offer, and done half a dozen jobs with competence enough to make a living at any of them (except the gambling; at that, he suspected, he would lose his shirt). The tracking of Gren Kenneally and his men, maybe he could put that behind him, but the experience of cooking for a trail herd on the long drive, of reporting for a small-town paper, of training and leading an irregular force of lawmen to attack a small army of bandits . . . the identities he had assumed to undergo those experiences would stand around mocking Cole Brandon's attempts to stuff himself back into the old self that had been his before Gren Kenneally took it into his head to hold up the CRI&P. The rain was coming down steadily now, but the trees he made his way through broke its force, and it was warm; his coat was tightly woven enough to keep it from soaking through, and he rather enjoyed the sense of being washed from above.

Ned Norland ought to have some ideas about how to come to terms with the life he would have to take up.

Norland had gone from fur trapping to trading to scouting to hunting to freighting to anything the West offered that would let a man earn some money and have a good time, including those offered by amiable Indian ladies. Not, Brandon considered, that he had any ambitions in that line—

He stopped short, and the valise banged into his shin. Oh, Counselor! he berated himself. You Goddamned fool, you are trotting around the edges of this and not paying attention to the most important thing. Counselor, what you set out to do is done, and you've lived through it. There is a future for you, whoever it is you've turned into, and this very damn morning you talked to Jess Marvell about that. You didn't say anything you could be held to, but does that matter a bucket of warm spit?

He pulled off his hat and let the rain wash down on his head, not caring that it was beginning to work its way past his collar and wick down his shirt. He grinned hugely, feeling the stretching of facial muscles long unused.

Now, Counselor, there's no choice there, is there? You're free to go to her, and she'll have you, as of last report, so that's all tied up. What'll it be like, I wonder? I don't expect that's important, though, how enjoyable it's going to be; the truth is that being with Jess Marvell is what makes the universe make sense, and it may be enjoyable or it may not, but not being with her, why, that's . . . unthinkable.

Brandon strode along in the drumming rain, lips too wet to whistle, but in a frame of mind to whistle dance tunes, even symphonies.

Of course, that elation about the future, the future itself, hung on how many bodies the police and firemen would find in the soggy embers of the shack in the quarry. Four, and the long hunt was done. Three or fewer, and it would go on. And Cole Brandon and what he hoped for, Jess Marvell and what she hoped for, would go back into the shadows of an uncertain future.

7

There were four, according to the next day's *Inquirer,* which Brandon read in the hotel dining room over a pot of coffee he was substituting for breakfast. The paper told most of the story in banks of headlines of gradually diminishing size, leaving the meager text the facts supported to reiterate them less colorfully:

Horror in the Hills!
Mysterious Explosion Kills 4
Gruesome Discovery
in Disused Quarry!

Fire Equipment From Two Townships
Responded To Nighttime Disaster But
Victims Were Beyond Help

Stored Blasting Powder May Have Been Cause;
Safety Precautions Are Being Investigated
By Fire Marshal

Remains Rendered Unidentifiable by Force of Explosion; One Bore Tattoo Marks, Suggesting Possible Anarchist Connection—Did an Attempt to Plant a Bomb at the Exposition Fail, With Fatal Consequences to the Perpetrators?

Brandon admired the impartiality with which the paper presented two contradictory explanations of the explosion, the second managing to drag in the Exposition with no justification whatever. He doubted that the actual connection, the presence of a denizen of the Hunters' Camp among the victims, would ever be made, since establishing that there had been four corpses had been difficult enough, without any question of identifying them. One unburned patch of skin had borne some crudely tattooed designs, but they had provided no clue.

The paper had no mention of an exhaustive search of the charred rubble, but even a cursory one would not have overlooked a chest holding one hundred thousand dollars in gold, and the heat of the fire and the force of the explosion would not have destroyed it without substantial and evident traces. Either Gren Kenneally hid it well away from the meeting place or, most likely, there had never been such a chest. Brandon wondered how he had proposed to flimflam the few who had survived to join him at the quarry—to spend, though they had not planned it, the rest of their lives with him.

Gren's scheme, however ingenious it might have been, had died with him, and Brandon decided he did not care what it was.

He sat back in his chair and poured coffee from the china pot the waiter had left on the table, and sipped at it. You have done what you set out to do, Counselor, he told himself, still finding it hard to believe. Gren Kenneally and the others who killed Elise and the rest, they're just as dead themselves now, and the ledger's balanced. Brandon had never really expected to reach this moment, not enough to have come to any opinion about what it would feel like, and he was surprised to find that he felt neither the satisfaction of consummated vengeance nor a belated remorse over the deaths he had dealt out. If there was a word for it, it was catharsis; he felt purged of something that had coiled within him since he had seen his wife's bloodied face and sightless stare at the night sky as she was carried out of the flaming house at Mound Farm.

The months he had spent in the pursuit seemed like a lifetime, or several lifetimes, crowded with curious and violent events, sending him across more of the country than he had ever expected to see, turning him into different men with different names and different jobs and characters. He was free now to find his way back to being Cole Brandon, if he could retrace that twisted and perhaps overgrown path.

He could think of Elise again without guilt or horror, and as her face formed in his mind's eye, he saw that it was calm but remote. He had loved her, he supposed she had loved him, but completing his self-chosen task had allowed what there was between them to recede into the past. Whether he had had to do it, whether it was worth doing, those were questions he had never asked himself, and had no intention of asking now. It was done, and what was important was what came next. . . .

The coffee tasted stronger and richer, and the dining room seemed more spacious and luxurious, than they had the day before; he seemed to sense everything more intensely and more clearly than he remembered, as if his eyes and his senses had been renovated and adjusted to their finest pitch. The sun struck in through the dining room's tall windows, laying down a gilded path that seemed to lead him into the bright day and everything that lay beyond. And, most particularly, to Jess Marvell. Maybe she could be convinced that the Marvel Hall display could do without her guiding touch for half an hour or so, and persuaded to take a walk around the grounds of the Exposition.

"I really haven't seen that much of it," Jess Marvell said, "but I'd say that I like seeing all the buildings and the crowds and such from a little away, like this, more than walking into each one of 'em and looking at what's there and making sure it matches the guidebook, then out again and on to the next building."

They were seated on the grassy slope that led to the creek on which the Hunters' Cabin was sited; Brandon could see that the two remaining occupants were doing their best to carry on without Hawken, presumably hoping that he would turn up any minute, since, going by the newspaper account, it would be a long time before the authorities would identify him, if they ever did. Across the valley the creek ran through, Brandon saw rising above the trees the imposing bulk of the Art Gallery and its annex, both of which, like Jess Marvell, he was perfectly happy to leave unvisited.

The air seemed to glow with the sunlight it contained, and it poured down the slope they sat on like a heady liquid. The light made everything seem newly created and remarkable, even the members of the crowds pressing determinedly along the paths and roadways. "It's a nice spectacle and I like being here, but now you'd best tell me what's so important that you've dragged me away from my exhibit and taken time off from your own business," Jess Marvell said.

"Ah, that's it, I guess," Brandon said. "My, uh, business. It's . . . it's finished."

Jess Marvell's head and hands had been in light motion as she fingered a blade of grass and looked around the park. Now she was frozen into the immobility of one of the statues stonily inspecting their passing viewers in the buildings across the ravine. What she was inspecting, Brandon could not tell, as she was facing half away from him.

"Cleared up," Brandon went on after waiting for her reaction. "I don't have to tend to it any more."

Jess Marvell remained marble-still, and Brandon was trying to recollect how Pygmalion brought to life the statue he was chipping out of stone, since he seemed to be faced with something of the same problem, when her head snapped around to face him as quickly and decisively as an owl's does; and her eyes were wide, luminous, and staring as an owl's.

"How did you finish it?" she said.

"I can't go into that just yet," Brandon said, realizing that he had not yet worked out what he would be telling Jess Marvell about his mission and himself, and when he would be telling it. Cole Brandon had a good many legal problems potentially hanging over him, and Jess Marvell and Rush Dailey had been abetting him for some time now. At the very least, there were some loose ends in St. Louis that he would have to see to before he was sure that he and Jess Marvell had nothing to fear from the law. "It's done, yes, but just some finishing off to do."

She looked at him thoughtfully, then said, "The explosion out of town last night, that killed four men, the papers said. Was that what ended your . . . business?"

"Ah . . . why would you think that?"

She shrugged. "If you've been looking for a gang of train robbers for more than a year, and yesterday you couldn't say when you'd be finished, and today you are, then something must have happened. And the biggest thing that's happened is the explosion, so it makes sense."

"Well, yes," Brandon said.

"Did you do it? Set off the explosion?"

"No," Brandon said. Not directly, anyhow, Counselor, which is what she likely means. As for shooting some of them first, I don't know I hit anybody but the one who screamed, and maybe he'd have survived if the others hadn't got cute and set that fire without thinking about the blasting powder. I could say that under oath and not be risking a perjury charge, anyway.

"I'm as glad," Jess Marvell said. "I expect they deserved what they got, but I'd have had to stretch some to be happy with the idea of your killing them all like that."

Well, I expect so, Brandon thought. But how about shooting Ed Marks off his horse, twisting Curly's head till the neck broke, killing Casmire in Missouri and that kid in Texas before they killed me? That'll take some getting used to, but we'd best wait a while before stretching you that much. He was suddenly appalled at how little closer finishing off Gren Kenneally and his gang seemed to have brought him to moving on to whatever there was going to be between him and Jess Marvell.

There was the matter of Casmire, moldering away in the earth at Mound Farm. Probably not much of a consideration, but if he were ever dug up and identified, the owner of Mound Farm would have some questions to answer. And then there was the tracking and destruction of the Kenneally gang. Jess Marvell had from the first accepted that he was doing something she didn't know the whole of, but her suppositions wouldn't be likely to come close to the actuality. The face he had shown her in their few times together had not been that of a man dedicated to implacable pursuit and wholesale killing . . . and, just then, he had not been such a man, nor the old Cole Brandon, but someone who existed only in those moments.

And there was Krista. Elise's sister, more spirited and ambitious, heir to the Ostermann commercial empire and doing a creditable job managing it . . . and, she had let Brandon know, ready to be a good deal closer than a sister-in-law, taking Elise's place in his life. Brandon had been attracted, strongly, but the tracking of Gren Kenneally overrode every other consideration; and now, only a couple of months ago, he had read a letter from Krista sent to his Chicago bank, saying in effect that she had waited for word from him as long as she was going to, and that she was prepared to make other arrangements for her life. Later, Brandon had linked that to some unconnected observations and for a while entertained the fantastic idea that Elise's sister was about to link herself to a prominent financier, one of the legion of legitimate businessmen with links to the Kenneally clan.

With time to reflect on the train ride to Philadelphia, he had rejected the notion, although it seemed clear that there was nothing to take up between Krista and himself; yet that had to be seen to and tied off. So did the remains of Cole Brandon's St. Louis life: the house in Walsh's Row, the suspended partnership in Lunsford, Ahrens & Brandon, Mound Farm. It was clear to him that he wouldn't be going back there to live, but he did not wish to leave ragged edges around his departure.

Cole Brandon's departure . . . but who would be on the train or boat when it left St. Louis? He had become the first of the many temporary successors to Cole Brandon when the upriver packet took him into the night toward Kansas at the beginning of the hunt, and he would revert to being Cole Brandon when he went back to St. Louis, but was there enough of the original article left for him to keep on being Cole Brandon away from St. Louis? And if there was, why? His recollections of Cole Brandon lay on the other side of a lot of travel and living and killing, and he had no special affection for the easygoing youngish lawyer back there. One thing that made it easy for him to assume all the different identities he had used was that there wasn't all that much to disguise; any mask he chose to put on seemed to have been as convincing as any other, and none of them contradicted by the personality of the man wearing them. . . .

Brandon came back to the here and now and saw that Jess Marvell was looking at him, calmly, unhurriedly waiting for him to say whatever he was going to.

"No, I didn't set off the explosion, but I was there and I saw it," he said. "So I know the business I've been at is done . . . in the main."

She closed and opened her eyes in a long blink and gave a faint smile. "There's a little more to do, then."

He gestured vaguely with his left hand. "Tying some things up, seeing to some matters that have been kind of lying around."

"Lying around where?"

"St. Louis."

"I'm off to Wyoming myself in the next day or so—Cheyenne," Jess Marvell said blandly. "That's where the Marvel Halls headquarters is, where I live, I expect, though I'm traveling most of the time." Her face bore a half smile, but her eyes were wary. She had sent the ball across the net, and was waiting to see where he would return it.

"I'll be in St. Louis day after tomorrow," Brandon said. "Three days there, four at the outside, four or five to Cheyenne, depending on connections. Ten or twelve days from now, then, I will see you in Cheyenne." It seemed to him that his face was mirrored in hers, that he must be wearing that look he saw, of hope and longing held back from expression for just a little longer.

"Ten days, twelve, call it two weeks if there's a hitch. Not very long," Jess Marvell said, and Brandon knew the statement for the valiantly extravagant lie it was; right now, ten minutes was a long time to wait for what was ahead of them, two weeks was a geological era. "If you run into John B. Parker, you might butter him up, put him in a good frame of mind. He's coming out to Cheyenne on railroad business, and I mean to waylay him and get him to put some money up for a bunch of new Halls I want to get started on. He ought to feel kindly toward you, if he remembers you saved him from the fellows who kidnapped him in Colorado."

"Maybe he does and maybe he doesn't, but he'll probably recall that I got him loose from some angry Grangers last month," Brandon said. He was not sure that the piratical financier, known to the newspaper-reading public as the Killer Elephant of Wall Street, and to a much smaller group as a hidden connection of the Kenneally family, would cherish fond memories of his rescue, since the terms Brandon had negotiated had included a substantial and irrevocable reduction in freight rates to the local farmers. "Where would I run into him?"

"St. Louis, he's visiting there, I hear," Jess Marvell said.

Brandon remembered Parker talking with admiration of St. Louis and its amenities, and grinned faintly at the bizarre fantasy he had allowed himself to fall into, a totally unwarranted linking of Parker's liking for St. Louis and its society with Krista's talk of finding a different focus for her hopes.

"Being nice to John B. Parker is kind of asking a lot of anybody," Brandon said mock-solemnly.

Jess Marvell gave him a steady look which, after a few seconds, seemed to pierce through his eyes and into wherever his thoughts and feelings were formed. "I don't mind one bit asking a lot of you," she said.

"Aren't you taking me for granted?" he said.

Now her smile was full, and she looked at him with the same warm delight that had nearly undone him at their last meeting in Kansas. Counselor, she's right, you *are* granted. And so, thank God, is she.

Brandon did not seek out Tsai Wang, but was not surprised to encounter him as he rounded a bend in the path he was taking back to the train station. Tsai Wang raised a hand in a ceremonious greeting, economically converting it into a gesture to his attendant to halt the rolling chair.

The tong leader looked closely at Brandon, then nodded. "I applaud your thoroughness and your resolution, Mr.

Brandon. I myself have a preference for a certain elaboration in these matters, so that the person chiefly involved has both time and motive to regret sharply the actions which have brought his present, if temporary, circumstances about. Yours is a younger civilization, which emphasizes efficiency and briskness, and in the end, even a few hours later, the result is the same."

Brandon was taken aback. "I'm not quite sure what you're talking about, sir."

Tsai Wang stroked his beard and rolled his eyes upward behind the glinting spectacles. "You know quite well what I am talking about, Mr. Brandon. What you do *not* understand is how I know what I know, though it is quite simple. One look at you tells me that you are not as I have seen you. Both two days ago and last year you were a driven man, a hunting animal if you prefer. Today you are not. Something has happened."

"And the only thing with a lot of deaths in it that's happened is the explosion last night," Brandon said, with a slight disquiet considering the idea that he was irredeemably in love with a woman whose mind seemed to work exactly like that of a crime-steeped opium merchant and whoremaster. It might be better to turn that around and credit Tsai Wang with the familiar if quasi-supernatural attribute of feminine intuition.

"I hope to hear your confirmation that one of those deaths was Gren Kenneally's," Tsai Wang said.

"I didn't see him blown apart," Brandon said, "and I gather that there's not much to know any of them by now, but he was there with three others, and there's four bodies, so it tallies. And just to set the record straight, thoroughness and resolution had nothing to do with it. The fools set the place on fire and it got to the powder stored there."

"The diligent man may strive and succeed or fail, but the fortunate man prospers regardless of effort," Tsai Wang said politely. It was a long time since Brandon had regarded himself as fortunate, but he supposed that finishing off the

Kenneallys, or being an audience to their self-destruction, counted as that, since it was what he had been living for these many months. And again, flowing past the specters of the dead outlaws, came the shining river of remembrance of Jess Marvell: oh, fortunate, Counselor, no question.

"You are looking considerable chipper, Brother Callison," Savvy Sanger said, coming up from behind Tsai Wang and his stolid attendant but ignoring the drably clad figure in the rolling chair. "A fair day for enjoying the fair, which I personally am doing considerably after some interesting conversations with Professor Bell yesterday."

"The gentleman who constrains the spirits of the lightning to convey spoken messages along a wire," said Tsai Wang. "When one considers what one most often hears, one may wonder if there is any great worth in hearing it sooner."

Savvy Sanger jumped as if tapped on the shoulder by one of the electrified spirits Tsai Wang had mentioned, clearly considered turning and running, as clearly decided that it would do no good—any attendant of Tsai Wang would probably be prepared to produce a hatchet from the recesses of his clothing and throw it with deadly effect at a fleeing man—and subsided into an attitude of resignation. "Tsai Wang, sir, ah, good to see you again," he said huskily.

"San Francisco has been less amusing since your departure, Mr. Sanger," Tsai Wang said. "I trust you found your term as mayor of that town in Arizona profitable, as well as your stays in Omaha, Minneapolis, Chicago, and most recently, I believe, Harrisburg in this very state."

Brandon had never seen Savvy Sanger, even in moments of crisis and danger, look stupefied, but he was seeing just that now, as Sanger took in the idea that his supposed nemesis had been aware of his movements since he fled San Francisco, and could presumably have taken his vengeance at any moment.

"I perceive that you have some fear of me, Mr. Sanger," Tsai Wang said.

"I did hear that you planned to cut me open, nail my bowels to a post, and make me run around it," Savvy Sanger said. "Not best pleased that I'd skinned Gory Kraft and he'd tried to recoup by, ah . . ."

"Skinning me, you need not fear to say it. He did so, and I admit that for a moment I was vexed, and would have dealt strictly with any who had even the slightest connection with Kraft, down to defiling the tombs of his ancestors and leaving their ghosts to harass him. But I have learned moderation in all things, and am content to confine my displeasure to Goren Kraft."

"Well, it's a relief to know I'm not in your bad books after all," Savvy Sanger said. "But now I got all the more room to worry about Gory Kraft. He ain't been heard from, and I've no notion where he might be, but he'd likely think the Maypole dance you had in mind was kid stuff."

Tsai Wang looked up at Brandon with a reasonable approach to a smile, then back to Savvy Sanger. "A fate more certain than any that Goren Kraft can deal awaits all of us; yours may well find you before he does, as his may already have found him, so that worry is a waste of time and effort." Brandon saw that Tsai Wang was not above allowing himself a little amusement in return for the slight vexation Sanger had cost him.

"Well, now," Savvy Sanger said. "You do have a wonderful way of turning up the bright side for a man to look at, Tsai Wang. I can now enjoy this wonderful raree-show all the more, sustained by the reflection that each sight might be my last. All the same, it's a great spectacle, ain't it? A whole hundred years of the country, all laid out for the world to see."

"A century," Tsai Wang said. He held his hands up, palms facing him, and opened and closed the fingers several times. "Twenty hand-counts of years, gone as fast as that. My homeland's history extends for fifty centuries. The sages had compiled the whole of human wisdom, complete with commentaries, when your ancestors lurked in the forests and conversed in grunts."

"True enough," Savvy Sanger said, "but you ain't there, you're here."

"Admittedly," Tsai Wang said, "it is a much better place for making money." He looked at Savvy Sanger. "This may often be done through elaborate commercial schemes of one kind or another, as you and I in our own ways demonstrate. But your country also manages to prosper through the contrivance and manufacture of ingenious mechanisms. . . . You mentioned Professor Bell. Have you acquired any knowledge of his device?"

"More than that," Savvy Sanger said. "I have talked the professor into allowing me to invest in it, which I expect will allow me the luxury of being an honest man in not too many years." He looked thoughtfully at Tsai Wang. "It's pretty handsome of you not to bear a grudge, but I'd be easier in my own mind if I was to do you a good turn by putting you in the way of a good thing. Bell's still got room for an investor or so, and I could set the thing up for you if you've a mind for it."

"Have you offered this opportunity to Mr. . . . . Callison?" Tsai Wang said with a faint smile.

Savvy Sanger shook his head. "No disrespect intended, Brother Callison, but I don't owe you anything special, and this is special. With Tsai Wang I feel the bond that joins one man to another man that's decided not to disembowel him, which you will see is pretty strong. Also, as you showed the other day, you ain't a man of vision and wouldn't spring for it. Tsai Wang here, he can see the glorious possibilities, and he ain't about to let them slip through his fingers."

Those fingers stroked the wispy beard, and Tsai Wang said, "Let us talk of this further. Mr. Callison has other matters to see to, I am sure." His nod and gesture dismissed Brandon politely but definitely.

Tsai Wang's calm assumption of control of the whole encounter nettled Brandon a little and prompted him to thwart the old man in his delicate tormenting of Sanger. "I don't owe you anything either, Sanger," he said, "but I'll do you a favor for nothing. Don't ask me how I came by it, but I have word you can trust that Goren Kraft is dead. And no, I don't want any stock in a talking telegraph for telling you."

71

"Is that the goods?" Savvy Sanger said, looking at Tsai Wang.

"Mr. Callison is a man of truth in important matters, though inclined to talk when it is not needful," Tsai Wang said. "We must not delay him further. I believe that you will find the weather in St. Louis less oppressive than here, Mr. Callison."

Brandon returned the nod and added another for Savvy Sanger, and turned and walked away. He was fifty feet on his way before he thought to wonder how Tsai Wang knew he was on his way to St. Louis. Hardly needs that fake voice telegraph to find stuff out, does he, Counselor? Don't expect he reads minds, though, but then how'd he do it? Hum . . . Well, yeah. He knows who I am and where I'm from, and with Gren and the rest out of things, it follows I've got to do what I am in fact going to do, go there and clear up the loose ends of my life. Pretty simple when you work it out, so the old fellow doesn't have to be that much of a mental giant.

Which he couldn't be particularly, Brandon considered, if he was letting Savvy Sanger spin him his yarn about the telephone and pull the resulting wool over his eyes. In a while Sanger would have separated Tsai Wang from a few hundred or thousand for a mythical share in an unworkable invention, and would have incurred the tong lord's implacable wrath, a pretty poor bargain.

I guess he's driven to con a mark whenever he finds one, no matter how dangerous it is, Brandon thought. Sort of like me and Gren and his men, and that could have killed me just as easy as swindling Tsai Wang's likely to kill him . . . but I'm out of that at last, and it's time for a new chapter in my life.

8

ell, I wouldn't mind a rest from my labors," said
Hercules.

Brandon chose to ignore the feeble joke, then realized he
wasn't sure if it was one. Captain Joseph Hercules of the
Second District of the St. Louis Metropolitan Police dis-
couraged playfulness about his name, though it was impossible to stem the press's jocularity whenever something
noteworthy in the police line came up in the Second.

During his dealings with the captain in the course of his
legal work, Brandon had been scrupulous about purging his
speech of reference to any Greek gods or demigods whatever, and he suspected Hercules was grateful for this unusual
forbearance. He had always been cordial to Brandon, who
had calculated that he would be likely to give a discreet
warning of any trouble Brandon might be in, such as county
authorities taking an interest in the discovery of a body at
Mound Farm, perhaps or perhaps not identified as the
William Casmire who had been tried and acquitted for
participation in the Mound Farm massacre, and shot at
several times in open court by attorney Cole Brandon,

whose violence (and bad aim) was charitably put down to agitation over what was generally accepted as an expensively procured miscarriage of justice.

Brandon had found Hercules at the district's substation in Lafayette Park and immediately learned what he had come to find out: Hercules's greeting held nothing of warning or of confusion at a social encounter with a man in whom a policeman should have a professional interest. Brandon decided to extend the encounter with an invitation to a saloon at the edge of the park, which Hercules accepted with the mild, perhaps unintended, joke.

As they strolled on the path under trees gilt-washed by the almost set sun, Brandon wondered why he asked Hercules to have a drink with him, then realized that he wanted to talk to somebody, completely casually, about as much of his recent life and future plans as he could comfortably reveal, and that a man who had known him slightly and didn't much care what he had done or would do was the ideal audience.

Brandon had already decided that finally severing his connection with Lunsford, Ahrens & Brandon had best be done by letter; a discussion with Jim Lunsford in person would be protracted, draining, and pointless, since the senior partner would never understand why Brandon would leave, and would insist on arguing forever, on invoking the memory of Brandon's father, even of Elise, both of whom he would portray as standing on the other side of the veil urging Brandon to have a little sense. Brandon had admired this technique when Lunsford employed it in court, though the departed were usually said to be exhorting the jury to credit the improbable account given by the defendant, but was determined not to have it applied to himself.

He had made no close friends in his earlier life in St. Louis, being occupied with his studies, the rigors of starting out in law practice, and his marriage. He and Elise had known many men and couples in the business and professional classes in town, but only on a casual visiting and entertaining basis; whatever connections there had been had withered from lack of use in his months of seclusion after Elise's death and the time his pursuit of Gren Kenneally had taken. Hercules might not be much interested in the doings of Cole Brandon, but neither would anybody else.

Except Krista.

Brandon knew he would have to talk to her before he left, give some explanation of what he had become and why—leaving out the matter of Jess Marvell, which was not necessary and might be distressing to hear—that person was not a prospective mate for Krista Ostermann. That might well be moot by now, of course, but out of all of St. Louis, Krista was the one who was owed a clear and honest (if not entirely complete) closing-out. Tomorrow for that, he decided, send a messenger to the house—no, the Ostermann main office, Krista would be likely to be there, keeping an eye on the firm's wide range of enterprises—and make an appointment to see her in the afternoon. There was something he had to see to that would take up most of the morning. Then on to Wyoming, leaving St. Louis, leaving Krista, leaving the past behind.

They entered the dark, noisy barroom, in function and looks much like many Brandon had seen across the West, but unmistakably St. Louis in sound and smell. For now, he decided, a heavily edited version of his recent life recounted to Hercules would create a past to leave; in time, he might come to believe it himself, and let the tracking, the hunting, the deaths, recede into the unreality of old nightmares. Already Gren Kenneally and the others seemed like legendary villains and monsters, now duly slain and gone as those dealt with by the original Hercules.

Standing at the bar next to Hercules, Brandon lifted his glass and nodded at his guest.

"They said you was traveling in Europe or so, to get over the, uh, sad business you had," Hercules said after his first swallow of whiskey.

"No," Brandon said. "Had that in mind but looked around the West instead. San Francisco, Arizona, Kansas,

Nebraska, Texas, New Mexico, Colorado. Amazing country."

He told of deserts, mountains, gigantic underground caverns, hot springs, lush farms; he told of characters he claimed to have met, a gambler, a range cook, a newspaper reporter, a fast-talking windmill salesman. As he spoke, he realized that the vast and varied land he had seen and the oddly assorted types of work he had done remained real and vivid in his mind, while the task that had brought him to that land and that work steadily receded into dusty oblivion.

"I expect you'll see more folks from here than yourself out there before long," Hercules said. "Some'll be looking for work, and others'll just have got tired of St. Louis. The depression ain't let up all that much yet, and that charity house Chief McDonough set up on Green Street to help the homeless folks get through the winter, you'll remember that?" Brandon nodded. "Well, that's jammed now, even in the summer, and there's men without work that can't find room there, and they're roaming the streets begging and so on, and St. Louis has come to be a sorrier kind of place than it was when you was last here, Mr. Brandon."

"I just got in about noon from Philadelphia," Brandon said. "Haven't had time to notice any changes."

"You been to the big Exposition in Philadelphia?" Captain Hercules said.

"Spent a couple of days going around it."

"That's a marvel to be sure," Hercules said, "and if there's any hope for ending the depression, I'd say that's it, boosting trade, showing off new wonders like the telephone, things like that'll do more for us than whether Hayes or Tilden gets elected." He lowered the level of whiskey in the glass substantially and looked at Brandon. "Did you, uh, get to the Wisconsin building?"

"I might have," Brandon said. "There's lots of state buildings, and I have to tell you, they don't all stick in the memory."

"You'd recollect this," Hercules said. "They have got Old Abe, that's an eagle that was regimental mascot of the Fifth

Wisconsin, there, that lived through many's the battle. And this Old Abe, he sits there and at feeding time they give him a live chicken, and snap! he tears its head off and gobbles it up. That's a sight a man don't often come across, and I would admire to see it."

A scatter of sparks hung in the air high above Brandon, and the wail of a steam whistle and a faint puffing came to him from above, as if some still-to-be-invented flying train or boat were passing over his head. He had seen nothing of the kind displayed at the Exposition, and in any case knew perfectly well that it was an ordinary train crossing the high-arched Eads Bridge across the Mississippi. It was just that, though the bridge had been finished before he left St. Louis, it was new enough so that this was the first time he had experienced a train actually using it, and as he stood in the familiar dankly odorous darkness by the riverbank, the train's overhead passage seemed incongruous and somehow threatening. It represented progress, not poverty and decay, but it reminded him of Hercules's comment about St. Louis being a sorrier place than it had been.

Brandon had been walking for perhaps an hour after leaving Hercules, along the waterfront and the mile-long granite wharf, not as bustling with loading and unloading as he remembered them, then along the riverbank to where the bridge bulked almost invisibly against the night. As he walked, he turned over in his mind how he would handle the talk with Krista tomorrow. Impossible to tell her that he had spent the time since he last saw her tracking and killing her sister's murderers or letting them kill themselves; that just didn't fit in with any universe Krista Ostermann could inhabit. Not quite as impossible, but difficult, to tell her about Jess Marvell, and he had already decided he was not going to do that.

Anyhow, the letter she had sent for his Chicago bank to hold for him said that she was about ready to take on a different partner if she didn't hear from him, and she hadn't heard, so there might not be that much to talk about.

Engaged young women usually didn't find explanations of conduct from former lovers—in Brandon's case, formerly potential lovers—worth taking time to listen to. He grinned as once again he recalled the kink his thoughts had taken in Nebraska, putting together Krista's letter with John B. Parker's suddenly expressed fondness for St. Louis and coming up with an impossible sum. Parker was old enough to be Krista's father, and a good deal less honest and amiable than Berthold Ostermann had been before Parker's remote cousin had slaughtered Berthold and the others.

Brandon turned over in his mind the St. Louisans he knew of who were of a proper age and standing for Krista, and wondered which of them she might have pitched on. Charley Withers or Heini Stolz looked like the best prospects; if it was either one of them, he'd be a changed man after a year of marriage to Krista, who was probably the strongest personality to come up among the Ostermanns in a century. Brandon thought detachedly that he probably would have been taken over by Krista if they had married after Elise's death; now, if it had worked out that way, it would have been different. . . .

The river smell, a symphony of different kinds of rot but somehow not unpleasant, at least to one who had grown up here, eddied around him as he followed a path under the bridge. Some distance off a tiny fire sent a pale splash of red to the underside of the shoreward arch. One, or a bunch, of the homeless Hercules had mentioned, cooking something begged or scavenged, maybe stolen. Brandon grinned as John B. Parker came again into his mind. Parker, his sometime bodyguard Jake Trexler said, lived in fear of being garroted by some resentful or rapacious unemployed man; coming behind a prosperous-appearing man and quickly strangling him, sometimes fatally, with a length of cord or wire, and relieving him or his remains of any valuables, was becoming a popular crime as the depression deepened, and John B. Parker was strongly aware of it. Trexler's opinion was that unemployment was not needed as an excuse, that any rational man, knowing John B. Parker, would like to garrote him, which made his own job lively and interesting. John B. Parker would have to be a fool, Brandon thought, to be walking in the dark down by the Mississippi, with the poor and presumably desperate lurking in the night. . . .

So, he realized as a smell of unwashed clothes and old sweat engulfed him and an arm enclosed in rough cloth clamped around his neck, would Cole Brandon.

The attacker would have done better to use piano wire, cutting off the blood to Brandon's brain in an instant and constricting his windpipe completely; only half-choked, he retained enough alertness to slip into one of the identities he had created in his quest for Gren Kenneally. Probably Craig Bascom, the wandering hardcase who had trained a bunch of New Mexico townsmen into an irregular ranger force and perfected himself as a lethal fighter in the process of teaching his men.

Brandon, or the being that now occupied his body, sagged as if he had been deboned by a swift and thorough cook, lifting both feet clear of the ground. Blue-green fireworks blossomed in his eyes as the choking arm bit harder into his throat; as his weight pulled himself and his attacker forward, he drove his right heel upward with all his force and felt it slam into a softer surface than bone. The man holding him squealed like a pig as the knife goes into its throat, or like a man who has taken a bootheel in the testicles.

The ground rushed up to meet Brandon, and he twisted to one side, then slammed into it, breath driven from him by the weight of his attacker. He followed the twist all the way through, and was on top, still in the clutch around his throat. He snapped his head back, and felt a yielding crunch under the impact of his skull, and the arm relaxed.

He twisted away and sprang to his feet; he could see the shadowy form of his opponent rising, though unsteadily, to grapple with him. The man was keening wordlessly, whether in pain or fury, Brandon could not tell, then managed to articulate: "G'me money . . . ereyekeeyou." It took Brandon a few instants to interpret this as a death threat, if a feeble one, since the attacker was wavering on his feet.

Brandon poised himself for a head blow that would end the contest quickly, but the shadowy figure collapsed to the ground and resumed the shrill moaning of a moment before.

Brandon stood over him, unsure what to do. With an animal in straits like this, the kindest thing would be a head shot, but that wouldn't suit this case; anyhow, he had not thought to go armed in his native city. Hercules had the right of it, apparently; St. Louis was sadder and meaner than he remembered it.

"Fucking *starving,*" the man on the ground wailed hopelessly. "No food two days, er I'd have had you. No work, and I cain't even rob good."

"You gave it a fair try," Brandon said dourly.

"You gonna call the cops, mister?" the man said. "Might's well, they'll feed me something in jail after as they kick my ribs in. And I won't notice that so much after what you done to me."

The river-smell and the new odor of bruised herbage from the grass torn and trodden in the brief fight warred with the reek emanating from the man huddled on the ground: long-dirtied clothing, the bodily pungency of accumulated layers of sweat and worse, and, perhaps imagined but powerful, the sour stench of utter defeat and despair. It seemed to Brandon that something of it clung to him where the man's arm had gripped his throat and his body had pressed against him.

"You could get some food at the shelter on Green Street," Brandon said, remembering Hercules's mention of Chief McDonough's project.

"Full up," the man said. "Said they was sorry, but too many folks in need, they got to take care of the worst off."

Brandon fished in his pocket for a match and thumbnailed it into flaring light; the sharp sulphur smell seemed to clean the air a little. The broad face looking dazedly up at him was dabbled with blood and badly puffed and abraded, and the upper lip was clearly split. "You look in bad enough shape that they should let you in."

While the match still burned, he eased a bill out of his

pocket and looked at it: two dollars, enough for a couple of good meals and cheap lodging for a few nights. "If they won't, this'll see you right for a few feeds," he said, and put the bill in the hand that reached uncertainly for it.

The match's flame was nearly at the fingers that held it; Brandon shook it out and dropped it and darkness came back, impenetrable for a moment while his eyes adjusted to the absence of the feeble light.

The man said nothing, neither "Why?" nor "Thanks," just breathed heavily. Brandon stood up, and could think of nothing to say himself. "Good luck" would be stupid; the best luck the man had had was being smashed up trying to rob Brandon, and it wasn't going to get any better. "Goodbye" meant "God be with you," which seemed a dubious proposition.

Brandon walked away, wondering why he had staked the would-be robber to the means of prolonging his misery awhile. The depression wasn't Brandon's fault, and being assaulted certainly put him under no obligation to his attacker. Maybe it came down to doing something that at least didn't add to the city's sorriness and meanness.

It occurred to him that he had not had that violent a physical encounter in the course of hunting the Kenneallys over the often lawless frontier, and he grinned. Best you get back to the Wild West, Counselor, where things are comparatively safe and orderly.

But before then, he decided, he would treat himself one last time to the one thing that was imperishably St. Louis's glory.

Brandon savored the bitter smell of the beer mingling with the flower-scented air of the spring night and warmed to the forgotten cheerfulness induced by the diffuse glow of hundreds of tiny lanterns that canopied the beer garden in a web of light.

Saloons, like the waterfront dives and the place he'd taken Hercules to, were for the volatile drinkers, the ones who might be morose or humorously argumentative or quarrelsome, or all of those in turn, and, whatever the Babel of languages among the customers, pungently male and American in atmosphere. The beer garden, certainly this one, was a lighter-hearted place, open to the sky and not closed in, thronged with women as well as men—wives, sisters, sweethearts, daughters, even mothers and mothers-in-law—in couples, quartets, and larger groups around the tables that stretched to the bordering hedges, a couple of hundred people anyhow, old and young, mostly looking happy to be there and to be drinking what St. Louisans modestly admitted was the best beer brewed west of the Rhine. Brandon had spent most of his time lately in places that could not be taken for anything but bare-bones America, and it was a shock to see how European, how lighthearted, the town he had grown up in could be.

Outside, it probably was, as Hercules had said, getting sorry and mean, but here was the old St. Louis, and the beer he remembered. He raised the heavy mug and took a deep drink. There had been some good beer in San Francisco, even in Santa Fe, and some remarkable German and Bohemian brews available at the Exposition, but this was the beer all the others had to be measured against.

Chatter, some of it rapid-fire bantering German, some of it the more staccato French, most of it in a range of dialects of English almost as dissimilar from one another as the French and German, filled the air around him, mingling with the strains of the jaunty song the brass band in the center of the garden was playing. Brandon recognized it as something Elise liked to hum; something about having to go to a far-off city but coming back again joyfully to a lover. Now St. Louis was the *stadtele hinaus* he'd come to briefly, and the journey away could indeed end in joy.

Wenn i' komm', wenn i' komm' wenn i' wieder, wieder komm' . . .

His thoughts had turned so strongly to Jess Marvell that it was as if some cooperative spirit had almost managed to bring her into being, standing before him, but had got the assignment slightly wrong.

"Mr. Brooks," Rush Dailey said. "An unexpected pleasure to find you here. A man takes a turn around a new city to drink in the sights and spectacles, finds himself sauntering amongst the pleasure-seekers in search of a table to share, and wouldn't you know the first vacancy that turns up is right next to, I won't presume to say a old friend, but certainly a cordial acquaintance and benefactor."

"Friend will do fine," Brandon said. "Sit down, Rush."

By the time Rush Dailey had settled into his chair, plucking at the knees of his pipestem trousers to keep them from bagging, and unbuttoned his tight-fitting jacket, the stout, aproned waiter had appeared, taken his order, and vanished on the run. Jess Marvell's junior partner was scarcely out of his teens but was decked out in a good imitation of a prosperous businessman.

"Unexpected," Brandon said thoughtfully.

Rush Dailey shrugged and shifted to one side as the waiter set a full mug in front of him. "Miss Marvell did wire me as you would be passing through town," he said. "But no further particulars, so it's only a horse's chance I'd run acrost you amongst almost half a million people. I figured if it was meant that I'd cross your path, so I would, and if it weren't, then I wouldn't, so I let it come about it would."

This was close enough to the principles Brandon had followed in tracking the Kenneally gang, drilled into him by Ned Norland—look into every trace and sign, and if there weren't any to follow, let chance take over and see what was fated to happen—to make him somewhat uneasy. He first knew Rush Dailey as a news butcher on a train, a vendor of magazines, fruit, drinks, sandwiches, shaving gear, and what other sundries bored or hungry passengers might conceivably buy, and had never entirely shaken off that early impression of a wide-eyed, slightly comically ambitious youth. But boys Rush Dailey's age were seasoned cowhands, lawmen and outlaws, and Rush Dailey himself had functioned with great capability in the founding of what looked to becoming a highly successful business, and it was reasonable that he would develop his own personal philosophical approach to life.

He was also devoted to Jess Marvell in ways that went well beyond the business, Brandon was pretty sure, and hoped that what was, or pretty soon would be, going on between himself and Jess Marvell would not throw Rush Dailey into too much disorder.

"You will be joining Miss Marvell in Wyoming," Rush Dailey said.

"That was in the wire?" Brandon said.

"Miss Marvell don't stint on telegraphy," Rush Dailey said. "Gets as much into a telegram as most would in a letter, so there's no mistaking what she means. I expect when they get the telephone spread around some she'll be on it half the day telling folks in all the Halls what to do."

"Are you going on out there?" Brandon said, wondering if he would be traversing half the continent in company with the young man whose hopes, however unrealistic they were, he would be blighting. Maybe he could use the journey to find a way to let Rush Dailey down easily.

"In time," Rush Dailey said. "I have business to see to here on Miss Marvell's behalf. Supplying all the stuff the Halls need is trickier than a horse, and I am trying to get it lined up to have one firm handle on as much of the supplying and shipping as I can."

Brandon looked at Rush Dailey with some interest. There were not many companies that could undertake the kind of effort he described.

"It is important business I'm seeing to," Rush Dailey said, "but I'll allow, Mr. Brooks, there is more to it than that."

"What more?" Brandon asked.

Rush Dailey drank slowly from the beer mug, either to enjoy the flavor more thoroughly or to hide part of his face from Brandon for a moment. He set the mug down and said, "Well, now. As you know, Miss Marvell is a pearl among women, and it ain't to be denied that I have entertained sentiments towards her deeper and warmer than those of ordinary friendship." Brandon recalled that Rush Dailey had softened the tedium of train journeys by browsing in the dime novels he sold; apparently the prose had worked its way into his brain, tainting his speech.

"But," Rush Dailey said, "it ain't to be. Miss Marvell is set apart from me as if she was smack-dab in the middle of a moated grange with the bridge up."

"The, uh, age . . . ?" Brandon said, estimating that Jess Marvell had at least five years' lead on Rush Dailey.

Dailey shook his head. "Naw, that don't count for much no more. If a man can do a man's work, that's enough these days, and . . . well, it works the other way too. But you know perfectly well, Mr. Brooks, that nobody ain't got a look-in with Miss Marvell with you around, even in the hit-and-miss way it's been, so I have let my thoughts and propensities wander elsewhere and otherwhom."

Brandon thought that he should not have needed reassurance of Jess Marvell's feelings for him, but needed or not, it warmed him to have Rush Dailey confirm them.

"How is the, uh, wandering going?" Brandon asked.

"Come to a halt and the team unhitched," Rush Dailey said, but not as happily as the news seemed to call for.

"Another moated grange?"

"And the moat with alligators swimming and snapping," Rush Dailey said. "Riches and power ain't that much of a obstacle, for I'm on my way to them, and she's the sort to appreciate that, running a big business like she does."

Brandon sat upright in his chair and looked hard at Rush Dailey.

"I been dickering and dealing with her," Rush Dailey said, "and we are twin souls, doing business like it was a waltz and us knowing the steps better 'n Fanny Elssler. I *know* I could be the man for her, and I have seen her looking thoughtful-like at me whenas she has pushed me up five cents a hundredweight on shipping charges, in a way that makes me think she sees that too."

"What's the moat and alligators?" Brandon said warily.

"She has plighted her troth to another," Rush Dailey said, his voice hollowed by the half-empty mug he held to his face, then set down. "And that other is not worthy of her—ain't worthy of a flea-bitten three-legged coyote with the mange and a note past due at the bank, if you ask me, or anybody who knows him, for that matter, which you do, in fact, and I look to you to agree with me."

Brandon stared wordlessly. The surmise he had been fighting off—in a way, since Nebraska—came rolling toward him, horrible as a tornado writhing across the prairie.

"What a prime-grade lady like Miss Krista Ostermann sees in John B. Parker I'll never know," Rush Dailey said mournfully. "Without you know about Miss Krista Ostermann, you can't understand how outlandish it is, so I will tell you about Miss Krista Ostermann."

"You do that," Brandon said faintly, feeling as battered and dazed as the man he had left in the mud of the riverbank.

9

Brandon could not remember the last time he had seen Mound Farm by sunlight. His last visit had been under a three-quarter moon, and the time before that, he saw the farm buildings in the light of the fires that were consuming them.

Now it was more like the days when Mound Farm was the country retreat of Mr. and Mrs. Cole Brandon of Walsh's Row, St. Louis, or an almost convincing imitation of those days. The old Indian mound that gave the place its name loomed as always—no visible scars at the top, where Casmire lay buried, Brandon was glad to notice—across the fields from the farmhouse, stables, barn, and outbuildings. To Brandon's surprise, the buildings were whole again, roofs restored and smoke stains cleaned from the stone walls. But no smoke came from the kitchen chimney and there was no movement about the place, and what had been cornfields and a half-acre vegetable garden was a single field of chest-high weeds. Past the buildings he could see the dense woods, stretching down to a creek and continuing on the other side, into which Gren Kenneally and his men fled after killing Elise Brandon and the others and firing the farm. He caught a flicker of movement among the trees, perhaps one of the deer that used to come out and treat the vegetable garden as a free-lunch counter.

Squinting, Brandon could almost imagine that Elise was waiting for him there, but with his eyes open he could see that the place was desolate, no matter what had been restored. That would be Krista's doing, he supposed. Mound Farm was his property, but he had left his affairs in her hands to conduct as she chose, and she would have seen to getting the place ready to sell; certainly no member of the Ostermann clan would ever use it as a holiday retreat again. For someone else, even someone who knew what happened there, it might do well enough. There weren't a lot of places around here that didn't have some horrors connected with them if you looked back a ways; and Brandon and the Ostermanns had never troubled themselves about what dark doings the old mound would have known—burials at best, human sacrifices perhaps—just admired its antiquity and the picturesque touch it added to the property.

The thought reminded Brandon of his business here, and he flicked the reins, stirring the rented horse into motion, drawing the buggy along the road, on the point of being overgrown with tough grasses, that led down the slope to the farmhouse. The man who hired out the horse and buggy back by the railroad station was a stranger, which suited Brandon quite well; on the train up from St. Louis he had anticipated with distaste the prospect of greetings and condolences and curiosity from those who remembered him, but so far he had not encountered any such.

He dropped the reins over the hitching post at the farmhouse porch, noticing that under a coat of paint it was, on the side that faced the house, scored with intersecting lines where its surface had been charcoaled by the heat from the burning building. He stepped down from the buggy and walked up the stairs to the porch and into the house.

His steps on the flagstone floor reverberated in the room

with a hollow quality occasioned by the lack of furniture or curtains to disperse the sound. This had been the parlor, where Elise and he and whatever family members had been invited, often enough self-invited, to join them had sat in the spring evenings—summers, they'd be on the porch unless the insects were troublesome—and talked, played cards or simpleminded family games, or sung while Krista played the piano. Some German songs, but also the American tunes, half of them at least by poor Foster . . . Brandon tried, but could not see Elise and Krista and the others in this empty box, its fresh-plastered walls awaiting a new householder's wallpaper. Not even enough left to keep a ghost waiting around.

Brandon walked through a rear door to the hall leading to the kitchen and looked around. Like the parlor, it was empty, but not as featureless. The fireplace and oven were part of the structure, and had been cleaned and repaired, and the iron wood stove had been polished; even without tables, chairs, icebox, or pantry, it proclaimed itself a kitchen.

The iron door to the oven gleamed. That was where Gren Kenneally had hidden almost an eighth of the loot from the CRI&P robbery, concealing it from his men with, fairly certainly, the intention of retrieving it later and swelling his own share of the pot. But one of his men, Casmire, had known of the held-out money, and had come back to hunt for it on his own after a few months. He had not had a chance to retrieve it before Brandon and Ned Norland captured it, but had the dubious pleasure of seeing them discover it a bare few minutes before he obliged Brandon to kill him.

Brandon had meant to return the money to the railroad, but killing Casmire meant that such a course would raise questions he would not want to answer, and he chose to use it to finance the beginning of his hunt for Casmire's leader and the rest of the gang. Brandon's lips twitched as he considered the fact that the disguises he had assumed to track the gang had helped pay the expenses of it: To disguise yourself as, say, a trail cook meant that you had to do the job well enough to get paid for it.

The floorboards looked new. Good. Casmire's blood had stained the old ones, but, caked with ash, the dark blotch would not have been noticed until someone tried to wash the floor, and that could have been awkward. On the other hand, enough blood had been spilled in that house so that more of it, anyplace, would have been no surprise. . . .

Brandon stiffened. He heard nothing, but had a sense of another presence, nothing so definite as a shadow or a sound, but something like the lightest touch of a finger on the hairs at the back of his neck or an indeterminate stirring in his belly. He remembered Ned Norland telling him, not all that long ago: "Wagh! Iffen I hadn't turnt off my brains and let my guts tell me what to do more times 'n not, I'd been scalped or a pauper or both back in Andy Jackson's time." Brandon's gut was telling him something, but the message was not coming through clearly, unless it was "Don't get careless."

And there was another thing Ned Norland said then: "That old-time coin you dug out of the mound when we planted that feller . . . that's powerful medicine, and you best pay it mind whenas it's got somethin' to tell you." Well, it had told him some things from time to time, sometimes feeling hot, sometimes almost electrically charged. Always, it could have been imagination, but sometimes the "medicine" seemed to have put him on a trail he might otherwise have missed. And Chief Atichke in New Mexico recognized the snake sign on one side of it as an old, old symbol, maybe older than his people, that suggested strongly that Brandon had some kind of fate to see through.

Well, he had seen it through, and had followed the way of the hunting animal that appeared on the disk's reverse side, accounting finally for each man of those he sought. The disk had nothing more to tell him now, and he had no need of it or any wish to have it around him. He could have dropped it into the woods at Fairmount Park or sent it skimming into the Schuylkill as it flowed by the park, but it seemed to him fitting to return it to where he had found it. He started to reach into the pocket he had placed it in this morning, then stopped at the clop of hoofs and the grating of wheels on the gravel turning space at the front of the house.

He stepped through the hall and the empty parlor and onto the porch. A woman in a trimly cut blue dress and jaunty hat was stepping down from a light buggy drawn up beside the one he had hired; that was it, then, he must have heard some faint noise of the buggy's approach some distance off. . . .

The woman turned to him as she descended. "Mr. Stewart, I didn't expect to find you here this . . . *Oh.*"

She stared at him with eyes so widened that white showed above and below the irises, and gave a single sudden powerful shiver as if galvanized by a dynamo, then fell still.

Only for the slimmest fraction of a second had the line of the back, the curve of the neck sliding into the upswept hair, the bend of the blue-clad arm at the side of the buggy, combined to sketch a picture of Elise, but it was enough to shake Brandon powerfully; then it was clearly Krista, so like her sister in many ways, but so definitely not her.

"Krista," Brandon said. "I didn't expect to find you here."

Krista took a deep breath and her face relaxed, her look at Brandon fading from its almost fierce intensity into friendly or sisterly cordiality. "You didn't, Cole. I found you. I thought you were Arthur Stewart, who's thinking of buying Mound Farm. I wanted to come out and look at it before he did, to see if there was anything that needed doing, or at least to see anything he might pick on to get the price down. You don't mind that I sell it? It's your property, but you left me to handle your business when you . . ."

"That's fine, Krista," Brandon said. "It's time it was sold, and I know you'll get a better deal than I could myself. I came out here to . . . well, to kind of close out the past before I went to see you."

"You *were* going to see me, then?" Krista said. "That is

good to hear. I would not have wanted to depend on this accident that we should meet." Krista's English, normally easygoing though scrupulously correct, would revert in moments of stress to the polite formality of the schoolroom lessons that had instructed her in the language back in Germany, and her Ws would move well along the line toward V. If she slipped into German words or phrases, it was a well-known signal that she was mad as hell, and prudent people found important business elsewhere.

"Oh, yes," Brandon said. "I sent a messenger around to the office, asking to see you this afternoon. But—"

"Clearly I left the city not long after you did," Krista said, "so I did not get your message. Very well, then, Cole. We have met, though a little earlier than you meant, so let us . . . talk about what we would have talked about later on."

They sat on the edge of the porch as the morning sun climbed in the hard blue sky, and talked. They were careful to avoid elaborate explanations or apologies for what they had done and not done. Brandon gave much the same account of his wanderings as he had to Hercules the day before, concluding with his plans to close out his connection with his law firm, leave St. Louis for good, and start a career somewhere in the rapidly vanishing frontier.

"I've got used to how things are out there," he said, "and I wouldn't be comfortable back here any more. I'm not sure what I'll do, but I've found I can turn my hand to lots of things, and I expect I could do even others if I had to."

"What you know best is the law, so I think that is what you will come to," Krista said. "You will never be content to do less than the best that is in you, and that means the law."

"Maybe."

Krista gave a brief account of how she had taken over the controls of her father's linked enterprises, won the respect of the originally dubious managers and foremen, and started them on what seemed to be a depression-proof increase in prosperity. That was how she had met John B. Parker, looking for some funds to finance expansion. She did not mention the letter she had sent to Brandon's Chicago bank early in the year hinting at a change in the course of her life that Brandon might prevent if he replied within two months. That deadline was weeks in the past when Brandon picked up the letter, and he had seen no reason to ignore the deadline, or to mention the letter now.

"Mr. Parker was surprised that a woman could deal with him on equal terms in business, and even avoid some of the traps that he so often successfully set," Krista said. "He took an interest in me, to see how my mind worked, I think, so that he could find out how to get the better of me, and he couldn't, so that made him interested in other ways. And . . . well, we are to be married."

"Yes," Brandon said. "Well. I, uh, wish you all the best, Krista." The best that's possible if you're married to John B. Parker, anyhow—my dear, dear Krista, how can you?

"It is not as in novels," Krista said. "Mr. Parker is not a man of romantic temperament. But we will deal very well together, and he has enough respect for my mind for finance and trade that I am to have a hand in some of his businesses. Since you . . . since I have had to take over Papa's companies, I have made my work my life, and marrying Mr. Parker will widen my horizons. You will understand this, Cole; you have discovered the satisfaction in many kinds of work. And Mr. Parker is not completely as the newspapers show him; if you knew him—"

"As it happens, I do, some," Brandon said.

"Oh." Krista seemed taken aback at this, perhaps seeing that saying anything favorable about John B. Parker would be less effective with someone who had personal knowledge of him. "I don't recall that he has mentioned you."

"I was tired enough of who I'd been to be tired of the name as well," Brandon said. "Parker knew me under the name of Blake, Calvin Blake."

"The newspaper reporter he rescued from bandits in Colorado!" Krista said. "He has told me of that, how he rode his horse down a cliff to intercept them and shot one from his horse and freed you."

"Something like that," Brandon said, deciding not to switch the roles of the participants back to what they had been in reality.

"You must come and meet him while he is still in St. Louis," Krista said. "He will be happy to reminisce of your exciting times together."

"Doubtless," Brandon said. "But I have business in Wyoming and I'll be on my way there tomorrow, so I can't have the pleasure."

"Mr. Parker is going to Wyoming also," Krista said thoughtfully. "Perhaps you will meet there."

Brandon stiffened at a faint scraping noise that seemed to come from toward the back of the house, then relaxed as he saw the wind stir the branches of a tree shading the porch; a tree limb out back scraping another, that's all it would be. "Maybe," he said. He did not feel that it would be useful to add that John B. Parker was going to Wyoming to be, among other things, persuaded to further the business plans of the woman who was sun, moon, and stars to Cole Brandon.

"I should perhaps be selling railroad tickets to Wyoming," Krista said lightly. "It seems to be a good business. There is Mr. Parker, and you, and also an amusing young man who has been negotiating very fervently with me, he is also going to Wyoming soon." As she touched on Rush Dailey, Brandon saw that her face softened and that the corners of her mouth turned upward. She would have been aware of his infatuation, any woman would, and liked it at least a little. Brandon did not know if that news would elate Rush Dailey or—since it did nothing about narrowing or draining the moat surrounding Krista—deepen his despair; in any case he had no intention of mentioning it.

What needed to be said had been said, or as much of it as ever would be. Loss, regret, anger, love, Brandon and Krista touched on none of those, and so could ignore any part they might have in their relationship. For another twenty minutes they talked idly and comfortably, bringing up family reminiscences, recollections of good times at Mound Farm, safe talk, ephemeral talk, drifting away from the mind as fast as from the ear. When Krista said it was time to leave for the train back to St. Louis, even though Mr. Stewart hadn't materialized, she did not object to Brandon's wish to spend another hour at Mound Farm and catch the next train down. Their time there had rounded off their chapter, and railroad-car chat would have been a pointless temporary resuscitation of something decently interred.

It was just past noon when she left, and the buildings, the trees, the expanse of weeds in the old cornfield, all left the smallest possible shadow. The trees cast bold pools of shade on the ground, but the weeds seemed to exist in light only, with no contrasting dark to define them; they were like a giant furry pelt of brown-green spread over the field, stirred by the wind. The mound glared in the down-striking sun, seeming insubstantial with no side of it molded by shadow.

Brandon walked through the farmhouse to the back door. On the way through the kitchen he noticed the oven door was a little ajar and pushed it shut, irritably rubbing off onto his jacket some smudges of stove blacking. Outside, he found a long-handled spade leaning against the back wall, picked it up, and began walking toward the ancient mound.

Last time, the moon had just set, and he had relied on Ned Norland's practiced night vision to avoid major obstacles, doing his best not to let the occasional stumble over a stone or being snatched at by branches distract him into loosening his grip on Casmire's limp ankles. Now the route was easily seen and traversed, and in a few minutes he was at the top of the mound.

A few seasons of growth and weathering had obscured Casmire's grave, restored almost to its pristine state by Ned Norland's careful replacement of its surface, sod by sod. Right at what he remembered to be the center of the excavation, the ground had subsided slightly. No coffin, and Casmire was probably now a compressed tangle of bones, distorted by the weight of the earth pressing down after his softer components decayed.

That was about where the disk had come from, but Brandon felt that returning it to the mound was the big thing, not to any precise location in the mound. He selected a site a few feet away and jabbed at the turfy surface with the spade until he cut a piece about half a foot by a foot and almost three inches down. It would do, just pop the disk onto the raw earth of the shallow pit, slap the turf on, and get about his business.

He fished in his left front trousers pocket for the disk, and found a pencil stub and a crumpled note saying *Buy socks, 2–4 pr, black, brown.* Brandon frowned. He could visualize himself, that morning, picking up the disk and slipping it into that pocket, so it should be there.

Perhaps he was mistaken. He checked his other pockets, trousers, jacket, and shirt, without success. Casting his mind back over the short journey from St. Louis, it seemed to him that at one point he had idly thumbed the piece, so it would have to be someplace on his person.

It was not. He felt in the sides of his shoes to see if the disk could have dropped there and flexed his toes to see if they encountered any foreign object. He walked back to the porch and inspected its surface and the nearby ground, and ran his finger around the upholstery in the rented buggy. It seemed definite that the worn old metal disk Ned Norland had been so enthusiastic about, that Chief Atichke had invested with mystery, that seemed to have in some measure guided Brandon, was not there.

After he accepted that, he decided that Ned Norland might say that the piece had done its work and decided to move on, perhaps to assist someone else with a reason and need to hunt and kill. Fair enough. He was done with it, and just as glad it was done with him.

When, on the train back to St. Louis, his fingers encountered the disk in his pocket, he was at first considerably irritated, then amused. He remembered how often an important file would be missing at Lunsford, Ahrens &

Brandon, be hunted for desperately by attorneys, clerks, and partners, and after hours or days be found lying in plain sight, as if some natural process had thrust it from the bowels of the earth.

All right, Counselor, throw it in the Mississippi next time you're down by the riverbank. If you remember.

10

Brandon had passed through Omaha twice, earlier this year, but had not taken notice of the depot. Now, perhaps because of his exposure to the buildings of the Centennial Exposition, the huge girdered shed with its narrow roof clerestory seemed to him like an exhibition hall, say the Transportation Pavilion, which there hadn't been one of at Philadelphia, as far as he could recall. The fancied resemblance stopped with the structure; instead of a variety of exhibits, there were three railroad lines feeding in from the east and one heading out to the west, with, usually, one or two trains standing in the station waiting to depart.

Brandon's was there, its locomotive breathing quietly, like an asthmatic bulldog, its fires banked but not cold, waiting to be brought to full steam at departure time an hour and a few minutes hence. Brandon walked along the platform past the express car and the first two passenger cars—their weathered, shabby siding and a generally decrepit aspect marking them as destined for the use of emigrants to the Black Hills and other areas of settlement—to the last car, which, even in the muted light that filtered down from the narrow roof windows, gleamed with fresh paint, buffed glass, and polished metal.

Two day-coach trips across Nebraska had given him a strong disinclination to spend yet another clutch of days in the same way. Prairie was prairie, and it got damned dull looking at it day after day. Spending a brief time as a windmill salesman in this territory had left him able to distinguish among the main types and brands of windmill as he saw them from the train, which he expected would ease the boredom of the journey by as much as half of one percent. He had decided that from Omaha on, he would spring for the expense of one of the UP's palatial Pullman cars in which, if the illustrated weeklies' reports were to be believed, one could be whisked along as in a drawing room, enjoying polite diversions of all kinds and having drinks and light meals fetched from the kitchen at the end of the car; and then, at night, the drawing room was converted into comfortable sleeping apartments. It would still be prairie passing by outside, but it would be easier to ignore it.

He stepped into the car and found a porter who would take his valise and assign him to a "comfortable sleeping apartment," which, as he had expected, turned out to be a berth that folded out from the wall and would be concealed behind curtains flanking the car's central aisle. All the same, the saloon area of the car looked spacious and the over-stuffed seats seemed luxurious. Brandon found that he expected to enjoy the trip, and after a moment realized that it was the first time in a very long while that he had considered enjoyment as an aspect of his life.

The porter accompanied him down the steps and said, "This is one fine car, I'll tell you. Latest and comfortablest there is, and a pleasure to work in." He stopped next to where a laborer knelt on the platform and pushed boxes into a compartment slung under the car, and kicked the cake of ice that lay in the center of a spreading stain. "You get that ice in there 'fore it melts away, man. We don't want to give the passengers warm wine."

Brandon admired the storage compartment, an elegant elaboration of the facilities of the chuck wagon he had commanded on the long trail drive from Texas to Kansas last year.

"Now here," the porter said, "is something as'll interest you, sir." He kicked one of the massive wheels attached to the swiveling truck under the car and said, "What d'you expect that's made of?"

"Iron," Brandon said, puzzled at the question.

The porter shook his head and said, chuckling, "No, sir! Paper, that's what!"

The longheaded fellows working for George Pullman, Brandon learned without any great wish to do so, had discovered that paper, if you handled it right, was immensely strong, and had the elasticity to handle the shocks of rail travel without the danger of fracture presented by metal or wood, and, edged with steel, made the best wheels you could want.

Brandon had always taken train travel for granted, and preferred to keep it that way. Now he could reflect either that he was hurtling along at twenty miles an hour or more in a steel and wood box supported by pasteboard disks or, in a less up-to-date car, by more conventional wheels that might at any moment choose to disperse into a shower of fragments. On the other hand, he had always managed to avoid worrying about derailments, fires, collisions, and boiler explosions, so he ought to be able to manage not worrying about paper wheels.

With almost an hour to fill, he left the depot and gave himself a look at Omaha. He had heard of it as a bustling town of some twenty thousand, but saw a discouraged-looking place with dirty streets and men standing around in listless groups or in the doorways of shops without customers. A public clock had no hands, as if it did not matter what time it was in Omaha. The depression seemed to have hit here harder than in most places Brandon had been lately, and he wondered if the election would make any difference.

Perhaps, he thought, if the Greenbackers or the Prohibitionists win, or pigs fly, which is about as likely; they'd certainly stir things up, anyhow.

Or if Victoria Woodhull's crazy one-woman campaign succeeded, that'd be a turnup, wouldn't it? Free love made legal and God knows what kind of monetary reform . . . He tried to remember what there had been about Victoria Woodhull and her sister Tennessee Claflin at the Women's Pavilion in Philadelphia—something, but nothing he could recall clearly. Free love might be fun, but then, no it wouldn't, would it? Not with Jess Marvell only a thousand miles or so of steel rails away. There was love there, being freely offered, but even if Jess Marvell did not demand it, there was a price: Everything he had or was would have to be hers as much as his; whether Jess Marvell wanted that or not, it was what the situation demanded.

Brandon's interest in Omaha ran out before the time available to satisfy it did, and he returned to the depot. The platform, almost deserted before, was filling up with a highly varied crowd, people of all ages from infancy to antiquity and dressed in almost anything except plain traveling suits or dresses; they reminded Brandon of the displays of national costume different countries were showing at the Exposition, though these were a good deal more workaday and shabby. Headgear ranged from kerchiefs tied around some women's heads to stovepipe hats, and an unmusical symphony of languages reverberated in the cavernous shed: German, French, Italian, and Spanish were easy to identify, and he thought he heard some words in whatever tongue it was the Wendish colony he had met in Texas used; the nasalities and drawls of different areas of the States had their part in the composition.

Some were making their way into the passenger cars to which Brandon's Pullman was attached, and others were coming onto the platform through doors at the side of the depot. Brandon made his way against the flow of the crowd and found himself in a crowded, high-ceilinged room. From toward the top of a square wooden pillar supporting a ceiling beam, the head of a massive elk stared glumly at him, the expression perhaps being the result of the lunch pail it held in its mouth; its many-pointed horns were festooned with pots and lunch pails, and a neighboring pillar bore the explanatory sign:

LUNCH BASKETS FILLED FOR 25 CENTS
TAKE NOTICE BLACK HILLERS

The crowd, though denser than on the platform, was thinning as more occupants of the room left to board the train. These would be the emigrants, people from the East and from beyond the Atlantic, heading out to take up free land from the government or cheap land from the railroads, some bound for Cheyenne and points west on Brandon's train, others headed north to Sioux City, the railhead for the Black Hills.

Brandon found that he was looking at the emigrants with a kind of double vision. Through one mind's eye, so to speak, he saw them as the people who were fulfilling the promise of the country's first century, abandoning lives of poverty and oppression to become independent and productive in a free land, very like what the papers were fond of writing about in connection with the Centennial Exposition.

Through the other he saw them as Ned Norland had, the formless regiments of the army that would settle on the wild lands he had been traversing and transform them as completely as the periodic plagues of grasshoppers changed a field of standing corn to a desert of stubble, only more permanently. In the comparatively short time he had been in the West, Brandon had seen wilderness turned to townsites, and remote valleys suddenly pierced with steel rails and fogged with smoke, and the mounds and drifts of rusting or still-glinting tin cans that marked the presence of civilization just ahead.

He decided that it didn't matter what he thought of the

emigrants. They were there, and they would be there in growing numbers; it was a fact of life that the frontier was vanishing, and that whoever lived out here, as he seemed to be working his way around to do, would have to accept it.

Some of the people in the waiting room were talking animatedly, some were sitting quietly in family groups, others were buying supplies at the long counter that ran the length of the room. At one end of the room, next to a massive stove, mercifully unlit on this sultry day, he saw a man perched on a high stool with a large pad of paper supported on his jackknifed knees, and thought there was something familiar about the mane of blond hair and the occupation he was engaged in.

Brandon made his way down the room and found that his long-distance recognition was correct. "Mr. Vanbrugh," he said.

The man on the stool looked over the edge of his pad at Brandon, lifted his pencil from the paper, and pointed. "Newspaperman, Spargill paper. Never forget a face, but I'm no good at names."

"Calvin Blake," Brandon said. In not much more than a week he had been Cole Brandon to Tsai Wang and to Krista and the others in St. Louis, Charles Brooks to Jess Marvell, Beaufort Callison to Savvy Sanger, now Calvin Blake to Nelson Vanbrugh (with, to be sure, a mention to Krista of the Blake identity, just to tangle things a little more).

"Ain't this something?" Vanbrugh said, gesturing around the room with his pencil. "A big, blooming, buzzing confusion for sure, every kind of folks you can imagine. Old Breughel never had this kind of stuff to work with, I'll tell you."

Brandon craned his neck to get a look at the sketch Vanbrugh was working on. It was the same scene Brandon had been observing, but it seemed to vibrate on the paper, to be more alive than the living people it depicted. Even the lunch pail-festooned elk was more vivid than in actuality, sporting a leer that seemed to suggest that all the bustling humans below would, one way or another, wind up nailed to a wall.

"That's the first go," Nelson Vanbrugh said. "Gets the feeling of the thing, and I'll try to keep some of that when I get to the engraving. You do a photograph of a scene like this, and then engrave from it, you'll get every last detail right, down to the nails in the siding, and it'll be dead. The engraving I'll make from this, it'll maybe have a few less people than there are here, and some of 'em will be in different places, but anybody who looks at it that's been here will know it right off, be able just about to hear it or smell it."

So they would, Brandon thought. He also thought that if he collected pictures, he would a lot rather have Nelson Vanbrugh's sketches than the engravings of which he was so proud. The engravings were good, the ones he had seen, but the sketches were outstanding.

"Willson send you here to get pictures of the new wave of settlement?" he asked. Nelson Vanbrugh had left a well-paid but tiresome job of painting attractive scenes of Western landscapes to promote John B. Parker's passenger and emigrant railroad enterprises to join Abner Willson on the Spargill, Colorado, *Chronicle* as news artist, steel engravings being his passion.

"No," Vanbrugh said, staring over Brandon's head and rapidly sketching in a seated woman nursing a child in the far corner of the room. "Did my time there and loved it, couple of engravings a day of tragedies and triumphs of Spargill life, from the *tableaux vivants* the ladies of the Browning Society put on to the inauguration of Mayor Gerrish." Brandon considered the last item with some interest. Judge Gerrish had, among other things, explained to him the various paths the Kenneally family had pursued in the worlds of commerce, politics, and the professions as well as crime, and in fact was the man who had handed him the list of Gren Kenneally's associates in the CRI&P robbery and the Mound Farm murders. So now the Kenneally tentacles, however lawfully they might be behaving, had grasped the town government of Spargill. And who knew what else and where else?

"But once I'd found I could slap 'em out fast and still keep 'em good, there wasn't much more to interest me," Nelson Vanbrugh said. "And with the paper Willson could afford to buy, first-rate work wouldn't show up as it should. Anyhow, when I left, he wasn't too sorry; said my stuff was great, but folks would get uneasy when the mayor came out looking like a fox or the Browning ladies looked kind of more naked under the drapery in the *tableaux* than they ought to. But all I can do is get the line down the way I see it, and there's no help for that. So I cut out a few months back and racketed around, did a whole raft of sketches, and when I've got enough, I'll engrave the best of 'em and go around to *Leslie's* or one of the other weeklies and see if my stuff don't knock their eyes out."

"I'm sure it will," Brandon said. "Be interesting to follow these folks out West and draw what happens to them."

"I've seen that already, and drawn it some," Nelson Vanbrugh said. "Some good, some bad. They take up Homestead Act land free or railroad land for five dollars an acre, eighty acres maybe, and go at it. If they get the right land and the grasshoppers don't chew them up, they can make a go of it. I've worked for John B. Parker, and you and I know that he is a miserable bastard, but I got to say that he's giving the emigrants a chance—ten years' credit at six per cent, so's they pay the farm off at about fifty a year."

Brandon had seen last month in Nebraska how John B. Parker made such apparent fair dealing pay off, raising freight rates the farmers paid to ship their produce high enough to keep them on the edge of poverty.

"Done it!" Nelson Vanbrugh said. He slipped the pencil into a jacket pocket, held the sketch up in both hands, squinted at it, nodded, and slid it into a large pasteboard portfolio that stood on the floor next to the stool.

He stepped down from the stool and stretched. "You like my stuff, Blake," he said, as if it were a self-evident proposition. "Let me show you some of the things I've been doing since Spargill."

He found an empty stretch at the end of the counter, set the portfolio on it, and opened it. "This here's in Cheyenne, miners leaving for the Black Hills."

Brandon saw a picture of a stagecoach with what looked like twenty people crammed inside and half that number clinging to the top, waving cheerfully; a crude Conestoga type of wagon piled with boxes and trunks and men, pulled by six mules agitated into motion by a bearded rider flourishing a twenty-foot whip; a pack-laden pedestrian with a long rifle on his shoulder and a spotted dog bounding at his side; bystanders perched on benches or standing by the road waving farewells; with a distant prospect of brooding mountains sloping in the background.

"Some of that bunch was dead not a week later," Nelson Vanbrugh said. "The Indians are getting touchy about whites coming into the Black Hills. Supposed to be their land as long as the sun rises and so on, but once they found gold there, that don't hold any more, and the prospectors keep pouring in, and the Indians are starting to kill 'em off when convenient. There's troops being sent in to discourage that, General Custer in charge, and I expect he'll settle that soon."

The hopes and plans of the emigrants and how they would fare at the hands of John B. Parker, the ambitions of the miners and the resistance of the Indians . . . Brandon sensed these floating in his mind, as if seeking ways in which to relate to each other. . . . As the frontier filled up, there would be more and more conflicts and problems that would have to be sorted out, either by the operation of law or by the law of force. A man looking for an occupation in that raw country could find something to keep him busy there. . . .

Brandon looked on as Vanbrugh turned over the sketches, giving a brief description of where he had done them. They were good, but Brandon knew that the train's departure time was coming near, and consulted his watch.

"Thanks, Vanbrugh," he said, but I've got to . . ." He stopped and looked at the sketch the artist had just turned over, feeling a chill seep through him.

"The Yellowstone Park," Vanbrugh said proudly. "Damned tough getting there, but it's worth it. Don't usually like to do pictures without people, but this is different. This one's what they call the Grand Canyon of the Yellowstone."

Brandon had seen the identical scene last month in a photograph in Carl Swanson's shop in Bigsbee, toward the western edge of Nebraska: in the distance a high waterfall, partly hidden by sheer faces of rock plunging down the right side of the drawing into a turbulent river which coursed between the slabs of rock to the right and an upthrust formation to the left. A jagged peak topped an overhang suspended above the rushing water like a balcony. Far off, a fluted wall of rock seemed to bar forever any human passage.

Brandon looked at the sketch as he had at the photograph, with a strong feeling of unease. Now, as then, what he saw impressed him as the setting for a drama too vast and horrible for a stage to hold. In Bigsbee he had associated it with his hunt for Gren Kenneally and the others, but that was over now; there was no reason for this view of a picturesque wilderness to trouble him. He found that his hands were in his trouser pockets, and that the fingers of the right hand were stroking the old Indian medallion, and tingling at its touch.

"Thanks," he said to Nelson Vanbrugh. "I'd like to see more, but I've got to catch my train. Good luck with *Leslie's* or whoever."

Brandon felt the coin as he hurried across the platform to the Pullman. He had meant to throw it from the train window on the way to Omaha, as they crossed the Mississippi, but had forgotten to do so. Maybe, if he and Jess Marvell ever toured the Yellowstone, that would be a fitting place to dispose of it, among the boiling springs and fuming cracks that led to the underworld.

11

Brandon supposed that the rules of social encounter in a Pullman drawing room might be something in between those suited to the public rooms of a hotel and those of a party in a private house. The train was a public place, but the enforced intimacy of travel in close quarters seemed to make a degree of familiarity acceptable.

In any case, the handsome woman of about his own age who sat on the pillowy divan next to him seemed at ease about doing so, and striking up a conversation. Brandon had been testing the proposition that prairie, seen through the haze generated by a good cigar and the glow induced by good whiskey, from a vantage of luxurious softness, wasn't nearly as tedious as usual, and made a gesture falsely indicating his willingness to extinguish the cigar if his self-invited companion wished.

"I admire the odor of a fine cigar," she said, the Southern tinge to her speech making it "seega'." She looked appreciatively at the plump, long brown tube, redly smoldering at the tip, that extended from Brandon's hand. "They're so . . . manly." Brandon was a trifle taken aback at the fervor of her tone, and reproached himself for the lewd speculation about what she found admirable that sprang to his mind.

The reproach faded as Mrs. Davenant, a "lorn widow lady adrift in the great world" by her own account, disposed her person, as opulently stuffed as the divan, in attitudes suggesting that she would be as comfortable as it to lie on, or with, and talked of the pleasures of "palace car" travel, of which she claimed great experience. In particular, she said, she had learned which of the sleeping apartments in this class of car was the most comfortable and afforded the most privacy, and had made sure to secure it for herself. Number four, it was, she said, a very easy number to remember, "don't you agree, Mr. . . . ?"

The fact that Mrs. Davenant's presence, style of conversation, scent, and evident accessibility were having a palpable effect on Brandon firmed his resolution not to let things go further. He was too old to have any sentimental feelings about holding himself relatively "pure" for Jess Marvell, but even a casual involvement on the way to her would seem silly and demeaning.

"Blake, ma'am, Calvin Blake," Brandon said. He felt in his vest pocket and, as he hoped, found a small oblong of pasteboard that had been there since Bigsbee. "My card, ma'am; as you'll see, I'm proud to represent the Nonpareil Wind Machine Company of Chicago, Illinois. I expect you've seen the many windmills embellishing the prosperous farmsteads along the route, but I don't guess you'll have reflected on how important those windmills are, uh . . . ." He reached back to recall what he had studied in Nonpareil's advertising leaflet, preparing to act as a salesman for them as his most recent Kenneally-hunting mask. "Powered by the providential powers of the winds of the air, they achieve their true triumph by making possible a reliable supply of water to the farms that have civilized the West in the first century of our nation's independence."

Brandon thought he might have garbled Nonpareil's text a little, but that seemed not to have diminished its soporific effect; Mrs. Davenant's eyes had a slightly glazed look, and she was breathing shallowly.

"It's the patent Catesby vane that gives your Nonpareil its superiority over the competition, Mrs. Davenant," Brandon said earnestly. "Keeps the fan, that's the part that spins, turned directly to catch the wind. Unlike your Halliday type of fan, that's got such a lot of slats to it, and a tiresome kind of machinery to make them all turn at once to get the wind, that's always breaking down. I can't, of course, fetch out my sample case and demonstrate one right here for you, for it'd be a mighty heavy case to carry!" Brandon laughed immoderately at this piece of trade wit, and was rewarded with a tightening of his divan-mate's mouth.

"I don't have a farm," she said, "so I don't need a windmill."

"Everyone who needs water needs a windmill," Brandon said firmly. "Even if you're on city water supply, pipes can break. A windmill over a well is your surety of life-giving, health-giving water at all times. The Nonpareil can also be adapted to grind feed or shuck corn, even gin cotton or saw wood, and what household does not have some such work to be done? I have drawings and specifications and order blanks back by my berth, and would be glad to fetch them out."

"Don't trouble on my account," Mrs. Davenant said. "I believe I see Mrs. Robichaux of Charleston, South Carolina, at a table yonder, and must renew my acquaintance; good day, Mr. Blake."

"Ma'am," Brandon said. He watched her sway across the car, and a primitive portion of him growled its regret. It would be nice to see Mrs. Davenant's smooth face red and sweaty and gasping, and creamy undersides of thighs exposed by knees drawn up to shoulders . . . but a lot nicer with Jess Marvell. He had never had a really specific sense of erotic attraction with her, or romantic attraction, for that matter; just a complete conviction that they were needed to complete each other, and could do nothing to alter that. The erotic and the romantic would be there, he knew, and, he suspected, with an intensity neither of them had experienced before, but they would be part of the whole thing, the undefinable but overmastering magnetism that was drawing him across half a continent.

Mrs. Robichaux seemed either to have departed suddenly or to have turned invisible, for Mrs. Davenant sat at an empty table next to a window and stared moodily at the unwinding vista of prairie.

Brandon smoked and looked at prairie, doubtless much the same from this side of the car as from Mrs. Davenant's, and let nonspecific but highly pleasing thoughts of Jess Marvell drift through his mind.

A man in a broadly striped suit and a soft hat sank into the portion of the divan vacated by Mrs. Davenant. Somewhat to Brandon's surprise, since he did not seem the reading sort—a salesman, of a good deal brasher kind than the comparatively restrained Calvin Blake of Nonpareil, he would have guessed—the man opened a thick, new-looking book and began to read with apparent interest.

This seemed to flag after a few moments, for the reader began leafing through the book, pausing every ten or twenty pages to scan the facing pages briefly, then pressing on. Once having passed through the book in this manner, he began reading from close to the beginning again.

But the book no longer held him, and he looked up at Brandon, grimacing irritably. "What a sell!" he said.

"What is?" Brandon said, knowing that there was no point in trying to stall him with silence. This kind would talk all the way through, once they were started; it was what made them good salesmen, if they were.

The man held up the book. "This! Banned in Denver for immorality, it said in the papers, so I got a copy in off a fellow I know in Omaha that's always reading and buying new books and foolishness like that, and figured to have some nice lively reading for the trip."

"And it's not that," Brandon said.

"Not lively the way a man likes it, if you take my

meaning," the disappointed reader said. "There is a lot of things going on in it all the way through, but none of 'em of that kind, if you understand me."

"What does it have in it, then?" Brandon said. "Ladies' stuff by Fanny Fern or such?"

"Not even that," the man said. "Some trash about a boy named Tom that's told off to whitewash a fence and tricks the other boys into doing it for him, and it seems to go on with this Tom and his pal Huckleberry and dumb kid doings for about three hundred pages."

"Nothing blue about it, huh?" Brandon said.

"No." The man looked thoughtful. "D'you suppose 'whitewashing' stands for something kinder salty? Something they get up to in high-class parlor houses that don't get generally knowed? Maybe if you was to know what what's wrote down here means all the way down, you'd find it was gamesome stuff after all."

"Could be," Brandon said. He nodded toward Mrs. Davenant's brooding, seated figure. "That lady's a literature hound, I happen to know. I don't doubt she'd explain any hidden meanings in the book to you, if you asked."

"If whitewashing and like that is something strong, I'd be kinder embarrassed to ask her about 'em," the man said. "A lady and all."

"Ladies that like literature are prepared for what's in it," Brandon said. "I don't expect you'll embarrass her."

As he watched the man make his way down the car, Brandon was not sure he had done either of them a favor, but was reasonably certain that they deserved each other.

He rose from his seat and walked back toward the bathroom. It was a luxury to feel like using the toilet whenever nature gave even the slightest prod. In most passenger cars, people preferred to wait until the absolutely last possible minute before rushing to the fetid closet that served their needs, praying that someone else had not reached that extremity just previously.

Back in the car he paused to inspect a table of four men of a tradesmanlike appearance playing poker.

"Join us, sir?" one of them called.

"Thanks, no," Brandon said.

"Why, damn your eyes," another man at the table said, his snarl slurred with whiskey, "ain't we good enough to play with?"

Standing over the seated men, Brandon could see that the last speaker affected a wider brim to his hat than the others, and had a gun belt around his waist, complete with holster and the protruding butt of a revolver. A hay, grain, and feed merchant from Omaha probably, but he'd traveled in the West, or wanted it to be thought he had, and he was putting on some bad-man attitudes.

"Good enough and more," Brandon said lightly. "But I don't care to play just now."

"Why, damn your teeth," the wide-brimmed man said, "you can't brush by us like that, a damned insult. You better take a hand in this game or be prepared to defend yourself."

Brandon did not consider gunplay a serious possibility, but he could see that the wide-brimmed man's companions were tipsy enough to be amused rather than shamed by him, and would not be much help in damping him down; there was certainly a good chance of a noisy scene, which might get the cardplayers thrown off the train, but could also subject Brandon to the same fate. Conductors were the autocrats of the trains, and there was no effective appeal to their decisions, which could be arbitrary.

Brandon had come up to the table more or less as Calvin Blake. It was time to turn the job over to Beaufort Callison, the itinerant gambler who had made a place for himself in the mining town of Kampen mainly by hardly ever gambling, for which he had little aptitude. Callison was in part Brandon's recollection of Dan Doyle, the icy-eyed professional gambler who had once owned the weapons he now relied on. Brandon recalled seeing Doyle cow a farmer who wanted redress after a game by a look, not menacing but avid, as if an aggressive move would please him above all things. Doyle's look had been backed by his arsenal, including the gun in the sleeve holdout, and Brandon was once again unarmed; but he calculated that getting into the part, as Edmund Chambers had advised, would work.

He twitched a chair to a vacant place at the table and sank into it. "Well, sirs," he said in a soft, almost whispering voice, "it's some time since those who know me have cared to ask me to play, and I appreciate the kindness." He looked from one to the other, keeping his eyes dead and cold, but letting his mouth open in a doglike grin that showed a little of his tongue, as if he found the four throats facing him somehow immensely appetizing.

"Uh, we, I'm afraid we, ah, don't know you. . . ." the man who had hailed him said.

"Beaufort Callison," Brandon said with a touch of impatience, as if his face should have been familiar to them, possibly from the *Police Gazette* or a Wanted poster. "Now that you know, I'll understand if you prefer not to include me in your game."

There was a silence as the four men, with Wide Brim suddenly looking close to sober, considered this statement and wondered whether it would be safe to ask why the name of Beaufort Callison should appall them, since the reason might include extreme irritation with people who were so ignorant as not to know of his infamy.

Brandon leaned forward and took the deck of cards from the center of the table. He fanned them, found the ace of clubs with a grunt of satisfaction, and creased it with a thumbnail. Four pairs of eyes watched him, fascinated, and four Adam's apples bobbed as the men swallowed in response to a sudden dryness of the tongue. Brandon looked up at them, glacier-eyed still, and slid the ace of hearts from the deck and creased it. "I always inspect the deck before I play to see that it's square," he said. "Any objections to my doing that?"

"No," one of the men said humbly and sadly, watching Brandon mark the ace of diamonds.

"I don't like markers, but I'll take 'em," Brandon said.

"It's sometimes troublesome, but I've always managed to collect. I'm agreeable to it this time, after you've run out of greenbacks and coin, as I don't travel with much spare cash, so I'll be anteing mostly markers, backed by some mining claims I have out in Arizona."

"Uh, how . . ." one of the men said, then fell silent, seeming to feel that continuing with "do we know the claims are worth anything, if they exist at all?" would not be prudent. There would also apparently not be much point to it, since this Callison did not seem to intend to gamble, as the term was usually understood; that is, indulge in a game in which there was some element of uncertainty or chance that he might have to make good on his markers.

Three of the men looked at their companion in the wide-brimmed hat, silently indicating that he had got them into this mess, and it was time he did something about it.

Brandon did not like Wide Brim, but had to commend the efficiency with which he handled the situation, grabbing his belly and squalling, "Get me to the crapper, boys! I got a raging attack of the squitters coming on!"

His companions sprang to their feet and, as if rehearsed in the maneuver, supported him under each arm and at the back, and bustled him off. One turned and said to Brandon, "Sorry to break up the game, Mr., uh, Callison, but it's distressful to all around if Charlie gets caught short with one of these spells."

Brandon nodded and said, "Another time."

The door to the bathroom closed behind Charlie and his friends. Brandon wondered if Charlie's malady were pure invention, or whether sudden apprehension had both provided inspiration for and added verisimilitude to the ruse. He riffled through the cards, found and extracted the queen of spades, and set it in the center of the table before rising and returning to the center of the car. Coming back and finding what was popularly known as the Death Card staring up at them should confirm their disinclination to have anything to do with Beaufort Callison.

* * *

Before he stepped down on the platform, Brandon slipped the .38 into his jacket side pocket. This bleak town in the hilly west of Nebraska didn't look as if it could field anything considerable in the way of menace, but that could be deceiving. A thug could appear from around a corner and do to a strolling passenger what the man by the river in St. Louis had tried to do to Brandon, and be away with his loot in seconds, and pursuit hampered by the victim having to be back on board and away in a few minutes.

He mostly stayed in the Pullman at these stops, but he hankered for fresh air and a walk on hard earth instead of carpeted floor. Also he had noticed a long lunch wagon, like the one Rush Dailey and Jess Marvell had devised and operated as the first step in the business that had become Marvel Halls; it would be interesting to see how this one was being run.

It was certainly drawing enough custom, for what seemed like most of the emigrants were pressed up against it, waving coins at the wagon's proprietor, who was grabbing and pocketing them and calling back orders to a man at the stove behind him.

"I don't see how you folks'll all get fed in the little time we're here," Brandon said to a man next to him who wore massive boots and a tall fur hat that seemed almost an extension of his luxuriant beard and mustache, so that the squinting brown eyes and button nose seemed to be all that was visible of the face of someone who had been swallowed by an extremely hairy troll.

"Condyuktr sad spatial lung stop," the man said. "Heff ar, planty time eat. We not had hot food a couple days now."

Brandon thought that they would need the full half hour, since the cookstove, though lit, did not seem to be doing anything much, and, he could see, drawing on his weeks on the chuck wagon, the food and utensils were not laid out for fast action.

As the emigrants' excited voices quieted, all having placed their orders and paid, a booming voice rolled across the platform: "Awaboooaard! Bort!"

Brandon swung around to see the conductor standing at the top of the steps of the front passenger car. "All passengers back on the train! Booaard!"

There was an instant concerted yell of protest from the platform and a knot of angry men and women formed in front of the conductor. Brandon pushed through the crowd, mounted the front steps of the second car, and stepped through the vestibule until he was almost next to the conductor.

"Can't help it," he was telling the protestors. "Train's late and we got to make up the schedule. It ain't my fault I couldn't get you the time I said—you can't argue with the engineer. Now you go tell your folks that don't know the language to get back on, fast."

"Money, our money, we got to get back from lunch man," a woman called.

The conductor shook his head. "No time for that, I'm afraid. Train's about to pull out."

Brandon's glance across the platform at the smug face of the lunch wagon proprietor and the knowing look he shot at the conductor confirmed what the conductor's lie had pretty well told Brandon. A train's conductor was its monarch, and it stopped when he signaled Stop and went on when he signaled Go on. Also, the porter two hours ago had proudly reported that the train was well ahead of schedule. The conductor and the lunch wagon man had devised a simple scheme to add to their revenues: Take orders and payments for food, whisk the customers away before delivery or restitution was possible, and split the proceeds.

He eased the .38 out of his pocket and stepped next to the conductor, tapping the side of the blue uniform jacket with the barrel. The conductor looked down at the weapon, then quickly up at Brandon, who moved the pistol so that its muzzle rested firmly over a kidney.

"You saw it, now you feel it," Brandon said. "Let's do this fast." Carter Bane had been a compound of Dan Doyle's menace and the general flintiness Brandon had seen in cowtown hardcases, and had been pretty effective both in coercing and in gunplay. Brandon stepped aside a little and let Bane take over. "These people paid to eat, and you're going to give them the time to do that," he said. "Cut the crap about the engineer. You give the orders and you know it. You go find a hotbox or a square wheel or something that'll take about half an hour to fix."

"You wouldn't shoot me in cold blood," the conductor protested.

"The only kind I've got," Brandon said. "Anyhow you'd sooner have me do that than yell down to those folks what you've been doing and then kick you off the steps and let them take you. They'd have their lunch then, raw and fresh, I wouldn't doubt, and they wouldn't mind picking the buttons out of their teeth."

The conductor paled and said, "Jesus! Hey, even if we stop half an hour, Grover ain't set up to . . . I mean, he wasn't figuring to actually . . ."

Brandon grinned. "I will help Grover. Could be I will show him a thing or two about how to feed folks." Chuck Brooks had fed a trail gang damned well for a long drive; time for Carter Bane to step back and let Chuck Brooks onstage.

Brandon sat back in the opulent chair and watched the hilly country that replaced the plains slide by, and grinned with satisfaction. Grover had objected to the change in plans only until a cast-iron skillet across the face had stifled him and it was made clear that the next correction would be made by submerging his head in the pot of grease simmering on the stove. Chuck Brooks's organizing skills had got food served out—not always what the patrons had ordered, but solid and well cooked, and when Grover's supplies had predictably proved to be insufficient, Brandon superintended a raid on the Pullman's underslung ice chest and made up the shortage. The conductor had raved, though quietly, since he was still hostage to Brandon's concealment of his duplicity.

All in all, it had been fun, and the emigrants had not

been embittered, perhaps permanently, by a heartless swindle. It occurred to Brandon that, since Omaha, almost all the identities he had assumed in the long quest for Gren Kenneally had come into play: the salesman, the gambler, the hardcase, the cook . . . everybody but the newspaper reporter.

A fruity blast of gin-soaked breath engulfed his head, fetid in his nostrils and even stinging his eyes. The conductor's rage- and gin-distorted face leaned close to him, speaking venomously but softly enough not to be overheard by the nearest passengers.

"You had the gun back there, and I done what you told me. But we're back on *my* train now, Mr. Weisenheimer, and the gun's no good. Just you wait here, or if you've a mind to make it easier on yourself, jump off the train. We're doing thirty miles an hour now, so you'll break your neck nice and clean."

As the conductor strode from the car, Brandon speculated on what retribution he might have in mind. Not hard to see; there was usually a railroad detective traveling with the express car, and the conductor would be summoning him to apprehend this dangerous malefactor and emigrant-feeder.

About the only aspect of what he had done that might prove ticklish was the raiding of the Pullman's supplies; the rest of it the conductor would have to be somewhat evasive about if his scheme were not to come to the attention of the railroad management.

As he expected, the conductor was returning, followed by a slender man in a derby hat, looking every inch a railroad detective . . . every inch a specific railroad detective, in fact.

"Mr. Trexler!" he called out as the pair approached his seat. "A pleasure to see you again after all this time! Calvin Blake of the Spargill *Chronicle,* remember?"

"Of course," said Jake Trexler, who had last seen Brandon indeed as Calvin Blake, but only a few weeks ago, during

Brandon's term as a windmill salesman. "How's the paper doing?"

"Fine," Brandon said. "I'm working on a special series, the emigrants who are building the West and the treatment they're getting."

The conductor, who had been swelling with triumphant rage as he bore down on Brandon with Jake Trexler in tow, deflated perceptibly at this exchange, and looked anxiously from Brandon to Trexler.

"I got to say, I couldn't make out what you were dragging me along here for," Trexler said, "but I thank you for putting me in the way of meeting Mr. Blake again. He is one newspaper reporter that it's best to stay on the good side of, and is personally known to John B. Parker."

"Shit," the conductor said.

"Yeah," Brandon said. "But you can lift yourself up out of it if you lay off fleecing the emigrants and get that Grover to give them fair dealings or get out of business. You do that and I just never heard about you, so there's nothing to write up in the papers or to pass on to John B. Parker."

The dawning hope, relief, and gratitude in the conductor's eyes would have done credit to a Chicago politician just learning he had failed to receive the endorsement of the Prohibition Party.

After the conductor left, Brandon summoned the waiter to bring drinks for Trexler and himself. When they came, Trexler sipped at his and looked closely at Brandon.

"Finished, aren't you?" he said.

Brandon saw no point in fencing with him. Jake Trexler had brought him to Mound Farm in time to see Elise's body being carried out; Jake Trexler had seen his subsidence into frozen apathy after Casmire's acquittal; Jake Trexler had seen him as Calvin Blake, reporter, and Calvin Blake, windmill salesman; Jake Trexler had known he was engaged in some desperate enterprise and had made sure not to know what it was; Jake Trexler was entitled to straight talk, if not yet the whole truth.

"Yes," he said.

Trexler nodded. "I almost didn't recognize you, Mr. Brandon—oh, you're still going by Blake, aren't you?"

"Doesn't matter," Brandon said.

"I guess it wouldn't. Thing is, you look younger, like a different man. A little the way you did when I came to you in St. Louis, before everything, but not altogether. A new man, somehow, I'd say." He looked questioningly at Brandon.

"It'd be good to think that," Brandon said. It was not the time to go into what it was he had finished; there could be too many things about it that a conscientious detective would have to take notice of. "Say, I'm surprised you're not traveling with John B. Parker."

Jake Trexler accepted the change of topic equably. "I'm more pleased than surprised. I am going to Cheyenne, to meet him there and take up the bodyguarding again. I would rather be chasing train robbers or checking on thieving conductors, but John B. Parker seems to think I can keep him from being garroted, so he keeps sending for me. I gather I'm to have double duty this time, for the old bastard's bringing along some lady who's had the bad luck to get herself engaged to him. I can't work it out whether she's blind and deaf and otherwise impaired, or will do anything for money. A Miss Otterburn, I think she's from your town, St. Louis. You know her?"

"Not Otterburn, Ostermann," Brandon said evenly.

"You know her, then? Hey, I'm sorry if I said anything to . . . Ostermann? That was your wife's . . . A relative?"

"Her sister. She isn't blind or any of the rest, and has more money than she'll ever use, so I can't come even close to figuring out why."

Jake Trexler drained half his glass in one gulp, then stared at Brandon. "It's a terrible thing to say of any man, Mr. Brandon, but you are going to be John B. Parker's brother-in-law."

It had never struck Brandon just that way, and he wished

it had not struck Jake Trexler. He would have to be a very new man indeed to get past that.

But it was remarkably interesting that Krista had said nothing to him of intending to accompany John B. Parker on his trip west, indeed had commented lightly on how many other people were going to Wyoming. She had made up her mind after she talked to Brandon at Mound Farm, that was clear. Why she had was not at all clear.

12

The Cheyenne night belonged to the saloons and gambling houses. Their glaring red and blue illumated signs,

KENO FARO ARCADE
MONTE SALOOON MONTANA
BELLA UNION

provided most of the light on Main Street, making the few streetlamps look like pale afterthoughts, there to show that Cheyenne *had* streetlights, just like Philadelphia or Denver, even though they weren't good for much.

The signs also had the effect of turning the pedestrians and the men who lounged in the doorways, doubtless harmless riffraff, into operatically menacing lurkers; even, Brandon noticed, Jake Trexler, whose face, next to him, was a pallid blue up to the middle of his nose, and diffuse darkness, shadowed by his hat brim, above, with the glint of an eyeball punctuating it.

"How many Ls in 'saloon'?" Jake Trexler asked.

"One," Brandon said.

"I *meant* O's," Trexler said, as if Brandon should have known. "Look."

Brandon checked the Monte's sign ahead and said, "I think they stuck an extra one in. Maybe they wanted to be sure nobody thought it was a salon, which they wouldn't want one of in a place like this."

"Well, we don't want to go to a place that gives itself an extra O, do we?" Jake Trexler said.

"Not when it's a block away and there's a place right here," Brandon said.

They stepped into the Montana and set about judging its beer. Whiskey in places like this was an uncertain proposition, and Brandon in any case meant to spend more time drinking tonight than hard liquor would let him. Beer had a safety-valve property, having to be pumped out before it could permeate the brain completely.

So far it had been a pleasantly drunk evening, like some that Cole Brandon had had with friends or colleagues in St. Louis, back in the Old Stone Age or some time that seemed as long ago, and not since. It was a strange feeling to be in one of these places and not be surveying drinkers, wondering if among them there was a man he was hunting, or a man who had some piece of information that would put him on the trail. Just leaning on a bar with a man he liked well enough, having a few drinks and being a little foolish . . . A long time since he'd done that, and he felt rusty at it.

Getting off the train, he had been unsure what to do next. Finding the Marvel Hall and presenting himself to Jess Marvell would be the logical thing, but the evening was already well advanced, and he felt gritty and stale after the long train journey, in spite of the Pullman's luxurious washroom. At Jake Trexler's suggestion, he took a room at the Inter-Ocean Hotel, which had a metropolitan look that contrasted with most of the rest of the town, and decided to call on Jess Marvell in the freshness of the morning.

That settled, he took up Trexler's suggestion of an exploration of Cheyenne's night life, which so far had found them sampling the delights of the McDaniels Variety Theater (extremely pretty girls serving drinks during a remarkable trapeze act) and the Bella Union (not-quite-as-pretty women dealing faro and lansquenet) and the spectrum of saloons, among which the Montana was toward the indigo end. Brandon sensed that this would be about the last stop; next, the journey, with considerable care to keep from weaving, back to the Inter-Ocean and deep sleep. And after that, another day, a day for opening a door and finding Jess Marvell behind it.

"What you said on the train, Trexler," he said, "about me being a new man, I get a feeling that's right. New, like I could be anything, and I have to figure what."

Jake Trexler pulled at his beer and sighed. "Brandon"— the "Mr." had fallen away early in the evening—"you can be anything, but only what you are, see what I mean?"

"Sure," Brandon said, impressed. Trexler's words seemed immensely significant, though he could not explain in detail what they meant.

"And whoever you're gonna be, you have to, have to . . . ah, drop the pack."

"Pack?" Brandon said dubiously. This was so significant that he couldn't make out what it meant at all, powerful stuff.

"What you carry on your back," Trexler said. "All the stuff you bring along, stuff you picked up, 's not you but what you been carrying. Got to take it off and leave it."

A chill wormed through Brandon, and he was suddenly sober. Whatever Trexler's beery philosophy might mean, his words faced Cole Brandon with a clear imperative: The only way out of the past and into a new life was to lay down the burden, and that meant telling Jess Marvell what he had been doing, what he had become. That was going to be harder than facing bullets, he suspected.

"You look as if you've had some hard traveling," Jess Marvell said.

Brandon nodded gingerly. He was not quite hung over, but a bath, a shave with hot towels, and a breakfast carefully chosen to be restorative without placing too strong demands on the system had not got rid of all the iron filings behind his eyeballs or evicted the small moths that had settled in his stomach, with a minor colony in his skull.

"Train wasn't so bad," he said, "but I got in last night, decided it wasn't the time to call on you, went out drinking with Jake Trexler—you remember him from Colorado, John B. Parker's bodyguard?"

Jess Marvell nodded, not seeming to mind it at all, Brandon noted with a touch of envy. "You need some fresh air," she said. She straightened the papers on her desk into two piles, except for one she impaled on a lethal-looking spike protruding from a metal base, and stood up.

"My doings are in order," she said. "I can leave my manager in charge. We'll take a ride out toward the mountains, up Crow Creek."

"A ride," Brandon said. He was certainly getting steadily back to normal, but jouncing on a horse for some hours didn't seem like a good idea.

"I have a very comfortable surrey," she said with a smile that acknowledged his doubts. "Or the Hall does, and as I'm the boss, I get to use it. I'll have the kitchen put something up for lunch, and we can have a picnic. You go for a walk and come back in half an hour, and it'll be all set."

"A light lunch, that'd be nice," Brandon said.

Jess Marvell drove expertly, and knew the terrain. "I spent some time out here last year, and found some nice places out in the country," she told him.

Brandon, seated next to her on the narrow front seat, felt the jouncing of the limber springs of the surrey acting on him like a massage, sorting his disparate constituents back into place. The motion also threw him gently but constantly against Jess Marvell, and he realized that he had never felt their thighs, their sides, their arms, touching before, and

127

even though there were at least five layers of sturdy cloth between them at any point, he was vividly aware of the warm flesh under that cloth.

It seemed to have been understood that the ride out was for casual conversation, mainly about how the Halls were doing, when Rush Dailey was expected, the weather, and such news of Cheyenne as might be of interest. "I don't expect you saw the posters, but those actors you met on the train to Inskip, Edmund Chambers and his daughter, they're coming to town in a day or so. I think they're doing dramatizations of some of Browning's poems."

"Be nice to see them again. I ran into them in Denver a while back," Brandon said.

"Uh-huh," Jess Marvell said, not adding, "I never knew you were in Denver."

"Here," Jess Marvell said. She pulled on the reins and the horse, already moving slowly, suspended his progress entirely. Brandon agreed that there could hardly be a better stopping place. A grassy bank sloped gently toward the creek, which here widened into a gently rippling pool that transmitted the rays of the sun to the golden sand and warm-hued rocks of the bottom and sent them shimmering up to dance on the trunks and lush young leaves of the trees. The blue mountains in the distance rose to a harder blue sky, and the air seemed to flow through the glade like the ghost of the most refreshing drink you could imagine.

They stepped down from the surrey and Jess Marvell reached in the rear and took out a large covered basket, which she handed to Brandon. "Over under the trees, I think," she said.

She followed him, carrying a large folded square of canvas and some cushions, and opened the canvas and spread it on the ground and set the pillows on it. Brandon put the basket down and sat on the canvas.

He looked up at Jess Marvell. The noon sun made the narrow brim of her hat cast a deep shadow on her face, but glinted on the green silk of her tight-waisted jacket and skirt;

she seemed to glow in the sunlight like a tree coming into leaf.

"There's talking to do," he said. "For me to do, anyhow."

Jess Marvell took her hat off and set it on the canvas, shaking her head. "Later. It's hot and we've driven a long way."

She pulled off her jacket and dropped it beside the hat. Her fingers went to her throat and he thought she was loosening the top buttons of her shirtwaist for air. He stared as she methodically undid button after button until she reached the waistband of her skirt, unfastened it, dropped the skirt and stepped out of it, and shrugged out of the unfastened shirtwaist and dropped it also.

Jess Marvell stood before him wearing only a cotton camisole and drawers, and in a moment not even those. She kicked off her shoes—no stockings, he saw, so she'd dressed for undressing, so to speak—and ran her fingers through her hair. "It's hot," she said again. She turned away from him and walked down the slope to the pool in the creek, crouched and slid into the water. "I always swim when I come out here," she called to Brandon.

He watched her pale body slide through the water, the sun dappling her and reflecting up onto the trees, and wondered what the hell she was up to. After a moment, he thought he saw.

A good deal more awkwardly than she had, he undressed. Women's clothes are more practical than ours in some ways, he thought. Anyhow, for getting off, which makes sense in a way. Peeling off his socks, he saw that there were holes at the heels, and was glad Jess Marvell was not close by to see them. There was nothing wrong with holes in socks, but this wasn't the time for them to be noticed.

When he stood up and felt the air rolling across his body, he had a stabbing moment of self-consciousness. Elise was the last woman to see him naked, and not very naked at that, there usually being a nightshirt, even though it got tucked up around the chest, as did her nightgown, during the proceedings. . . . No, he was wrong, there was that time in the cave in Arizona with Rebecca Jenks, days underground, when they'd had to swim across a lake and it had seemed silly, in the heat and dark, to put their clothes on again. There, being naked had seemed like a birth into a different kind of life, and it hadn't seemed strange at all.

He walked down to the creek, not disturbed by Jess Marvell smiling up at him, and stepped down and let the water embrace him.

They swam, saying little, moving around and toward each other, but not touching, and Brandon felt as if a thick, gritty crust around him were dissolving, so that he could move freely once more and sense and feel what was around him.

As if they had both heard the same signal, they turned to the bank and climbed out. Jess Marvell's nakedness seemed unremarkable to Brandon, as did his own. They walked slowly to the canvas under the trees, letting the air dry them, and sat down, about four feet apart.

Brandon looked at her and felt a flood of . . . not desire, as he had expected, but a sharp yearning, then deep relief as he acknowledged that what he yearned for was there.

Jess Marvell looked at him thoroughly and appreciatively, and gave him a broad smile. "Oh, yes," she said. "It'll be fine. But now, my dear, now it's time to talk."

Right, Brandon thought with delight. You saw how it had to be. Every covering stripped away first, then we can get to revealing what else has to be revealed. No collar to fiddle with to gain time to evade, no pockets to root in, no shirt to sweat into at the thought of telling something he didn't want to . . .

Jess Marvell lay back with her head on a cushion and looked up at him. "First thing, dear Mr. Brooks, very dear Mr. Blake . . . what's your name?"

Shadows lay across Jess Marvell and Brandon and the debris of their lunch, consumed with absentminded relish as he went through his narrative: Mound Farm and the murders, the capture, trial, and acquittal of Casmire, the bizarre mountain trip with Ned Norland, the killing of Casmire and the commitment to kill the others, Inskip and meeting Jess Marvell, Texas and one kill, Arizona and a death he had no hand in, Colorado and Jess Marvell again, and train robbers claiming his intended quarry (and the bizarre aid offered by the Kenneallys in hunting down their renegade kinsman), New Mexico and letting Gren Kenneally's brother ride away rather than fail men who trusted him, Texas again, and the long drive that had ended in a death that was as much mercy as vengeance, Nebraska and a killing he had tried to back away from; and finally Philadelphia and the catastrophe that finished it.

The air had cooled, not to a chill, but to less than hot, during the long unburdening, and the sun was moving down toward the distant mountains.

"All that," Jess Marvell said, speaking for almost the first time since Brandon began his story. "Oh, dear Cole, all that. What it must be to have gone through it, to have done those things, to have lived so."

"It . . . wasn't all bad," Brandon said thoughtfully. "Aside from bringing me you, even. Having to be those people, wear those masks, I don't know, it taught me something. I mean, I liked being good at those things, even though it wasn't important, say, that I do a good job as trail cook, but it meant something to do it. And I wasn't a half-bad reporter in Spargill, you know that, and I sold some windmills that'll be bringing up water where it's needed for years. I used to think that being a capable lawyer, clever when it was called for, was the best thing a man could be, but I've come to see that damn near anything can be good to do if you do it right."

"I didn't think it was bad," Jess Marvell said. "Strange, often terrible, but bad, no. What you did, I don't know if I would have felt I had to do that, in your place, but I'm not you, and I don't have anything to say about what you did. Good, bad, neither of those has anything to do with that."

With that, Brandon seemed to feel the last of what he had

been carrying since he saw Elise's bloody, sightless face staring at the fiery skies above Mound Farm slip away from him, as if he had dived once again into the cleansing water. There was nothing now separating him from Jess Marvell, no fabric, no secrets, no guilt.

She smiled as he moved to her. "Getting cool," she said. "Warm me."

Brandon could just see the outline of the Laramies against the darkening sky, and the air was cooling him as it dried, yet again, the slickness of sweat from his skin.

"Agh," Jess Marvell said thickly, her eyes managing to focus on him. "Oh, my." She lay sprawled and breathing heavily, her paleness seeming to glow of itself in the twilight. Brandon could not see her altogether clearly now, but it seemed to him that her body was engraved on his eyes, his fingertips, his whole body, with a detail and precision Nelson Vanbrugh could not have equaled.

Nelson Vanbrugh would have loved to sketch Jess Marvell as she was now, and then engrave from the sketch. Brandon thought that it would be marvelous to have the sketch and the engraving, though he would regret the necessity of having to kill Nelson Vanbrugh for making them. . . .

"I hate to leave here," he said finally. "But it's getting late, and we'll be hungry by the time we get to town."

"Another basket in the back," Jess Marvell said. "Ham, cold beef, potato salad, beer. Also coffee and coffeepot, a slab of bacon for breakfast. Blankets and another canvas, loaded rifle in case of curious bears. Marvel Halls stand ready to fill the traveler's every need."

Brandon fished in his folded trousers, found a match and a cigar, cracked the match to life and lit the cigar. Jess Marvell's body glowed briefly in the match-light and points of light glinted in her eyes. "You figured it'd work out the way it did?"

In the near-dark she was silent for a minute. "Once in a while, maybe once in your life, you want something so hard that it *has* to happen, not should or ought to, but has to, and you know it's going to, and it does. I don't think I wondered about it or worried, really, because it couldn't not have happened, not in this world."

Brandon puffed at the cigar, bringing Jess Marvell briefly into dim view as the end glowed, then letting her recede into the shadow. "I guess it couldn't," he said.

13

It was very nearly a scene of cozy domesticity such as Currier & Ives were doing so well at printing and selling: Brandon in his shirtsleeves, settled back in a yielding chair in the parlor of the owner's apartment above the Cheyenne Marvel Hall, reading the local newspaper and sipping an interesting fruit punch that the day's customers hadn't ordered as much of as expected; a small fire burning in the grate, since the nighttime temperature was close to twenty degrees lower than the day's; Jess Marvell, in a pleasantly loose-fitting housedress, curled on a settee with a lapful of women's work.

The work, though, was not a basketful of sewing, such as some socks that needed darning—she had been sardonic about his as he pulled them on, that morning out by the creek, but had not offered to mend them—but a thick ledger, a pile of papers, a sheaf of sharpened pencils, and a contraption consisting of wires stretched across a wood frame with thick wooden beads strung on them. Brandon had seen Chinese laundrymen using them in some manner in the course of business before stating the amount he owed, and had vaguely thought they were some appurtenance of whatever exotic religion the Chinese practiced.

Jess Marvell set him right on that. "Cheaper than a Babbage calculating machine, and works faster," she said. "Do any kind of ciphering like a breeze." She demonstrated how she could multiply large numbers on the abacus and come out with the answer about the time Brandon had finished writing down the first steps in the process.

Now she flicked the beads back and forth, shuffled papers, wrote in the ledger, hummed abstractedly. Brandon looked up from the paper and studied her. Would you want a woman who'd sit there doing needlework or snapping beans or something ladylike, Counselor? (*Someone like Elise?* a faint voice in the furthest corner of his mind whispered, and was silent.)

"You have to go in a while," Jess Marvell said.

Brandon nodded. The owner of the Marvel Halls could absent herself from her premises overnight, with no one to quiz her about her comings and goings or to do anything but assume she had been on some sort of business trip; but that owner could not entertain a man in her rooms overnight without it being noted and entered in the reddest of inks in the invisible social ledger. Women were more independent in Wyoming Territory than almost anyplace else in the country, but not independent enough to behave as freely as men in their amours. Brandon would have to return to the Inter-Ocean for the night, and unless Jess Marvell, "heavily veiled" as the more lurid newspapers liked to describe clandestine ladies, chose to sneak past the desk clerk to join him, he would have a solitary night.

Considering what the day had been, beginning with a sunrise awakening like nothing he had ever experienced and going on to what had happened after breakfast, what had almost happened in the surrey on the way back to Cheyenne, and what had happened during the course of the afternoon and evening, in intervals between business claims on her attention, a night with Jess Marvell was likely to be as

celibate as one without her. But, after last night, remembering a brief coming awake to sense the slowly breathing
warmth beside him and the almost painful shock of delight
that ran through him before he drifted back into sleep,
Brandon knew that the only thing that made separation
from her bearable was the certainty of reuniting with her.
There was something about that in Shakespeare, he thought;
Edmund Chambers would know.

"You said you were thinking of going back to law," Jess
Marvell said after a moment of clicking the abacus.

"Only thing I know, though I'm not sure I'm suited to it
any more."

"You know a lot more now," Jess Marvell said. "You've
been a newspaperman, salesman, cook, so on."

"I don't see myself hiring out to pilot a chuck wagon on
the long drive again," Brandon said.

"No. You'd have to take me with you or I'd kill you, and
the owner wouldn't allow a woman along. But, Cole, the
things you know, the lives you've led, even the lawbreaking
you've done, it seems to me they'd go to making you the best
kind of lawyer there could be for out here. Whatever the
local statutes are, you can learn them, but you know your
way around the law and how it works as much as any man
can, and now you know how people live in the West and the
kinds of problems they have to face. Before, could you have
represented a gambler or a gunman in trouble the way you
could now? Or a farmer or a cowboy?"

"Something in what you say," Brandon said dubiously.
"But . . ."

"Think about it," Jess Marvell said.

Brandon nodded. "Wonder what the prospects for a
lawyer will be after the election. Hard to say what whoever
gets in will do about the depression. The paper's guessing
Tilden and Hayes will get the nominations, but I wouldn't
know which of 'em would make a difference."

"Neither, probably," Jess Marvell said. "My business is
inching up, so I'd guess we're on the way out of it, but
slowly. Me, I'm voting for Victoria Woodhull."

Brandon was not sure which part of the last statement was the more astonishing. He could see after a brief reflection that the flamboyant Mrs. Woodhull would appeal to Jess's sense of independence, so took up the other shocker. "Vote? But you're, um . . ." After last evening, this morning, and this afternoon and evening, to point out that she was a woman would be supremely fatuous.

"I'm surprised that your legal cronies in St. Louis weren't tut-tutting and bemoaning and deploring when women got the right to vote and sit on juries in Wyoming seven years ago," Jess Marvell said tartly. "You folks back there may not have been paying attention to what's going on out here, but there's more happening than gold rushes and fighting Indians. Victoria Woodhull hasn't got a chance of winning, but she'll be heard from, and the women who support her will be heard from, and women everywhere will get just a hint that they don't have to be quiet and put up with everything any man decides to do to or with them."

Brandon knew enough not to say anything at all at this point. Jess Marvell laughed. "That's not aimed at you, Cole. Being a woman and running a business, sometimes it's like pushing boulders uphill, and I get snappish. But it's something, being in a place where I've got the same legal rights as a man, and that's why I run the Halls from here, and live here, and mean to go on."

Brandon had not until now looked closely at the shape of the future. Jess was in it, of course, in fact she *was* it, pretty much, and his occupation was the rest of it. Jess Brandon, helpmeet and housewife . . . That was how it worked, wasn't it? Looking at Jess Marvell, Brandon found it hard to fit her into that picture. And it was clear that she had no intention of stepping into the frame. "You'll, uh, want to go on with the Halls, even after . . . I'd sort of thought . . ."

"Oh, yes," Jess Marvell said sadly. "I'm going on with the Halls, and I'm going to make them hum. And to do it the best way I can, I have to be here. I know that means I'm asking you to accept that I'll have my own life, and that if you want me, you'll have to do what you're going to do here, at least for a while. And if you can't accept that, if you have to own me as well as love me, if you have to go someplace I'm not going to go, why, that'll break my heart and my whole self, but it'll have to be that way."

She stood, setting aside the ledger, paper, pencils, and abacus, and came to stand over him. "But we'll be . . . Hell, Jess, we haven't talked about it, but I want to marry you. You'll be my wife. So keeping up the business . . ."

Jess Marvell put her hands on his shoulders. "I love you, Cole Brandon, right to my toenails. And that's who I love, Cole Brandon. And you love Jess Marvell. Not Mrs. Cole Brandon, there's no such person, no matter what the marriage certificate's going to say. And Jess Marvell is the inventor and proprietor of the Marvel Halls, that's as much a part of her as loving you is."

She bent close to him, and her scent—hair, a faint hint of sweat mingled with soap, an undernote of musk—seemed to stroke him like a lightly touching hand. "Cole, I will be your wife, your lover, your comfort, your whore, I'll take you into my body and my spirit, and I'll accept everything of yourself you'll give me . . . but never, never, never will I be your . . . Missus!"

"Brandon," Rush Dailey said. "Now, that is a good kind of name, suits you better than Brooks or Blake, which is what I've knowed you as. And nice you can go back to it, with your detectiving done after all this time." He gulped at his beer and eyed Brandon with curiosity.

When Rush Dailey returned to Cheyenne on the morning westbound train, Jess Marvell and Brandon gave him an edited version of how the job detective Charles Brooks had asked them to help him with in Kansas long ago was finally completed, and how the Brooks and Blake (Callison, Bascom, and Bane had not come to Rush Dailey's attention and could be ignored) identities could be retired, allowing the genuine article, Cole Brandon, to resume his place.

Jess was steeped in Marvel Hall business and had no

immediate need of the services of Brandon or Rush Dailey; at Brandon's suggestion, they went to the Inter-Ocean's bar for some before-lunch drinks.

"All the bad men safely under lock and key?" Rush Dailey asked.

"More or less," Brandon said. The door they had passed through had never yet been known to unlock, unless you credited the mediums who claimed to bring back the spirits of the dead to communicate complete balderdash to the living.

"And now you're free as a horse, primed to commit entangling alliances with Miss Marvell," Rush Dailey said. "And I am staring at the woman I prize above rubies— which ain't saying much, as I don't believe I've seen a ruby, but I read it someplace and it was meant to be strong stuff—acrost a . . ."

"Moat?" Brandon said.

Rush Dailey shook his head and drank from his mug. "Moats ain't in it. A tempest-tossed ocean, with the sea serpent ready to eat the voyager alive or the giant kraken to drag him to the depths, that's about it. Pledged to John B. Parker, and anyhow back in St. Louis, where I doubtless won't get to go to again in some while."

"Well, she's coming here with . . ." Brandon said, then realized he was opening a door he had not meant to.

"Here? With who? John B. Parker?" Rush Dailey looked sharply at Brandon, registered his slow nod, and went on to the obvious question. "How d'you know that?"

"Ah . . . she mentioned it to me in St. Louis," Brandon said.

"You know her? Well, damn, of course you do or you wouldn't be chatting about travel plans and what all with her, would you?" Rush Dailey said. "How come you didn't mention this to me when we talked in St. Louis?"

"I hadn't seen her yet," Brandon said.

A deep flush spread over Rush Dailey's face. "Damn it, I mean that you knowed her! I told you how I felt about the woman, and you just sat there looking like a stuffed horse and said nothing! That ain't friendly doings, Mr. Broo . . . Brandon!"

Brandon sighed. "That was it, Rush. I wasn't Brandon then, not yet, and I couldn't be frank about Cole Brandon's life." This was perfect nonsense, and he hoped Rush Dailey wouldn't see that it was. The history that lay behind Brandon's shock at Krista Ostermann's engagement to John B. Parker was something Rush Dailey would not be happy to hear. "I'd better tell you now, though. Miss Ostermann is my late wife's sister, that's how I know her." *No need to say she was close to being my late wife's replacement.*

Rush Dailey looked into the depths of the almost empty mug for a long time, as if some configuration of foam might spell out the answer to a very complicated question. "Well, it's as queer as a horse," he said, after a while. "A man don't know whether to be heartbroke or puzzled the more. Now, you said as how Miss Ostermann is coming out here?"

"Yes."

"Traveling with . . . ?"

"Yes."

Rush Dailey looked thoughtful.

"Maybe," Brandon said, "it'd be an idea for Miss Marvell to, uh, find something for you to do at one of the Halls in Colorado or what. Until they've gone, that is; it might be easier on you not to . . ."

"Well, no," Rush Dailey said. "I am not a tender plant that withers in the burning winds, no sir. I only met John B. Parker the once, that time over in Colorado, and I didn't see what in him that would gain the regard of a lady like Miss Krista Ostermann. I have me a mind to renew the acquaintance, and take his measure. A man can learn a lot from studying the likes of John B. Parker."

"A man can learn a lot from hanging by his heels through a privy seat," said Jake Trexler, coming up to their table in time to catch Rush Dailey's last few words. "But that isn't to say he'll like it. Dooley is it, no, Dailey, right? I remember you from Spargill. Saw you here, Brandon, and thought I'd join you if it's all right with you and Mr. Dailey."

"Sure," Brandon said. "Mr. Dailey's Miss Marvell's right bower, as you'll recall, the steam in the Marvel Halls' boiler. Rush, you'll remember Mr. Trexler was guarding John B. Parker."

"From the justice of an outraged Creation," Jake Trexler said cheerfully, sitting down and signing to the waiter to bring him a beer. "The Killer Elephant of Wall Street, that the papers call him, that's kindliness and flattery. Hydrophobia Skunk of Wall Street, that's more like it, or Slimy Python or Unwashed Warthog, anything from the parts of the zoo they don't let the kids into. I can tell you all you want to know about John B. Parker, Dailey, for I'm not his man again until tomorrow, and can speak frankly. Thanks." He sipped the beer the waiter had just set down and turned to Brandon.

"I'm sorry to say this about the man who's going to marry your sister-in-law," he said—Rush Dailey winced, and Brandon was glad he had explained Krista's relationship to him; Trexler's offhand statement would have been a hell of a way to learn it—"but John B. Parker is a turd with ears. About the best I can say is that when the time comes, the Widow Parker will be the happiest woman you can imagine. Here is a thing that will show you what John B. Parker is like. . . ."

Brandon considered kicking Trexler under the table to try to pinch off this vein of conversation, but limited himself to grimacing meaningfully. Not meaningfully enough, since Trexler took no notice and went on about the appalling nature, manners, and actions of John B. Parker through another round of beers.

"I'd best go now," Rush Dailey said, and stood up. "Things to see to at the Hall. John B. Parker'll want to look it over, along with the books, when he talks to Miss Marvell tomorrow. So long."

He left the room slowly, looking, Brandon thought, sad as a horse.

"One man in his time plays many parts," Edmund Chambers said. "He that was Brooks, let him be Brandon, it matters not. Pleased to meet you again, whichever."

Brandon and Jess Marvell had met Elaine and Edmund Chambers just outside an ice cream parlor, an enterprise that did not seem typical of the nighttime Cheyenne Brandon had seen, but was certainly welcome on the dry, warm day, just short of summer by the calendar, well into it by the thermometer. Greeted as Charles Brooks, he had set the nomenclature straight, arousing no great curiosity in the actors. There were no figures on the prevalence of aliases in the West, but it was not remarkable to deal with men who changed their names more often than their drawers, and the Chamberses clearly did not consider the matter worth wondering about—a good deal less so than the ice cream, which rated close attention.

Advised by Jess Marvell, Elaine Chambers chose the strawberry and found, as promised, that it was flavored with the tiny, sweet wild berries just coming ripe on some south-facing slopes. Brandon relished the bitterness of chocolate, and Edmund Chambers dug into a dish of vanilla. "Hardly any taste," he said cheerfully. "That's as it should be. I can flavor it as I will by the exercise of the imagination: peach, orange, or, say, brandy or champagne."

"Or turkey," Jess Marvell said, licking a berry embedded in the ice cream on her spoon in a way that gave Brandon a feeling of sudden melting in the pit of his stomach.

"Well, yes," Edmund Chambers said, looking at the dish with diminished avidity. The trouble with imagining flavors is that once something like turkey ice cream has been presented to the imagination, it is equally difficult to forget or to relish it.

The Chamberses suggested a stroll about town to pass some of the afternoon before their performance. "You'll come to the first night?" Edmund Chambers said as they walked down Central Avenue, the two women a few paces ahead of him and Brandon. "Elaine is spectacular in 'My Last Duchess.' Sometimes she's the woman, sometimes she's the painting, and she breaks your heart when I get to 'Looking as if alive,' so still and remote."

"How I do that is, I think about the manager in Phoenix who ran off with the receipts in seventy-three," Elaine called back. "I went all dead inside, scared and shocked, and all's I have to do is remember how it felt, and there I am, hanging upon the wall. Do come."

"Tomorrow night," Jess Marvell said. "Mr. John B. Parker will be in town, and Mr. Brandon and I will want to show him the best entertainment Cheyenne has to offer."

"We are that," Edmund Chambers said. "John B. Parker, eh? We'll have to exert ourselves for such a notability, see if we can draw an approving trumpet from the Killer Elephant of Wall Street. Perhaps," he said to Brandon as the two women's heads leaned together in conversation, "you would bring him to the green room after the show. I gather that he's the sort of fellow you wash in carbolic after you shake hands with him, and I'd like to pick up some character touches from him. I can see using some of that as Macbeth. . . . No, the Thane's a little watery for it, Richard the Third would be the one, do him as a moral monster and forget the hump."

Brandon saw that Elaine Chambers and Jess Marvell were talking earnestly, then that one of them, then the other, would turn and glance at him fleetingly before returning to the conversation. Life with Elise, general observation, and the complaints of male friends had taught him that there was nothing to do about the appalling intimacies women exchanged, often enough about their men. A trill of laughter from Elaine Chambers drifted back, and he earnestly hoped it was about the holes in his socks, though he feared not.

"I think about retiring sometimes, you know," Edmund Chambers said. "From the stage, not, alas, from the necessity of earning my bread. But Elaine and I have a bit put by, and we could purchase and run a superior theatrical board-inghouse, a leisurely and undemanding enterprise. And we could, day after day, be ourselves." He looked down at the pavement as they walked. "Always assuming that there are selves to be, of course. As far back as I can remember, I, and Elaine after she was old enough, which was about seven, have been regiments of other people, night after night. And between, we've been playing the roles of aspiring actors looking for work, or, when we're alone, those of The Father and The Daughter. I mean, no matter what we're doing, every once in a while there's the smell of greasepaint, the limelight, we know the gestures to make with every situation and emotion, and we make them, even to each other."

He looked ahead at his daughter and Jess Marvell. "I think I'd really like Elaine if I knew her. Not just love her, I know I do that, but like her. I hope she'd like me. Maybe we'll come to that in time, after we've set all the masks aside long enough. Or maybe not, maybe the faces underneath have been molded by all the masks. They that live by the mask shall die by the mask, it says in the Scriptures, or almost."

Thank you, God, Brandon said silently. I got my masks off in time, and don't have to wear them ever again. Whatever Jess Marvell's getting, it's me and no one else.

"—and we'll take them over to the barn and warehouse we want to lease to provision the Black Hills trade," Jess Marvell said. "It's not going to last long, either the gold'll give out or they'll put a railroad through, but it'll be profitable while it lasts, and it'll back up the regular Halls business. Miss Ostermann will be interested, since you've been talking to her about us getting supplied from Ostermann storehouses in Wyoming and Montana."

Rush Dailey nodded. The yellowish lamplight in Jess Marvell's parlor, or perhaps dispiritedness, made him look five or so years beyond his age.

144

"Maybe Miss Ostermann'd rather leave that stuff to John B. Parker," he said. "A lady gets tired of business, even if you don't—oh, Lord, I didn't mean it that way, and you know it—but she'll likely be vaporous after the trip, and I could show her the sights and superfluities of Cheyenne. . . ."

"No, Rush," Jess Marvell said gently.

"Oh," Rush Dailey said. He looked at Brandon. "Well, I guess you had to tell her, course you did."

"Yes, Rush," Jess Marvell said. "I can't tell you how to feel or even what to do, except about Halls business, but it was something I had to know. All I can say is that things work out the way they're going to, and even the longest-shot horse sometimes wins."

The two men and the women sat around the table, staring at the yellow glow of the lamp, each considering what the coming of John B. Parker and Krista Ostermann would mean:

For Jess Marvell, a source of financing that would put the Marvel Halls five years ahead in one step;

For Rush Dailey, the torment of seeing the woman he adored basking in the company of a man it was hard to find animals repulsive enough to compare to;

For Brandon, the final sad closing out of the past as he saw Krista companioning a man connected, however remotely, with the monster who murdered her sister . . . and perhaps the solution to that nagging minor problem of what had prompted Krista to complicate a couple of lives with her sudden decision to accompany Parker to Wyoming.

He slouched in his chair and looked at the others, locked in their thoughts, and slid a hand into a trousers pocket. The old Indian coin was there, though it seemed to him that it hadn't been the last time he had probed the pocket, but that was the way with small objects; they came and went according to some arcane laws, and there were probably dozens of collar studs and cuff buttons that had successfully made their escape from him over the years but sometimes come back weeks later, perhaps lonely for the bureau drawer. Anyhow, here it was, and once again giving his fingertips that queer, tingling sensation; the next time he was by a suitable place, he would get rid of it for good and all.

14

White clouds from the cylinders steamed the waiting party on the platform as the locomotive drifted past them, then the tender, the express car, the two passenger cars, and, as on the train Brandon had taken, a Pullman, but one noticeably longer and more richly decorated, even palatial. Jess Marvell, Brandon, Jake Trexler, and Rush Dailey had stationed themselves toward the rear of the platform, the normal stopping place of the last car, but the Pullman rolled past them.

They turned and trotted after it, looking, Brandon knew, slightly foolish. Jake Trexler swore and said, "I should have known. John B. Parker don't figure to walk an extra step— he'd told the engineer to pull up ahead so's the Pullman will be right at the waiting room!"

When the got there, John B. Parker had already descended to the platform and was looking impatiently at Jake Trexler and the others as if, predictably, the mental defectives he was forced to rely on had once again failed him.

He turned as they approached and strode through the waiting room door, leaving them to follow him. As they did so, Brandon saw through the waiting room window Krista and a younger woman being helped down the car steps by a porter. Other porters had organized a human chain and were passing an impressive quantity of boxes, trunks, and other luggage to a rapidly growing pile on the platform.

"Miss Marvel. Trexler. Dailey," John B. Parker said, either greeting or labeling. "And . . . Blake, that's it; what're you doing here?"

"Consulting with Miss Marvell on business matters," Brandon said. "And the name's Brandon, Cole Brandon, sir. In Nebraska and Colorado, the exigencies of the moment obliged the use of Blake."

John B. Parker grinned thinly. "No matter; I've had reasons to appear as other than Parker now and then, facilitates business wonderfully at times." Brandon´ reflected that his need for aliases had been imposed by the determination to hunt and kill—if need be, murder outright—but that John B. Parker's motives were probably worse.

Krista and the young woman came into the waiting room. Trexler looked at her with pity mixed with disapproval; Jess Marvell surveyed her and gave the faintest smile, knowing that this woman was no threat to her and, no matter what Cole Brandon might think, never had been; Rush Dailey looked at her in a way Brandon hoped John B. Parker hadn't seen, though Krista seemed to have.

The waiting room door opened and a face peered in, received a wilting glare from John B. Parker, and vanished. Brandon could hear the crowd of passengers on the platform moving away. A bulky shadow slowly passed the waiting room window.

"My dear, this is Miss Marvell," John B. Parker said. "Miss Marvell, my fiancée, Miss Ostermann. Those are Trexler, the bodyguard the railroad insists I have, Miss Marvell's assistant, Dailey, and this is that newspaperman I helped out in Colorado, Blake, only his name's Brandon, Claude or something. Gentlemen, Miss Ostermann." It was not polished, but it was a better job of introducing than Brandon would have expected from Parker.

Krista stepped forward to Brandon and held out both hands. "But how delightful to see you, Cole. I had no idea you would be here." No idea anyhow that I'd be back to being Cole Brandon, he told himself sardonically, but she's adjusting to it smoothly enough.

She turned to John B. Parker and said, "I think I've mentioned dear Cole to you—my sister Elise's husband."

"Um," John B. Parker said, "of course. Mrs. Brandon here with you, Brandon?"

"Cole is a widower," Krista said, her lips thinning.

"Sorry to hear it," John B. Parker said. He looked past Elise to the young woman who stood quietly, twisting a pair of gloves in her hands. "That's Rosa Zweibel, Miss Ostermann's paid companion and watchdog. Rosa, you heard who these people are, so I don't need to bother going over them again."

"Rosa is my friend," Krista said hastily, "and kindly agreed to accompany me on this trip so that neither Mr. Parker nor I would be troubled by perceptions of impropriety."

"Now, what have you got set up for me?" John B. Parker asked Jess Marvell, considering that the social niceties had been fully seen to.

Jess Marvell began giving Parker the itinerary she had prepared for his inspection of her enterprises; Krista moved to Brandon. "I'm glad I don't have to call you Mr. Blake, Cole. I'm not a good actress."

"Did you not tell him about Elise, about what happened, or did he for God's sake forget it?" Brandon asked. "Mrs. Brandon here with me, Jesus!"

Krista looked at Jess Marvell. "He may be right about that, given a little time, I think, no? Never mind, Cole, we don't have to talk about that now. What it is, Mr. Parker doesn't listen very much except when it's a matter of business. I did tell him I inherited the business when Papa died, and that I had a sister who died, and he doesn't seem to have remembered that awfully clearly. But no, I didn't tell him about how Elise and Papa died, about Mound Farm.

Sometimes I thought I would, but when I would think of how to start, I would see that he is not the kind of man you talk of such things to."

But he's the kind of man you're marrying. Oh, dear Krista, why? Did you give up on everything but business, figure that's all there was to life?

To one side, Brandon saw Rush Dailey, next to John B. Parker but looking toward Krista with a hunger that seemed to reach out with desperate fingers. Krista could have seen it, perhaps not; she gave no indication Brandon could pick up.

"That is the regular Marvel Hall dollar lunch," Jess Marvell said. "Beef, ham, chicken, fish, or pork regularly, antelope or buffalo, prairie chicken or passenger pigeon, when available, two vegetables, bread and butter, pie, coffee or beer. The conductor gives the passengers a bill of fare from a pad I give him, they mark their orders, and they're wired ahead from the train, all ready to serve when it pulls in. I can feed eighty head—eighty customers in twenty minutes, fifteen if they'll do without the coffee, or take it away in a tin cup if they're carrying one. Food costs about thirty cents a meal, wages and overhead in general another forty, leaving thirty cents profit and return on investment."

It was early for lunch, not much after ten, but the meal made a pleasant late breakfast, and it made more sense to demonstrate the Marvel Hall's capabilities to a potential investor when it was not crowded with eighty or so head of fast-feeding passengers. John B. Parker had insisted on coming straight from the station, as if hoping to take the Marvel Hall staff off guard and engaged in some wastefulness or depravity. If so, he was disappointed, since the untimely meals were prepared promptly and served cheerfully, and were, Krista claimed, the equal of what had been served on John B. Parker's private Pullman.

"That chef costs me ten dollars a day," John B. Parker said.

"Then Miss Marvell is getting more value for her money, and you will do well to invest in her business." Somewhat to Brandon's surprise, Krista had taken to Jess Marvell immediately, and seemed to be developing a genuine fondness for her.

Rosa Zweibel apparently enjoyed her meal as much as anybody, but kept quiet about it. She looked like the sort of person John B. Parker would step on automatically, without noticing it.

Jake Trexler, flanking John B. Parker, ate with an air of apparent distraction, caused by his steadily moving gaze, covering the entrances to the Hall's dining room, including those from the kitchen. Once John B. Parker was in his care, his personal views went into storage and he gave the job his best.

Rush Dailey could have been eating swill or ambrosia; he was opposite Krista and enjoying the bliss of being in the one place in the universe he should be, sharpened by the knowledge that the moment would end soon and might never be repeated. Luckily he was seated next to Trexler and out of John B. Parker's view. Since he could see Krista, she could see him, but did not seem displeased by what she saw.

"Not bad food," John B. Parker said, wiping his mouth, then his nose, with the napkin and spitting into it. "Charge a dollar and a half and you'd be making above fifty percent profit."

"Fifty-three and a third, and business would drop off badly," Jess Marvell said. "In a Hall in Kansas I tried raising the price ten cents to see what would happen, and what happened was that orders went down by a quarter. Until times get better, a dollar's what folks will pay."

"Huh," John B. Parker said. "Now, what's next?"

"After you've got settled in the hotel and had your real lunch, I thought we would take you to the buildings we want to rent for the Black Hills trade. The folks going out there need every kind of supplies, and the business will be fine as long as the gold rush lasts. You'll be interested, Miss

Ostermann, for we'll be looking to your companies for lots of the stuff we'll want."

"I'll leave that to Mr. Parker," Krista said. "I want fresh air after all those days on the train. I'd like to hire a gig and take a drive out in the country with Rosa."

Jess Marvell considered this for a moment, concluded that there was no point in objecting, and said, "I have a surrey, or anyhow it belongs to the business, and you'd be welcome to use it."

"I will go along and see no harm comes or insult offered to you ladies," Rush Dailey said. The words were ordinary, but the delivery had the fervor of the tenor's declaration of undying love in the second act.

John B. Parker looked at Rush Dailey, then at Krista. Krista looked at Rush Dailey and quickly at and away from John B. Parker. Jess Marvell looked at the three of them in turn. The impact of the looks seemed palpable, like that of billiard balls set in motion and crossing paths as they rebounded from the cushions.

Brandon saw with dismay that Krista seemed to be considering accepting Rush Dailey's offer; then Jess Marvell said, as she had the night before, "No, Rush. We'll need you for a lot of the details, things only you'll know. Mr. Brandon can escort Miss Ostermann and Miss Zweibel."

"I don't need escorting," Krista said shortly. "This is not Sicily or Morocco. You'll need Cole for your discussions just as much as Mr. Dailey, I'm sure."

In the end, it was fixed up that the stable hand who tended the horses would drive the surrey, not so much as an escort but for his knowledge of the country. "You can head west and northwest along Crow Creek," Jess Marvell said, "or north past the lakes. I'd say the lake way would be more interesting." And would not, Brandon thought, present him or Jess Marvell with the picture of Krista perhaps pausing to rest where the grass was probably still disordered, he could fancy scorched, from their passion.

As they left the dining room, John B. Parker gave Rush Dailey a long, speculative look, as if a kind of person he usually didn't take notice of had become noticeable and would have to be taken into account.

Brandon had no interest in lunch, and no part in the discussions Jess Marvell was holding with Rush Dailey and her bookkeeper, and so found himself drifting through Cheyenne's better section, then quickly enough, its worst. The places he'd drunk at with Jake Trexler looked diminished in the daylight, and bogus, like poor stage sets depicting saloons and gambling houses rather than the real thing. He turned back toward where the Inter-Ocean thrust up its full three stories toward the sky, debating whether a couple of drinks in the bar or stretching out on his bed would be the better preparation for the afternoon.

At the hotel entrance a slightly built man stepped forward and stopped him. "Sir? A word?" The voice was husky and slightly muffled. The man was slightly built, and fashionably, even garishly, dressed, inappropriately so for his years, which appeared to be advanced. He wore a plug hat and seemed to have weak eyes, as they were covered by blue-tinted spectacles. His face was seamed and leathery, though now flushed, very likely by the hot towels that had accompanied an evident recent shave; the odor of bay rum rolled off him like a gaseous avalanche.

"Can I help you, sir?" Brandon said.

"Is there a branch of the Young Women's Christian Association in this city, do you know?"

"I don't," Brandon said. "You, uh, have a granddaughter you'd like to get settled in there, perhaps? The desk clerk at the hotel here might know."

"No," the old man said. "All those pure girls, herded together like that, there's bound to be a few that's contrary enough to be looking to get corrupted, and I figure to go down to the corral and cut out a few likely lookin' fillies."

Brandon looked sharply at him and said, still half-incredulous, "Ned Norland?"

The old man nodded. "In the flesh, what there is of it, though not the hair, which is mostly gone, beard and all, now bein' swept up by the swamper in the barber shop. It's hard to be changed so, but gratifyin' and encouragin' that you don't reckernize me through it."

Brandon had once seen the old frontiersman cleaned up for presentation in court, but never had he been so far translated from his wispy-bearded, ragged-haired, odorous buckskinned self. "Are you getting married? You look respectable enough for it."

Norland shook his head vigorously. "No sir, far from it. Vice and verses, like they say, but what dirty poems has to do with things bein' contrariwise, I don't see and don't expect to. Take me in to this fancy place that I'd be thrown out of if I was in my right self, let me surround a drink or so, and I will tell you the sad story of a man that loved not wisely but too damn often."

With the first tumbler of whiskey downed like lemonade, Ned Norland relaxed and looked around the room. "Respectable and elegant, the kinder place I don't git a look at very often. Warms my heart to think what the trappers and the mountain men, the fellers that was at the last rendezvous, back in thirty-four, the shape they'd have this place into in not above ten minutes, broken glass like snowdrifts and splintered furniture in heaps and strong men sobbin' in the corners. I put it down to the Yellowstone country."

"Put what down?"

"Why, the plight I am in, ain't you listenin'?" Ned Norland said severely. "The Yellowstone country ain't like no place else on earth, and that's what done it."

Ned Norland had guided a party of easterners up from Green River City, over in the western part of the Territory, up to Yellowstone Park, nothing unusual for him except the composition of the party. "Women to a man," Ned Norland said. "Eight women, from New England and New York and Pennsylvania. Strong-minded ladies and experienced riders, wantin' to see the new national park. I studied out the propernesses of it some, but then seen that each of the ladies had seven chaperons, and what could be more iron-bound than that?"

"Makes sense," Brandon said.

"When you get a setup with women and it seems to make sense," Ned Norland said, "you have made yourself the wick in a shit candle. Women don't operate on the basis of good sense, like you and me, Brandon, there is tides that runs in them like the ocean, and sap that rises in them like in the trees, and the sensible man treats 'em with respeck and awe, and sails upon 'em or eats of their fruits, but he don't never hope to use the instruments of common sense and logic upon 'em."

"The Yellowstone," Brandon said. "What about it?"

In Ned Norland's view, the dramatic scenery of the park, the peaks, the canyons, the falls, played on the women's minds. "And then the boilin' springs, the geysers, the sulphur fumes, the crazy colors. Maybe they felt they was halfway to hell, and it was sinnin' time."

Shortly after they got to the Yellowstone, one of the women visited Norland in his tent at night. The next night another came, and so on until all had been accommodated, or Norland had been accommodated eight times, whichever way you looked at it. "By the time that was done, we was on the way back, and I thought that was all, and a nice diversion of the kind I've always a fancy for, as you know. But the first lady come back, and the night after that two of 'em at oncet, and the next day it was off the trail with one of 'em at lunch halt, and crazier after that. And back at Green River City they fell to arguing about which was to have me for good."

Some had suggested drawing lots. A small faction suggested going west to Utah and setting up a polygamous marriage, but most felt that making an honest woman of one of them was all that could be practically demanded. "The others was willin' to be bridesmaids," Ned Norland said morosely.

He had left Green River City on a night freight he had flagged down and come to Cheyenne, assuming his disguise in case any of the women came after him. "I'd have gone further east, but I'd like to find work around here. Too late to go on up to Montana and scout for Custer, he's well into the campaign; but I got a notion to go up to Deadwood and see what's to do. Bill Hickok's there, I hear, and he's got a way of knowing where there's money to be made."

Brandon remembered Edmund Chambers's scriptural misquotation about dying by what you lived by, and decided not to burden Ned Norland with a relevantly changed version.

"And now," Ned Norland said, "gimme the detailin's of how as you finished off Gren Kenneally. Miss Jess didn't say nothin' on that score whenas she tolt me your whereabouts, but last I saw you, you was goin' to Philadelphy to settle him, and you're back here and whole, so I got to assume the settlement's done. I was at the commencin' of it, so it'll satisfy me to here what the concludin' was."

"There is lots of storage space, and the floor's off the ground, so air will circulate and grain or whatever won't rot," Jess Marvell said, gesturing around the empty warehouse at the north side of Cheyenne.

John B. Parker looked at her with the practiced sourness of the man who does not intend to be sold whatever is being offered. "Owner's asking too much," he said.

"For property in Laramie or Rock Spring, yes," Jess Marvell said. "But this is Cheyenne, and the reason we want it is that it's worth something. Fill this with goods for the Black Hills trade and farm things for the emigrants, and you'll have to refill it every week, folks'll be storming it to buy. That place downtown, it's got awful stuff and they charge two prices for it, and still they sell everything they've got, isn't that so, Rush? Rush!"

"Oh, ah, yeah," Rush Dailey said. He had been abstracted since the four of them had met to conduct the afternoon's business, five, counting Jake Trexler, who said nothing and did his best to look alert. Brandon thought Rush Dailey was still in spirit seated across the table from Krista, or perhaps riding in the surrey with her, ectoplasmically disregarding Rosa Zweibel and the stable hand.

156

"And on the next lot there's a barn and a yard that I can see as a kind of wagon lot, wagons for sale right at the beginning of the road to the Black Hills," Jess Marvell said. "We could . . ."

She paused and cocked her head, and Brandon heard a disjointed rumor of sound, distant shouts, then closer, and a shriller note that fretted his eardrum like the whine of a mosquito.

He and Jess Marvell walked quickly to the door and outside. John B. Parker followed as if reluctant to be drawn into any action, Jake Trexler looking around as if to see if whatever was going on threatened Parker, Rush Dailey as if he were unaware he was moving.

From the few houses nearby a small crowd of men and women were rushing toward or running beside the Marvel Hall surrey, being pulled along by a horse stolidly ignoring the bloody-faced woman in the driver's seat who held the reins loosely as she screamed steadily and hoarsely, and ignoring also the man's bloodied upper body that dangled from the surrey's rear, swaying as the springs responded to the rough road.

The screaming woman was Rosa Zweibel. The evidently dead man was the Marvel Hall stable hand.

Krista Ostermann was not in the surrey.

15

Rosa's screams echoed stridently in the street, mechanical and inhuman, infusing the same urgent sense of catastrophe as a constantly ringing fire bell.

Jess Marvell gave a swift glance of horror and regret at the corpse of the man she had ordered on the journey to his murder, then ran to Rosa and, with Jake Trexler's help, lifted her down from the surrey and held her tightly. Rosa twisted in Jess Marvell's grasp, even as her screaming diminished, and streaks of blood spread on Jess's dress. Brandon saw now that Rosa's shirtwaist was torn apart, baring her almost to the waist, one small breast, laced with gouges, visible, the other concealed by a creased piece of dirty paper stuffed into the garment. Her skirt was bunched up around her thighs, marked by brown smears of dried blood.

"Keep 'em back!" Jake Trexler called to Brandon and Rush Dailey as he and Jess Marvell carried Rosa into the warehouse and the crowd in the street surged around them, some peering avidly into Rosa's distorted face or at her bloody bosom. Brandon and Rush Dailey cleared a free passage for them; then Brandon told one of the more responsible-looking men to drive the surrey to the police station and have some officers sent up right away. There seemed no point in keeping the corpse here to titillate the crowd or horrify Rosa anew when she came to her senses. You weren't supposed to move anything at the scene of a crime, but this scene could move on its own, and doing so would not make the police's work any harder.

John B. Parker had stood as still as an ugly statue during all this, from the moment he had seen that Krista was not in the surrey. He turned and jerkily followed Brandon and Rush Dailey as they stepped into the warehouse; Brandon snapped the latch on the door and placed a timber balk across it in case the crowd's curiosity got intense.

Rosa was sobbing more than screaming now, and then the sobbing gave way to a kind of rasping wheeze as she breathed openmouthed, making a sound like a fireplace bellows, staring up at the ceiling.

Jess Marvell cradled her, leaned close, and said softly, "Rosa, it's all right, Rosa, dear, you're all right, you're safe, Rosa . . ."

"Get her to tell what happened," John B. Parker said harshly.

Jess Marvell looked up at him. "Not for a while," she said. "Whatever it was—well, my God! It was at least poor Tom getting killed next to her! Whatever else, she's escaping from it now, and I don't know when she'll come back."

"Damn," Brandon said. "I should have sent word to the police to bring a doctor."

"They'll know to when they get the story," Jake Trexler said. He reached over and pulled the paper away from Rosa's chest; Jess Marvell made a gesture of protest, then nodded and pulled the torn fabric across the exposed flesh.

"Shake it out of her if you have to, damn it!" John B. Parker said. "We have to know what's happened to Miss Ostermann!"

"This tells us more than the girl can," Jake Trexler said before Jess Marvell could fry Parker with the lightning bolt her thundercloud face suggested. He held the paper out, and

Brandon, Parker, and Rush Dailey craned to read what was written on it.

Literate thug, carrying a pencil, Brandon thought, then remembered Krista always had two or three pencils in her handbag in case she wanted to take note of something touching on Ostermann business.

> PARKER
> IF YOU WANT YOUR WOMAN BACK THE
> WAY SHE WAS IT COSTS $5 THOUSAND, GET
> IT TOGETHER, TELL YOU LATER HOW TO
> PAY, ASK THE GIRL IF YOU WANT TO KNOW
> WHAT HAPPENS IF YOU DON'T PAY, WE
> MEAN BUSINESS

"The cops, the detective agencies, we've all been afraid of something like this ever since Charlie Ross got taken two years ago," Jake Trexler said. "Gang stole a three-year-old boy, demanded twenty thousand for him, and nothing seen of the kid since. Only a matter of time before others tried it, and now they have."

"Well, we got to pay!" Rush Dailey said. "Miss Krista in the hands of that gang, ready to treat her like they done poor Miss Rosa, which we don't even know what it was, for she can't tell us. . . ."

Brandon glanced at Jess Marvell and saw her eyes close and her face tighten with grief as her head shivered in an almost imperceptible negation; what had happened to Rosa was plain enough.

"It ain't a matter of pay and get the person back, that's the thing," Jake Trexler said. "Hasn't happened often enough so there's rules, but you could say that paying's just the signal for them to . . . dispose of the person and cut out, or you could argue that paying's best after all, and is worth a try. I couldn't rightly say which I'd advise."

"There's no question of paying," John B. Parker said flatly. "Pay ransom and you never stop. They know who I am, that's why they took Miss Ostermann in the first place.

If I pay up, there's no end to what or who they'll take and want to be paid for. Yes, they may know who I am, but if they're looking for money from me, they'll by God find out *what* I am!"

A really big cinder if Jess had her way, Brandon thought; sliced, roasted, and eaten by cannibals if Rush did; garroted with cheese wire, that's Trexler's vision. Me, I'd want it he'd never been born, just subtracted from the human equation so's I wouldn't have had to know about him. And because we're civilized folk, even Jess . . . though there's wildness there I wouldn't have looked for in one of those Sandwich Island girls that swims out to the boats to pleasure the whalers . . . we don't say anything, just look at him like one of those old dinosaurs, hard to believe in but right there before your eyes.

"Now, you're paid to be a detective, Trexler," John B. Parker said. "You and these men go out and find where this gang is holding Miss Ostermann and get her away from them. The police are blunderers, and I don't propose to bring them into this business. Blake or Brandon or whatever, he's resourceful, I know, and"—he gave Rush Dailey a searching gaze, omitting to notice the returning look of anguished fury—"I know you'll do your best for her, young fellow. When Miss Marvell gets some sense out of that girl, you'll know where to start looking."

He turned and left the building, dismissing them as effectively as if he had waved them out of his office.

"It makes me puke to say it," Jake Trexler said, "but he could be right about how to handle it. Except that I am a detective and not a Pawnee scout, to go reading trail sign and say that four horses and a mangy mule went that way last Thursday." Rosa's bellows-breathing had been a steady accompaniment to all that was said, but they found themselves disregarding it, as if it had been the reiteration of waves breaking on the beach.

"I know something about that," Brandon said. "But there's a man in town who knows everything."

* * *

"The thing is," Brandon said, "we have to wait till Rosa comes out of her fit and can tell us where she drove with Krista and that Tom. They were going north and the surrey came back from that way, but that's all we know, and there's a couple of roads they could have taken."

He had been lucky enough to find Ned Norland sunning himself on a bench in front of a saloon, scanning the passersby through his tinted glasses to make sure no matrimonially predatory ladies were combing Cheyenne in search of their misguided guide. Norland had instantly accepted Brandon's plea to join in the hunt for Krista.

"No need to wait till the poor thing's herself agin," Ned Norland said. "Wagh! 'Less it goes a mile and some in runnin' water, a wagon or a carriage ain't hard for even a child to track. Come on and let's git at it whiles we still have daylight."

Brandon looked at the sky and was shocked to see that it was not much beyond the midpoint of the afternoon. Four or so. Enough time seemed to have passed since the lunch he had not had so that it should be midnight. "Jess said there's four horses the Hall keeps that we could use," he said. "The others are over there now, so let's join them."

As they walked toward the Marvel Hall, they heard shouting from a saloon half a block behind them, then a shot and some more shouting. A town policeman ran past them, gun unholstered, toward the disturbance. He threw them a sour look in passing; Brandon recognized him as one of those who had come to the warehouse to investigate a reported crime and been treated like witless underlings by John B. Parker and refused by Jess Marvell any access to the one witness they had. If they had known of Krista's kidnapping, there would have been more than sour looks.

Ned Norland nudged Brandon into an alleyway and cocked his head to listen. After a moment he said, "Calmed down enough, not likely stray bullets'll be rovin' the balmy air seekin' a lodgin' in the tender parts of innocent strollers," and emerged into the street.

Brandon glanced over his shoulder and saw a man, bent

over and holding his thigh, being led away by some others; the cop was still inside, at a guess securing his prisoner. He pulled a cigar from his vest pocket and searched in his trousers pocket for a match. In amongst a scatter of them his fingers found the Indian coin. He had thought to just send it spinning into the night when he left Jess Marvell's quarters last night, but either had forgotten to or couldn't find it. Whatever kind of nervousness afflicted him with it sometimes had returned, and the metal seemed to vibrate against his fingers. He pulled out the match and lit the cigar.

"We'll likely be out all night and some," Ned Norland said.

Brandon nodded. "Jess knew that. She's rounded up blankets, cooking gear, and food."

"Handy to be sparkin' a lady with her own restaurant," Ned Norland said.

The far mountains were hazed and glowing, as if carved out of rich light, and the grass and trees through which the four men were passing seemed, too, to glow of themselves instead of by the rays of the sun, not quite setting but dropping toward the high horizon to the west.

Ned Norland, in the lead, seemed on the point of falling from his horse as he leaned far over to one side or the other, checking the rutted roadway. Brandon thought he could see wheel tracks from time to time, but not clearly or anything like continuously. Norland, like the vegetation, was enriched by the westering sun, and seemed like a figure of myth, some forest spirit or centaur, though he still wore his fashionable clothes and plug hat, but not the tinted spectacles.

Brandon saw that Rush Dailey, a little behind him and to one side, and Jake Trexler, bringing up the rear more than a hundred feet back, had the same aspect, more strongly colored and dramatic than in real life, so to speak. The things that had happened to Rosa, and of course, Tom, and what might happen, or have already happened, to Krista were horrible, but there was no denying that there was something exhilarating in being on the hunt again. Gren Kenneally was gone, but this gang seemed deserving of Kenneally fates, ranging from the bullet-abetted common catastrophe that killed the last of them to the ocean liner's stern wheel that chewed Peter Kenneally to tatters, and it would be satisfying to help deal out those fates.

It was a queer thing, outfitted and provisioned by one woman he loved to hunt for one he might, if things had gone a little differently, have married. He estimated the chances of finding Krista and getting her out alive at somewhere under even, and considered the further queerness of going after someone to deliver her to John B. Parker. Worse for Dailey than it is for me, though; whichever way it goes, he loses out on the thing he wants most in the world.

Norland looked back, checked his followers' positions to make sure they were deployed effectively, poor targets for an ambush and ready to fire in any direction without endangering one another, leaned down again, and said, when he straightened up, "Thought I seen this a ways back, but ground's dusty 'cept when it goes over rock, and this is the clearest yet."

The others came up to where he was, and looked down. Brandon saw the wheel marks and the, to him, random scatter of hoofprints from the horse drawing the surrey, just as he had when Ned Norland pointed them out just about the town limits. "About what we've seen, isn't it? Shows we're still on the right track, anyhow."

"Here." Ned Norland pointed at a hoofprint that blotted out part of a wheel mark. "Followin', a'most the same time. A guess, I'd say just out of sight."

"Trailing them, scouting for the gang," Brandon said.

"Maybe," Ned Norland said.

Half a mile farther along, he stopped his horse and leaned down nearly to the ground, then pulled himself upright. "Cut off to the right here, over this bank. Surrey followed the road, so you fellows keep at it, you in the lead, Brandon, and be on the *kiveeve*, like the old *voyageurs* useter say, for I think we're comin' to whereat this business happened, and them that done it could be hard by."

The light lay almost level across the roadway, and where trees or a bank did not block it, threw the shallow marks of the surrey's wheels into sharp relief, penciling the way ahead.

A few hundred yards along they came to a place where the road wound through a thick stand of trees, out of which Ned Norland came to rejoin them.

They did not need the evidence of the following horseman's trail returning to the road at that point; what had happened there was plain without it. The ground was disturbed and scored with the hoof marks of agitated horses, agitated by a sudden stop, perhaps, or the thunder and stench of gunfire, by screams, by the powerful scent of fresh blood, and crosshatched with wheel marks, showing where the surrey had been halted and turned. There was a patch of churned earth near an irregular dark patch about two feet across. "Clawed the ground some before he died," Ned Norland said. "Not for long, though."

The last of the sunlight revealed the scene with the clarity of stage lighting. Norland stepped around the area light-footed, avoiding the traces in the dirt and grass, crouched low and forward, humming and muttering as he inspected the ground, lean and lithe as a questing ferret. After a few minutes, he straightened up and said, "Hum. Was beginnin' to think so, and now it's sartin. No gang, one man."

"You sure?" Jake Trexler said, a question Brandon would not have wasted breath on; he had never known Ned Norland not to be sure.

"Onliest hoofprints is them from the surrey and the man follerin'," Ned Norland said patiently. "Follerer eels off onto a side trail some ways back, moves faster, comes back to the road jist here, shoots the driver off the seat, grabs the ladies, does what he does with the young 'n—yonder, where them yarbs is all flattened and corkscrewed, I'd guess—and then rode off north and some east, horse carryin' about a hundredweight more on his back than before. Plain as if 'twas wrote in a book."

Brandon had no trouble believing Ned Norland, and neither, apparently, did the others. How the kidnapper would have immobilized Krista while he was dealing with Rosa and whether her violation was the only outrage to disorder the grass and weeds were questions Norland might have been able to answer or guess at if asked, but Brandon thought that he, Trexler, and Rush Dailey very much wanted not to know the answers.

"Don't look like he went on a reg'lar trail," Ned Norland said, "but he'll be easy enough to foller, long's there's light. About a hour and a half, then we camp, go on at first light. He's about six hours ahead of us, if he's kep' goin', but movin' slower. If we push it now and tomorrer, we'll catch him up soon enough, or come acrost him if he's stopped and forted up."

"We could ride through the night," Rush Dailey said. "There's 'most a full moon, and it'll be light enough after maybe ten."

"Not to see his sign," Ned Norland said. "A b'ar or such you can track through the night, for he's got a powerful stink that clings to the trees and weeds he pushes through, but a man on a horse ain't that obligin'."

Brandon thought that a biting fly was prospecting on his thigh and slapped, then realized that it was the Indian coin, angled by the jackstrawed matches in his pocket to dig into his skin. Here might be the place to throw it away. . . . No, later, maybe at the camping place.

Brandon fingered the coin again, wondering if it had picked up some heat from the fire as he hunkered by it before rising to move to lean against a tree at the edge of the clearing. Tired through after a long day capped with hours of riding, and fed well enough by the dinner Rush Dailey had put together from Jess Marvell's supplies, and soothed by a half tumbler of whiskey supplied by Jake Trexler, he should have been asleep an hour ago, but found himself consumed with a restlessness he could not understand or overcome. He knew he had to get a decent sleep to be in shape for tomorrow's riding and, perhaps, fighting, but knowing that didn't keep the eyelids closed.

The moon, enough past the full to take the shape of a fat pumpkin seed, worked its way up through tree branches. Brandon looked at the other three, blanket-wrapped bundles faintly traced by the light of the cook fire, banked to burn slowly through the night. Not three, two, he saw, just as Rush Dailey moved up beside him.

"Couldn't sleep neither," he said. "Don't see how's they can."

"They know they need to, for what we've got to do," Brandon said. "So do we, but it don't do much good, does it?"

"I guess it's that Miss Krista's more to you and me than to them," Rush Dailey said. "She's about what family you got left, and me . . . well, you know about that." He spoke flatly, but Brandon felt an undertone as deep and somber as a tolling bell.

"If we walk a bit, maybe that'll get us readier to sleep," Brandon said. "Moon's up, we can see enough so's we won't break an ankle or a neck."

"Yeah," Rush Dailey said after a minute. "A walk, that's a idea."

It seemed easier to walk toward the rising moon, its rays creating a lit pathway through the rough country, giving them the false sense of a destination. Brandon felt drawn ahead, toward the moon, as if some tinge of the seas in his blood still responded to the tidal pull. A glance at Rush Dailey's set face suggested that he too felt that trace of attraction; get tired enough and you're open to any sort of suggestion, Brandon thought.

The moon caught a low, strangely shaped hill off to the left; as they approached it, Brandon saw that it was closer and smaller than it at first appeared, and not a hill but a house or shed, with the roof collapsed at one end. Some rancher or farmer's investment of hope and time, lost, with only rocks and weeds for the dividends.

"Let's look in there," Rush Dailey said.

"For what?"

"Maybe that's where the gang's holding Miss Krista!"

Brandon sighed. "First, there's no gang, just one man; Ned Norland saw that in the tracks. Put 'we' in the note to make us more cautious, I'd guess. And, man or gang, they're not going to be stopping this close to where they, he, caught Krista. And if they or he did, why, then, they're looking out from that place with a gun trained on us right now. So if you're right, Rush, we've got about three seconds to live, and if you're wrong, we might as well just walk on down the path."

Rush Dailey ignored him and moved toward the building, moving with the intensity of purpose Brandon had seen earlier in Ned Norland as he prowled the scene of Krista's abduction. He followed, picking his way carefully among the tenacious weeds and jutting rocks.

Rush Dailey stood in front of the house, the empty doorway a dark oblong in the faintly moonlit plank wall. "Let me light a match before you step in there," Brandon said. "Floor could be rotten and drop you into a cellar, if there is one."

He moved to the doorway, rummaged a match out from his pocket, having to work to get it past the Indian coin, which seemed to be perversely obstructive in the way that inanimate objects have, and thumbnailed it alight.

"Here." Rush Dailey peeled a long sliver from the dilapidated doorframe and held it to the match flame. He held the burning splinter high, looking around the room it feebly lit.

A mean enclosure, about twelve feet on a side, the floor pounded earth, walls partly covered with the remnants of newspapers put up for decoration and insulation, some broken furniture, an overturned planking table leaning against the rear wall, nothing else.

"Not the place, Rush," Brandon said gently. It was empty

of everything but a faint, sour odor of old sweat and dirt, the smell of defeat lingering surprisingly long. . . .

Rush Dailey jabbed the end of his improvised torch into Brandon's hand, sprang forward, and pulled the upturned table away from the wall.

Wrapped in crisscrossing rope like a parcel wrapped by a slovenly shopkeeper, her clothing disordered and stained, Krista Ostermann lay wedged in the angle between wall and floor. Above a dirty rag wedged into her mouth by a cord tied around her head, her eyes were closed, but Brandon could see the ropes that crossed her chest moving as she breathed. The smell was stronger now, and Brandon thought he caught the acrid scent of mortal fear. Whether Krista was asleep or in faint, she had been better off than waking.

Rush Dailey knelt beside her and pulled the gag from her mouth. It fell open and her chest heaved as she breathed in deeply; her eyelids fluttered.

"Get on back to the camp, Rush," Brandon said. "Bring Norland and Trexler back, and my horse, to carry her, water, and, yeah, Trexler's whiskey, might need that to bring her awake."

"You go," Rush Dailey said, cradling Krista's head and stroking back the hair matted across her damp forehead.

"But I should . . . She's my, uh, relative, and—"

"You go." The words were as final and unyielding as a closed fortress door, the kind you might find on the far side of a moat.

When Brandon returned with the others and his horse, Krista was awake enough to greet them, though dazedly. She gulped the water gratefully, then shuddered pleasurably as she sipped the whiskey. She threw a brief, wondering glance at Rush Dailey, who seemed to Brandon to be years older and somehow a good deal more solid than he had only hours earlier.

Rush Dailey mounted the horse and lifted Krista, firmly and tenderly as a parent would a child, onto the saddle in front of him, swinging her skirted legs to one side and holding her head against his chest. "I'm sorry . . . I know I stink," she muttered.

Rush Dailey looked down at her as if he did not know what she was talking about.

Jess Marvell's practicality had run to providing a change of female clothing, and after a sketchy bath, during which the four men found a convenient smoking room a hundred yards off through the trees, Krista regained enough composure and sense of herself to tell them what had happened— not much more than twelve hours ago, Brandon was amazed to realize. She insisted on it, saying that she wouldn't be able to sleep until she had got it off her mind.

The ride had been pleasant, and Rosa's spirits had expanded at the absence of John B. Parker's repressive thumb. Neither had ever been in the West, and the ordinary trees, wildflowers, and distant mountains had been novelties they enjoyed pointing out to each other. Neither knew many of the birds found in St. Louis by sight, but were sure that any they saw here were new and remarkable.

"Once Rosa looked back and thought she saw a cloud of dust way behind us," Krista said. "Another horse, we thought, or a gust of wind; we didn't think anything of it. We weren't afraid. . . ."

Until there was suddenly a man on a sweating horse facing them in the roadway, two flashes and thunderclaps as Tom dropped the reins, screamed, clapped his hands to his blood-spouting throat, and thrashed out of the driver's seat to fall to the ground, moaning and writhing.

The rider sprang from his horse, ran to the surrey, not even pausing as he casually fired another shot into Tom's head, dragged Krista from the back of the vehicle, and slammed her on the side of the head with the still hot revolver.

"It knocked me out," she said, "not long, but a few minutes or so. When I came to, I was tied up, and he had

Rosa, he . . . She screamed so, then she was quiet. And he took a piece of paper he found in the surrey, and he took a pencil from my bag, and he wrote, I don't know what."

"A note to John B. Parker demanding money for your return," Jake Trexler said.

Krista gave a faint smile. "He wouldn't care for that."

Uncomprehending, she watched as the killer stuffed the note into Rosa's torn blouse and threw her up into the driver's seat and slapped the horse into motion on the road back to Cheyenne. As an apparent afterthought, he grabbed Tom's body and flung it into the back of the surrey. At the impact, Rosa had begun to scream, as she had been screaming when the surrey reached town.

"Then he came over to me and I began screaming, too. And he hit me, not with the gun again, but his hand, but it hurt as much, and nearly knocked me out, and I kept quiet then. And he threw me on the horse behind the saddle, like a sack, and lashed me there, and he got on and rode off with me."

Brandon stirred uncomfortably. Krista's story was terrible enough, but there was something about it that added an extra element of uneasiness.

"What was so awful was that I didn't even feel he was doing it to *me,*" Krista said. "Tom, Rosa, and I, we weren't people to him, just things he was using as he wanted." Not too far off from John B. Parker, come to that, Brandon thought wryly, but could not repress a rankling in him that was moving past unease and toward dread.

"He head straight for that place, like 'twas whereat he'd planned to stow you?" Ned Norland said.

"No. He was just riding along, and he stopped and gave kind of a grunt, as if he'd had an idea or just decided something, and then he turned off the way he was going."

He had pulled her off the horse, found a foul bit of cloth in his pocket to gag her with, pushed her against the wall with the toe of his boot, and then, presumably as a precaution against accidental discovery, upended the table over her.

She heard him riding away, then spent she had no idea how many hours in a fog of fear and misery before unconsciousness blessed her.

"And then Mr. Dailey found me," she said simply. Rush Dailey looked at her with a calm, contented gravity that Brandon thought he could read. The morning would see Krista redelivered to John B. Parker, and likely never free again, and Rush Dailey's life would be bleak and barren for a long time, but he had crossed the moat and saved his love, and that was reason enough to have lived.

"Curiouser by the minute," Ned Norland said. "Left the lady in the first shack he come acrost, never come back to see to her, also nothin' to show he knows the country hereabouts."

"Don't forget, he knew Krista was close to John B. Parker," Brandon said. "I don't think there was anything about that in the papers, so it wasn't known in Cheyenne. Another reason to think he's not a local man."

"Maybe somebody from St. Louis," Jake Trexler said. "With a grudge against the railroad or against John B. Parker, knew about you, and determined to get revenge or money or both. Did he look as if he might be anybody you'd seen or knew?"

Krista shook her head. "No. That was one thing that frightened me when I thought about it, that he wasn't wearing a mask. He wasn't worried that I would ever be able to tell anybody what he looked like, and if I did, I don't expect it would be hard to identify him, such a strange-looking man."

The dread was rising higher in Brandon now, and he saw that Ned Norland was shifting on his haunches as if troubled; he looked at Brandon and quickly away.

"Strange how?" he asked.

"A big man, bulky, but he moved fast, God, how fast! Eyes like a beast's, sunk deep in his face, and a nose like a rug-cutter's knife or hawk's beak."

Krista faltered, and seemed agitated. She rejected suggestions that she lie down for a moment and said she needed fresh air, and a little exercise; her legs were stiff.

A word or so before she finished her request, Rush Dailey was helping her to her feet and walking with her to the edge of the circle of firelight and then beyond it.

Looking after them, Brandon had not known his hand was in his pocket, but the Indian coin seemed to push against his fingertips, and he could feel clearly the endless circle of the self-devouring snake.

The face he had seen in the shack outside Philadelphia re-formed in front of him as Krista spoke. Four men had died in the shooting and explosion there, but one of them was not Gren Kenneally. Who the fourth one was, was a puzzler, but unimportant. Gren Kenneally lived, and Cole Brandon's hunting was not yet done.

"So he ain't dead," Ned Norland said slowly.

"Who?" Jake Trexler said.

"Gren Kenneally."

"For sure it sounds like him," Jake Trexler said. "Savage beyond most, the eagle beak, it's nine parts a certainty. But I didn't know he was supposed to be dead. . . ."

He looked speculatively across at Brandon, then nodded slowly, as if understanding something that had been unclear for a long time.

16

Rush Dailey pushed strongly for the idea of riding back to Cheyenne to get a comfortable wagon to serve as an ambulance for Krista, and berated himself, Brandon, Jake Trexler, and Ned Norland—and just stopped short of including Jess Marvell in the list—for not having had the foresight to include one as part of the expedition's outfitting.

"You don't go after kidnappers, whether a covey of 'em or a singleton," Ned Norland said, "with a horse and buggy trottin' along with the posse. You needs all the men you has ready to move whereat and when they got to, afoot or mounted, stealthy as a painter, not rumblin' and crunchin' over the ground on four iron tires. We had dumb luck that Kenneally went away and ain't come back yit, the which he ain't goin' to unnoted with Trexler sentryin' out on the trail, but if he'd been to home or had friends there, why, we'd have had a fight on our hands, with them gettin' in the first fire soon's ever they heared the buggy."

Krista insisted that she was well enough to sit a horse and, now that she was cleaned and rested, would rather do that and get back to Cheyenne as soon as possible than sleep now and return to town in the morning.

The moon was bright enough to make night riding safe, and Rush Dailey, faced with the prospect of holding Krista in front of him for some hours in the moonlight, was willing to fall in with her wishes. There was no thought in any mind there that Krista would ride with anyone but Rush Dailey.

Ned Norland went down the trail to where Jake Trexler had been posted as guard; Brandon and Rush Dailey broke camp, loaded gear onto the horses, and killed the fire. Brandon saw Rush Dailey look at Krista time and again as he worked, and wondered if Edmund and Elaine Chambers's Browning dramatizations included "The Last Ride To-gether":

> To be together, breathe and ride,
> So one more day am I deified;
> Who knows but the world may end tonight?

"Now, Mr. Brandon," Jake Trexler said quietly, "I don't want to pry into your affairs. You ain't involved in any case I'm investigating, and I don't know of anything you've done that it would be my professional duty to take notice of and report to the authorities, and I believe that not knowing what you've been about since you left St. Louis is the best road to keeping things that way. You understand me?"

"Clearly," Brandon said. He rode beside Jake Trexler at the rear of the small procession. Ned Norland, as before, led, and Rush Dailey, with Krista on the saddle in front of him, held the middle. The moon had passed the zenith but seemed whiter and brighter as it slid toward the horizon, and the air grew steadily chillier. Brandon could see that Rush Dailey was holding Krista tightly enough to assure her both shelter from the cold and a source of warmth.

"What I am concerned about is this abduction of Miss Ostermann for ransom," Jake Trexler said. "It goes with guarding John B. Parker, though I will say that my heart is more in it. But there is something that smells of old fish about this business, and I got an idea that you could tell me some things about it. And if you can do that without touching on matters I'd be obliged to take action on, that'd suit me fine. Both of us, I daresay. There is a tie between you and Gren Kenneally and between you and Miss Ostermann, so I wonder if that's where I have to look first."

"I wouldn't think so," Brandon said after a moment's thought. "Gren Kenneally doesn't know about me, I'm pretty sure; he's never seen me." Except as a pair of eyes over stretched cloth and a gun muzzle spouting flame, he did not add; that wouldn't change the basic fact, and would only give Jake Trexler the kind of knowledge he was working hard to avoid. "I think it's that he happened to be in Cheyenne when John B. Parker and Miss Ostermann showed up, recognized Parker, who's had his picture in the papers many's the time, saw they seemed close, kept his eye on her for a chance, and when it came, followed the surrey and kidnapped her."

"And killed the stable hand for convenience and raped the girl so we'd take him serious," Jake Trexler said. "Whatever it is you've been doing I don't know about, I wish it had been more successful. Gren Kenneally is an affront to every decent man alive."

Brandon thought over very carefully what he had the notion of saying, and decided that Jake Trexler had the need, and therefore the right, to know something more than he now did. "Ah . . . not only the decent ones, as it happens."

"What do you mean?"

Brandon explained that Gren's excesses had gone too far for even the more conventional thieves and murderers in his family to accept, and that he had become an outcast. "They, ah, didn't mind that someone might be after Gren and his gang, and weren't above, say, lending a little help. Information and such. Or that's what I heard," he added, seeing even in the moonlight that Jake Trexler was uncomfortable at getting information so precise that a presently dormant professional inquisitiveness might soon be roused to action.

"I see," Jake Trexler said. "Well, no, I don't. What's this got to do with what we're in the middle of?"

"Well, Gren could sort of have a grudge against the Kenneallys, the rest of them, if you see what I mean."

"Even less than I did," Trexler said. "What's Gren taking a dislike to his kin have to do with the price of eggs or John B. Parker or Miss Ostermann?"

"Well, he is," Brandon said. "Kin, that is. Distant, some kind of cousin, but there it is, some kin of the main fellows, old Peter and Quint."

"John B. Parker is a *Kenneally?*" Jake Trexler's voice rose and cracked like that of a boy whose passage into puberty is about to exile him from the alto section of the church choir. "Brandon, you're crazy! In spirit, sure, I can see that, but . . ."

Brandon explained to Jake Trexler the story as the Colorado judge had given it to him: the realization that the vast proceeds of crime had to be made use of if they were not to go to waste, and the decision to invest them in the reasonably honest and occasionally profitable enterprises that thronged the frontier. "And then later elsewhere," Brandon said. "Factories, railroads, banks, stockbrokers all over the country. In a while, there were Kenneallys who weren't Kenneallys, so to speak, in just about every line of trade or the professions, even politics—some of the inner family members but also cousins, in-laws, distant connections, men who'd never had any known connection to them. Probably there's a lot more of that kind than the old-fashioned criminals, and they're making more money."

"I see where this is going," Jake Trexler said, "and I don't like the scenery."

"It's the way it is," Brandon said. "And you're right, John B. Parker is one of that bunch. I don't expect he even thinks about it much, looks on himself as a law-abiding man except in the way of business. If he needed a certain kind of help fast, though, like breaking a strike on the railroad, he'd know where to turn, but he wouldn't admit to himself that it was a family matter."

Jake Trexler looked ahead to where Rush Dailey and Krista formed a single shape atop Dailey's horse. "That's a strange connection, then, your wife's sister about to marry a man that's connected to those that killed your wife."

"When you think about it, the worst thing about John B. Parker is that he's John B. Parker, not that he's a remote kin of Kenneally," Brandon said.

"Yeah," Jake Trexler said. "And . . . yeah, what you're saying is that Gren has a down on the rest of the family, and he knows about Parker being his sort of kin. So the kidnapping's revenge as well as business."

"I'd say so," Brandon said. "Spur-of-the-moment thing, poorly organized, no provision made for getting the money he demanded, and Krista left unguarded, so it's almost certainly a single-handed job, which is stupid for this kind of thing."

After a moment Jake Trexler said slowly, "He could have figured that John B. Parker would come boiling along after Miss Ostermann, and planned to lie in wait along the trail and bushwhack him."

"Not if he knew Parker well," Brandon said. "But there could be something in it, yeah. If that was the idea, Gren didn't get to carry it out. I can't see him trailing us or waiting for us, then letting us get to Krista."

"Maybe bit by a rattlesnake and twisting on the ground someplace, waiting for the poison to get to his heart," Jake Trexler said. "Or stuck in a crack in the rock with his leg broke, where the sun'll bake his brains when it comes up and the ants'll eat him before he's dead. It's nice to think that might be what's happened to him, even if his views on John B. Parker are sound."

At the outskirts of Cheyenne, Ned Norland and Brandon rode ahead, Norland to the Inter-Ocean to wake John B. Parker and tell him the news of Krista's rescue, Brandon to the Marvel Hall to do the same for Jess Marvell. She was awake in an instant, blew the banked wood stove to life, put coffee on to boil, then dressed; Brandon admired her choice of what to do first. Ned Norland and a hastily dressed Parker arrived just before the remainder of the party rode into the stable yard.

Jess Marvell ran to help Krista down from the horse and caught her as she swayed after stepping to the ground. John B. Parker went to her and said, "You all right?"

Krista lifted her head from Jess Marvell's shoulder and nodded. "Now."

Parker patted her on the shoulder and said, "Good."

"Mr. Dailey found me; I was all tied up and unconscious, but he found me and saved me."

"Grateful to him," Parker said.

"Of course I am!" Krista looked at him with surprise.

"I meant *I* was grateful, that he'd got you back, d'you see?" Parker said testily. "Obliged, Dailey, very much obliged!" he called to Rush Dailey, who nodded acknowledgment.

"He was—" Krista began, but Jess Marvell interrupted her.

"There's a soft bed and warm covers upstairs, Krista. Let's get you on up there and into bed right now." She put her arm around Krista's shoulders and led her into the Hall's living quarters. She called back to Brandon to take Parker and the others into the kitchen for coffee, which should be ready by now.

Brandon set out cups, the sugar caster, the milk jug from the icebox, spoons, sniffed the coffeepot and judged its contents properly brewed, wrapped a rag around its handle and poured it out, all with an unthinking brisk dexterity that drew curious looks from Parker, Trexler, and Rush Dailey, and an amused one from Ned Norland, the only one of them who knew of the weeks Brandon had spent as a trail cook, one of that breed that dishes out coffee automatically at any lull in the activity of the moment, as other men whittle or swap lies.

"You'll want to know all about it," Ned Norland said, after a moment during which Parker had made no move to acquire that knowledge. "Well, trailin' the surrey out weren't no great doin's, for a horse and four wheels makes tracks you cain't lose. But along the way, wc seen sign, a horse that was follerin' them. And then . . ."

Ned Norland gave the story fairly accurately, though he shaded it to suggest that he played a smaller part, and Jake Trexler a larger one, than was true. Since Ned Norland would cheerfully inflate his exploits until they were in danger of bursting like an overblown balloon, Brandon was at first puzzled, then caught on. There was no fun in impressing, falsely or otherwise, someone like John B. Parker, because Norland could not possibly care about Parker's opinion of him. But poor old Trexler was Parker's man, so long as he took Parker's pay, and Parker's good opinion had solid value for him, if for hardly anyone else.

Trexler glowered briefly, but gave a silent sigh and fell to listening with the rest.

". . . and then I come and woke you up, and thar's the whole boilin' of it," Ned Norland finished. "And you got the lady back, hale and blithesome as ever, so it's like them old-timey tales about the girl that gits took by a big kinder winged sarpint and a prince or a pig herder or such goes after and gits her back safe."

He paused abruptly, and in the moment of thickened silence that followed, Brandon thought that everyone in the room was dealing with the recollection that the rescuer in those stories, swineherd or royalty, usually wound up with the princess. At any rate, Parker looked like a man who finds that the apple he bit into now contains half a worm in the area opened by his bite, and Rush Dailey looked like one of those men in another kind of story who spend a night in the realms of magic and are cast out in the morning, forever haunted with memories of glory. Jake Trexler glanced quickly from his employer to Rush Dailey, and looked more somber than ever.

"Safe," John B. Parker said heavily.

"She is that, now," Ned Norland said. "And I'm glad and proud to have played what part I did in that, little though it was."

"Safe, yes," John B. Parker said. "But how was she when you found her? Her clothing . . ."

"It was a mess," Brandon said, "all dirty and crumpled; she'd been tied up for a long time." And a longer haul from dainty than she'd ever been since she got out of diapers, poor kid.

Parker looked stonily at him. "Washing sees to that, or new clothes. There's other kinds of dirtying. We know what kind of man this is, what he did to that girl, what's-her-name—"

"Rosa," Jess Marvell said as she reentered the room. "Rosa Zweibel, traveled with you all the way from St. Louis. If you were wondering, she was screaming till the doctor gave her something that put her to sleep, and she still moves and moans a little while she's sleeping."

"Sorry for Rosie, of course," John B. Parker said. "But that's the thing. . . . Well, you took her up, Miss Marvell, you, ah, helped her. . . . Was there any, ah . . . that she'd been . . ."

"Outraged like poor Rosa?" Jess Marvell said, a touch acidly, then softened as she went on, "No, that at least she didn't go through, poor soul. She was afraid of it, and she was working out if she could hurt him enough to make him kill her if he did, but no, it didn't come to that." The trace of warmth in the look she gave Parker suggested to Brandon that she was pleased and surprised that he cared enough about the woman he was marrying to ask the question, or at least come close enough to asking so she could answer. Rush Dailey, he saw, seemed to be staring into a magic-lantern show, visible only to himself, of varied scenes of life in Hell.

"Good," John B. Parker said. "Would have been . . . well, difficult, begging off now, though she'd have understood, not made trouble, I'm sure. She'd have seen that it wouldn't have done, no doubt about it, not for Mrs. John B. Parker. Very sensible woman." He turned to Jess Marvell, who, if

181

not gaping outright, certainly had some slack in her lower jaw. "Now, keep close accounts on the care you're giving her, Miss Marvell. John B. Parker pays for value, no question about it, but I don't care for being fleeced, not that you'd be likely to try, but I believe in being particular about even small expenditures, so the more details the better, if you can justify 'em. I'll call round in the morning and look in on Miss Ostermann, some time after breakfast, I'd guess. Night to you, ma'am, gentlemen, Trexler."

Brandon realized that Parker was summoning his bodyguard to follow him, not distinguishing him from the mass of men you called "gentlemen" as a matter of form, until you found a reason not to. The two men left the brightly lit room; Brandon could see faint light in the doorway, showing that dawn was not far off.

After the door closed, Brandon waited for the extravagant spate of imaginative invective from Ned Norland, the volcano of outrage from Jess Marvell, the howl of outraged chivalry from Rush Dailey, or even the acrid rangeland expletives he had been unconsciously gathering in his travels for employment on an occasion like this. Nothing came; the three men and the woman looked into one another's eyes, sharing consciousness of an enormity they had not expected to find. Brandon thought, but did not say, *That Parker's a dandy—even Gren Kenneally wouldn't care to acknowledge him as kin.*

After searching his redolently virulent vocabulary for something vile enough to say about him, Ned Norland found it: simple, inarguable, and loathsome.

"John B. Parker," he said slowly, drawing it out so that it could slide coldly like a water moccasin across his hearers' minds. He shook his head wonderingly and said it again: "John . . . B. . . . goddamn *Parker.*"

"Krista got a look at the man," Jess Marvell said. She was adhering warmly to Brandon down their sweaty torsos as they lay in her second-best bed, the prime article now enfolding Krista down the hall in the master bedroom.

182

"Good enough description, they ought to be able to pick him up, even if he's in another state. What he did to Rosa, that's a hanging offense here. And of course, killing Tom and then trying to get money for kidnapping Krista."

"Hang him for Tom, hang him again for Rosa, then life in prison for Krista, that's a heavy sentence to get," Brandon said. Once alone in the kitchen, they had looked at each other and gone up quickly to the vacant bedroom, undressed quickly, and made love more quickly than they had become used to in this short time. It seemed to Brandon that they were looking for reaffirmation and reassurance, to celebrate that they lived and had the capacity for love, and that there was a lot separating them on the evolutionary scale from John B. Parker.

Brandon had no idea whether Jake Trexler had by now told John B. Parker that the kidnapper was Gren Kenneally; they had not discussed what use to make of the identification, particularly since Brandon's conviction would probably not be enough evidence to persuade the authorities to take action, such as it might be. He was convinced, though, that Gren Kenneally was alive, and that the job he had set out to do was not, as he had believed, finished.

Hearing that would distress Jess Marvell considerably, and it would be easy to keep that knowledge from her; neither Ned Norland nor Jake Trexler were going to bring it up to her. As soon as he had formulated the thought of concealment clearly, he said, "Her description was very clear. I don't think there's any doubt it's Gren Kenneally. There must have been a fifth man there, in Philadelphia, and he got killed and Gren got away."

Jess Marvell closed her eyes and her face looked old, and Brandon knew that he had done the right thing; he could hurt her if that was what was called for, and she could take it, and it was better than keeping things back from her. When she opened her eyes and looked at him again, he saw the hurt, and a new level of trust. "You must feel horrible," she said. "Thought you were done with all that, and you're not."

He closed his eyes and ran her words through his mind again. They rang flatly. He did not in fact feel horrible, even aside from what he and Jess Marvell had just been up to. . . . *And you're not.* Well . . .

"When I thought I was done, that Gren was dead, I didn't feel victorious, triumphant, anything like that," he said slowly. "Happy, yes, because I was through with something that had been keeping me from you for a long time; that was the strongest thing I felt. About Gren and the rest, it was just finishing something that had to be finished, and when it was, or I thought it was, it was a weight lifting off me, not much else. So I had whatever it was I was going to get from doing that, and if it's still to do and I do it, that's all I'll get. And, with you, with getting on with life and the work I'll be getting at . . . I don't know, it doesn't seem to make sense. When I was doing that, tracking them, I was the man who was doing that tracking, and now I'm not, and I don't find it in me to turn into that man again."

"Elise," Jess Marvell said.

"What is it now, ten men dead?" Brandon said. "Gren's a walking dead man, somebody will have to kill him soon for being what he is, it's a matter of time only. Maybe it's already happened, that's why he never got back to ambush us or keep Krista captive. And, you know, dear Jess, I'm finding I don't give a damn. My wife, her aunt, her father, and the farm people, they're dead, they've been avenged more than most, and I don't think it's done them a damn bit of good. I won't say I regret what I've been doing, any more than I'm proud of it, nothing to do with pride or regrets. There's some people in Texas I stayed with that had stories from Europe about men that turned into wolves at the full moon, then back. You could say I turned into a wolf for a lot of moons, but I'm turned back."

He laid his face on her hair, ran his hand down her ear, feeling its fragility against the bone that cradled whatever it was that made Jess Marvell Jess Marvell, and was moved at the strength and fragility of the ear and of the skull.

This was a new quest, a different kind of quest, and one

that had no ending in view, cherishing Jess Marvell and receiving her cherishing. That was his job now; unfinished or not, the other one was closed down.

"Now," said John B. Parker, "we can't get much forwarder with this, for I deal with principals, and Miss Marvell's tied up, and you have God knows what standing in this whole business."

"I advise Miss Marvell on the legal aspects," Brandon said.

"Huh," Parker said. "Well, in any case, she ain't here, and that Dailey kid's not authorized to speak for her. And I want Miss Ostermann to see this, she's set on being involved in this part of the business, and she's got a head for it."

They were back at the warehouse from which Rosa Zweibel's hoarse screams had drawn them yesterday, Rush Dailey showing off its points to John B. Parker with the heartily sincere manner of a horse trader at a county fair.

Now Parker had sent Rush Dailey off to stand by the door as he talked to Brandon; Trexler joined him.

"Miss Ostermann, Mrs. Parker she'll be then," John B. Parker said, "she'll be out and around these parts a good bit. She's taken a shine to Miss Marvell, and expects to like working with her. That is a thing you see with women that go into business, Brandon; liking who you work with counts with them. That is why women, even the intelligent ones, aren't going to get to run a business of any size. You look, you'll see that the big businesses are mostly run by men nobody likes, and just about totally by men who don't like anybody." He shifted his weight on his feet and once more looked at Rush Dailey.

"Went to the show last night," he said after a while. "Nothing to do while you fellows were out of town, and it seemed like it might be interesting. It was. There was this old man and this young woman, and they did sketches from some poet. And there was one about this duke fellow that had a wife and she took a shine to a fellow he had working for him, and he didn't care much for that kind of goings-on, which who would, and now there's nothing of her left but a picture hanging on the wall."

" 'My Last Duchess,' " Brandon said.

"Good guess, that's just the way he put it. What was interesting was that the fellow had the right instincts, for you don't let someone tamper with your property, but he was too dukish about it, and he wound up with just a picture, not the woman. Dukes don't wonder about where the profit is, they just go for feeding their pride, which is a hard beast to stable, I will tell you. Now, a man that can see where the profit is in a situation, a man that knows how business works and how money works and how people work, why, he can work out how to get the kind of profit he wants in about any situation."

He looked over again at Rush Dailey. "Now, that's a sharp young fellow, that could go far. I'd say he's wasted working for Miss Marvell, capable of a lot more than that. I'd say he could do well at my company's London bank, learn his way around there, then come on to New York for real work. It'd be a pleasure to me to see him prosper so, after what he done for Miss Ostermann, and I'll see to it that he accepts. I'm sure Miss Marvell will push him if he don't care for it when I put it to him."

John B. Parker looked around the warehouse. "I'll think about this, go over the figures again with the ladies. Come on."

He strode toward the door, Brandon behind him. Jake Trexler and Rush Dailey moved apart to let Parker through, then Trexler fell in beside Parker. Brandon had noticed throughout the expedition that Trexler had stuck closer to his boss than usual, and wondered if his near-idle speculation about Gren Kenneally harboring spite against Parker as disapproving relative had energized Trexler's sense of duty or perhaps just his interest.

The sky today was gray, and the wind raw, with a hint of rain splatting on them from toward the south. The trees that stood on the vacant land past the warehouse were dark as winter evergreens, and birds swooped distractedly toward them, sending tiny ripples of apparent movement over the thickly bunched leaves.

Something moved among the tree trunks—a deer? Brandon saw what could be a moving stick, and a metallic gleam running along it.

"Trexler!" he called. "In the trees, man with gun!"

Brandon saw the rifle, its wielder still shadowed by the trees, come up and point in their direction. Trexler slammed John B. Parker back toward the warehouse door, yelling, *"Inside,* damn it, Mr. Parker!" and firing his revolver at the trees. Brandon stepped aside to let Parker in. Parker turned to look outside, and Brandon heard what sounded like a small, nearby thunderclap with an instant echo, more of a thud than a thunderclap.

Next to Brandon, John B. Parker gave a moaning belch and leaned backward very quickly, leaving red spray from his throat hanging briefly in the air.

The floor transmitted a strong vibration as he hit it, which continued as he thrashed, beating his hands against the floor and drumming on it with one leg. The blood spouted from his throat in two more pulses, then ceased, as did his movements.

Jake Trexler and Rush Dailey burst into the warehouse, Trexler howling curses, which changed to a long cry of anger, disgust, and sadness when he saw Parker's sightless stare and the blood-soaked throat and chest.

"I let the son of a bitch down, damn it!" Trexler said, kneeling by the body.

Rush Dailey stared sickly at John B. Parker's body, looking almost as young as when Brandon first knew him.

Rush, you are very lucky, Brandon thought. If this hadn't happened now, you could have been the one doing it.

17

One of Jess Marvell's kitchen workers both had a dark-colored suit of clothes and was slightly built, so that Ned Norland could be fitted out to make a respectable appearance on the station platform. His own town clothes, cut from cloth woven in finger-wide green and ocher stripes, were not suitable for what was, if not a funeral, reasonably funereal.

"In the baggage car ahead, like it says in the song," he observed, looking at the windowless car the small party was standing by. "The mortal part of John B. Parker going to his long home, while behind the heedless passengers enjoy the jollities of modern train travel. It makes you think, I expect."

It made Brandon think that it was time for the train to start so that they could leave the platform. He was not sure who had decided that John B. Parker should be seen off, but it had over the last couple of days become an accepted fact, and even Ned Norland accepted his regarding and attendance without protest. Probably Jess's notion, he guessed; women tended to set the rules about those things.

He stood next to Jess Marvell; Rush Dailey stood next to

Krista, who had insisted on coming; Jake Trexler and Ned Norland formed a less well-suited third couple. All of them looked at the vertical slats of the car and studied the green and gold paint of the line's painted name with apparent concentration, since it was not a time for looking around and commenting on what points of interest the Cheyenne depot afforded, or on the fact that there weren't any. Also, looking around would involve meeting the sour looks of the delegation from the Cheyenne police that had escorted to the train the men from John B. Parker's companies who rushed west to arrange his packing and shipment home for burial.

The police had not cared for John B. Parker much after his dismissal of them in the matter of Rosa Zweibel, and they had been outright enraged when he had got himself killed, perhaps by Rosa Zweibel's assailant. If they had known of Krista's abduction and rescue, very likely, Brandon thought, they would have thrown everyone who knew John B. Parker in jail for interfering in police business, and been all the more savage because the effort had been successful.

Leaving Krista out of it also meant leaving Gren Kenneally out of it, but Brandon, Jake Trexler, and Ned Norland had agreed that naming Kenneally would not advance the hunt for Parker's killer appreciably. "And what's to say it's Gren?" Ned Norland said. "Killing John B. Parker ain't something that'd occur to jist one man in the history of the world, no, sir."

What had happened at the warehouse was clear enough so that the survivors' story was never strongly questioned, and the police gloomily made ritual efforts at finding the man who had, from evident traces, concealed himself in the trees and put a bullet through John B. Parker's throat.

The locomotive's whistle shrieked imperiously, the conductor clanged bells and bawled, and the pistons pushed the driving wheels shuddering through their first laborious rotation, drawing the train slowly along. Brandon looked sidewise at Krista and saw that her face was expressionless.

The baggage car moved past them, and then the passenger cars. From the forward car, John B. Parker's recent associates looked down at them without the outright irritation of the police, but without friendliness, especially when their gazes drifted across Jake Trexler's face. They had let him know that a bodyguard who let his charge become a dead body was not, in their view, giving value for money, and Trexler was unsure of what his future as a railroad detective, at least with this railroad, would be.

Brandon noticed that the passenger cars on this train were day coaches only; no palatial Pullman. John B. Parker was leaving Cheyenne with a good deal less style than he had entered it, but his requirements were less now.

When the train was dwindling eastward down the track and the taint of the engine's smoke had mostly dispersed, and the police delegation had done the same, Brandon and the rest relaxed, Trexler and Brandon asking and receiving from the women permission to light cigars.

Rush Dailey looked after the train. "The butch on that'll do good business. After a doings like that, those fellows that worked for Mr. Parker, they'll be wanting drinks and sandwiches and fruit and things to read. They get nervous and reflective, and they'll buy kind of anything, even combs and ready-threaded needles for small repairs, to keep from feeling solemn and uneasy."

"It is marvelous, how you know the details of even that kind of business," Krista said. She was holding Rush Dailey's arm with her right hand as if it provided sure and comforting support.

"Not so marvelous," Rush Dailey said. "I done that work for some years when I was younger, and it taught me a lot of stuff that's come in handy as a horse for the Marvel Halls later on, how to make sure people get what they want, for instance. Or anyhow, how to make them think that what they get is what they want."

"You put that so well," Krista said. "It is wonderful to be able to turn experience to account, to continue to learn throughout life." She laid her left hand on Rush Dailey's arm and clasped it over her right. Brandon thought that the slightly throaty German tinge to her speech was coming back perceptibly, and remembered that had always denoted a sharpening of Krista's focus on something.

"Well, a fellow that can't learn, it's like a horse with blinders," Rush Dailey said.

"It's past noon," Jess Marvell said. "We need some lunch, and I don't think this is a Marvel Hall sort of occasion. Let's go to the dining room at the Inter-Continental and give ourselves a . . . have a good meal." Brandon agreed that "treat," the obvious finish to her suggestion, would have sounded odd under the circumstances, though understandable.

"I am tired," Krista said. "It would be nice, but I cannot join you, Jess. I will go back to the so-comfortable room you are too kind to tell me to leave, and rest."

"Welcome to stay as long as you like," Jess Marvell said. "No question of you leaving, 'specially while poor Rosa's still there."

The Cheyenne Marvel Hall had been built with the idea of doing some accommodations business, but Jess Marvell had decided against it for the moment, and the bedrooms on the second floor had gone unused until Rosa and then Jess, turning her own room over to Krista, had occupied them. Rosa was now waking and sleeping normally, and moving around some, but still weeping a lot and disinclined to be near anyone.

"I will see Miss Ostermann back," Rush Dailey said. He spoke without the almost defiant firmness of such statements a few days ago, in the period immediately following John B. Parker's murder. Back then, it might happen that Brandon or Jake Trexler, or even Ned Norland, might offer to escort Krista someplace, but they gave that up in the face of Rush Dailey's implacable determination to see to all and anything Krista Ostermann might need or want.

Jess Marvell chewed on a mouthful of her antelope steak and swallowed it happily. "Better than in the Halls, I don't mind saying. Meat's as good both places, but if you can take the time to cook it just to order, it makes a difference." Her chin and part of one cheek gleamed with grease, and she had a pleasantly sated look that Brandon had become familiar with under other circumstances. It's a blessing to be paired to a woman of hearty appetites, he thought. Running the Halls, she can see to one of 'em on her own if she has to, but I seem to be needed for the other, thank God.

"Well, here's to the founder of the feast, so to speak," Jake Trexler said. He lifted his tumbler of wine. "John B. Parker didn't pay for it, but we wouldn't be here together right now if it wasn't for him getting killed, so it's kind of a wake for him, I suppose."

"Solemn thought," Ned Norland said around a bone he was stripping bare with his teeth. "Large as life one instant, full of pizen and fire, and the next returnt to the inanimal clay of whence he come. Happens all the time, accourse, but it's the size that makes the impression. Papers called him the Killer Elephant, and they was kinder right, he took up a lot o' room. I knew a feller oncet that traveled in Afriky and seen elephants a-many, and he tolt me of one he'd seen that'd got mazed and run off a high cliff and fell a long ways. Burst like a bomb made o' meat when it hit, he said. Stuck in my mind when he tolt me that, and now it'll come to me whenas I think of John B. Parker."

"A preacher couldn't have put it better, or not the same, anyhow," Brandon said, interested to notice that Jess Marvell continued to cut, chew, and clearly enjoy her rare meat, unperturbed by Ned Norland's vivid word picture.

"You could say he had a lot to live for," Jake Trexler said pensively. "He told me he was waiting for the conventions to see who'd get the nominations, then he'd pick the man he could get coziest to and push for him. Said it'd be a sure thing, with the papers and the telegraph, you can get whatever word you want all round the country in no time and make sure the voters go the way you want. It's a matter of knowing where the money'll do the most good and putting it there."

"Why not try to rig one of the conventions so a man he'd want would get the nomination?" Brandon said.

Jake Trexler shook his head. "Parker said that trying to control party delegates was like herding worms on a trail drive. The electorate's bigger, he said, but they bunch up better 'n cattle or sheep if you know how to drive 'em."

"And nextest thing, they're on the cars to Chicago or Kansas City and the man with the sledgehammer and knife waiting," Ned Norland said. "Or they got a new president and Congress, which is a slow way of gettin' the same place."

"He was a character," Jake Trexler said. "Nothing quite like him."

"I imagine you'll miss him, in a way," Jess Marvell said.

"Well, no," Jake Trexler said.

"I wonder if Krista will," Brandon said. "I never could figure what made her take an interest in him."

"He took an interest in her," Jess Marvell said. "Times in a woman's life, that's a very important thing." She looked levelly at Brandon, who knew then that Krista had gone into her history thoroughly enough to get to Brandon's role, or nonrole, in it, and that Jess Marvell did not propose to fetch it up again. "And for Krista, the other important thing was business. She took over the company her father left her and made it hum, even in the worst part of the depression, and she turned the men who'd distrusted and despised her into loyal managers and supporters, and that's something a lot rarer than catching a man is. It's like having a wine that's stronger and more delicious than anything that's for sale, and knowing that you're one of the very few that has it."

Well, yeah, Jess would know about that, Brandon thought dourly. Then he caught her fondly amused look at him and read it: Oh, yes, I have that delicious wine myself. And I have you, and that makes it five times more delicious, my dear.

"Parker admired her as a woman, and he respected her as a businesswoman, that was what drew her," Jess Marvell said. "And he knew what would catch her. He showed her some ideas that would expand the Ostermann businesses tremendously, and he made it clear that she'd have a voice in his businesses, the banks, railroads, factories, everything. She would have been the most powerful woman in the country."

And turning Kenneally money to the most profit of anybody in the country, Brandon thought.

"D'you suppose Gren Kenneally knew Parker was tied to the family?" Jake Trexler said, giving Brandon the startling impression that his mind had been partially read. "Pretty secret stuff, since I didn't know it, and I'm in the detective business, or maybe not, depending on what I hear from the railroad. But if he didn't know, it's hard to see the motive."

"You fellers never saw the shooter," Ned Norland said slowly. "And you and me, we never saw the one that took Miss Krista. And there ain't anything even that ties the two of 'em together."

"Krista described Gren Kenneally!" Brandon said.

Ned Norland shook his head. "She described a man that had a nose and a body like Gren's and acted the way we'd expect Gren to act. You know how far that'd take you in court, Brandon."

"This isn't a court!"

"No, 'tain't. And I'm a man to go with what my nose tells me and what my belly or liver tells me if there ain't what for the nose to pick up, and the fall of a feather or what I see if I chew on a peyote button if there ain't nothin' else. But I also know you cain't build a bridge by pickin' up a stick and lashin' another stick to it and another'n to that, and layin' the bunch of 'em acrost a crick. You got to have more sticks and they got to fit together better if you want to git over the water dry."

"I think you're right," Jake Trexler said. "It could be Gren Kenneally both times or one or neither, and nothing to go on either way. And if it is, he's killed Parker, for whatever reason, and he's got nothing to hang around for, so he's well away from here and good riddance." He got up out of his chair. "I better get to the telegraph office and see if there's a wire for me. If I still have a job, it could be to kick hoboes off the freight trains without getting cut in two sliding under the wheels."

"You think that the man Krista saw could be just some brute that has something of the look of Gren Kenneally?" Jess Marvell said.

Brandon sighed. "He could be, of course. And you're right, Ned, there's nothing to show he isn't. But Trexler's right, if it is Gren, he did what he wanted to and he's gone. I'd say it could be him, and he got mad at Parker for being in the part of the family that's turned against him and took Krista, then got madder when his plans failed, and got his revenge. Doesn't hold water all that well, but he's crazy, don't forget, and crazy people do crazy things; that's how you know they're crazy."

He sipped at the last of the wine in his glass. It was warming and delicious, gentle and stimulating, at the same time, like Jess. "But it's like I told you the other day," he said to her. "I don't care if it's Gren Kenneally or not. Maybe it is, or maybe he's dead and buried in Philadelphia. Whichever, it's over as far as I'm concerned. Gren and his men killed Elise and the others, and either they've all paid or there's one that hasn't, and I'm not concerned with making all the sums add up any more. Any time I spend worrying about Gren Kenneally is time taken out of my life, and I don't want to give them any more of that."

Ned Norland looked at Jess Marvell's radiant face and nodded. "You could be right. I hope you are." He took one of Brandon's cigars and lit it from the candle in the center of the table. "Somethin' that comes to mind," he said. "That old-timey Injun coin or what that you dug outer the mound, back on the farm? Seems to me it brung you luck or somethin' in some way I disremember. If you won't be needin' that kind o' luck, p'raps you'd keer to lemme have it as a play-pretty."

"Why not?" Brandon said. "I keep meaning to throw it away anyhow, but it never seems to be on me when I remember about that. It's like collar buttons and penknives, you know how stuff like that seems to come and go, no matter where you think you put it last."

"That's about how I'd expect that coin to be," Ned Norland said.

". . . a seahorse, thought a rarity,
Which Klaus of Innsbruck cast in bronze for me,"

Edmund Chamber said with a venomous silkiness that set Brandon's neck hairs abristle. You could believe he had taken a hideous revenge on his errant wife and her young lover, and that Elaine Chambers's staring beauty was that of a memorial portrait, not a living woman.

He bowed to a round of fairly substantial applause. Robert Browning's poetry was not a major enthusiasm of Cheyenne's theater patrons, but Edmund Chambers was known to provide robust, if not always understandable, drama, and Elaine Chambers was well worth anybody's two dollars to look at, especially as her notion of a Renaissance "Last Duchess's" costume involved swaths of loosely draped silk and velvet and provided a lot of looking area. Brandon considered that the visible area of her bosom was pleasant, and not half as alluring as Jess Marvell's, mostly covered in blue silk though it was at the moment.

"That is one prime woman," Ned Norland said, beating his hands together vigorously. "You goin' backstage to hello them folks?"

"We thought we'd pay a short call," Brandon said.

"I will company you and convey to these greasepainters my admiration for their dramantics," Ned Norland said.

A few minutes later, Norland was conveying his sentiments fairly vigorously to Elaine Chambers in one corner of the boxy space next to the dressing rooms while Brandon and Jess Marvell told Edmund Chambers how much they admired his adaptations and his performances of them. Norland seemed to be on the topic of admiration as well, judging by the smiles and laughter he was drawing from Elaine Chambers.

"I saw John B. Parker in the audience the night before he was killed," Edmund Chambers said. "Did he by any chance mention the performance?"

"It made a powerful impression on him," Brandon said. "Said it showed how poetry could mean something in real life."

"Glad to hear it, though he's in no position to give recommendations now, poor chap," said Edmund Chambers.

Jess Marvell remained behind for a moment's talk with Elaine Chambers while Brandon and Ned Norland strolled out into the alley behind the theater.

"That is some young lady, that Miss Elaine," Ned Norland said. "Her and I is to have a late supper after the show tomorrer night, and there's nothin' to say breakfast mightn't come into it."

Looking at the wizened frontiersman in his incongruous finery, lacking even the raffish distinction of his usual dirty buckskins, Brandon would have dismissed his statement as senile boastfulness, but he had seen enough of Ned Norland to know that his success with personable women was not illusory, even if it remained unfathomable.

Jess Marvell came out of the darkened stage door and took Brandon's arm. The three of them walked to the Inter-Continental, where Norland had decided, as he said, to "fort up" for the rest of his time in Cheyenne; then Brandon and Jess Marvell walked on toward the Marvell Hall.

"Norland claimed he, ah, made an impression on Elaine Chambers," Brandon said.

"Oh, he did," Jess Marvell said.

"Said something about supper after the performance tomorrow."

"A girl gets hungry after that kind of work. Feels like getting fed, relaxing, loosening her stays."

"You mean that metaphorically, about the stays," Brandon said.

"No."

"Oh. Damn," Brandon said reflectively. "Ned is a grand old fellow, but not what you'd expect the ladies to favor. What d'you suppose it is?"

"Well, he wants them," Jess Marvell said. "Not to make toys out of, not to be some kind of doll that looks pretty, not to make up for what some other woman wasn't, or couldn't or wouldn't do, all that mixed-up business that men get into with women, and Lord knows women do it worse with men, but he just . . . wants them the way they are. He doesn't care that Elaine's an actress or even, much, that she's pretty, he let her know he's taken with everything about her, that's what she told me. And she's interested in finding out what that adds up to."

"Told you all that about him, did she?" Brandon considered that if Victoria Woodhull did get elected president, political and diplomatic secrets might be a thing of the past, and maybe not a bad idea. No, women could keep secrets as well as anybody; it was just that they had unsettling notions of what not to conceal. If Ned Norland did get to breakfast with Elaine Chambers, Jess Marvell would know all the prebreakfast details within a day, Brandon was sure.

"And one thing more. Said he reminded her a little of you."

Brandon wished Jess Marvell had spoken with at least a touch of incredulity instead of mild amusement and apparent understanding.

This train had a Pullman, and Rush Dailey was at its door down the platform, superintending the loading of Krista's luggage and Rosa Zweibel's, and Rosa herself, onto it.

"She's not her old self, and I don't know if she ever will be," Krista said, "but she is better. Maybe being home will help her. I have told her I will not tell what happened to her, and she had better not, either, not even in confession. It is not her sin, and she need not bother a priest with it. If she says nothing, she may come to believe it never happened."

She looked down the platform and sighed. "Rush is so helpful, so kind, so smart. I will miss him, and I feel badly to be leaving him."

"Well, I suppose he was a big help to you with all the troubles," Brandon said. "But you're past them now, and you're your old self again, Kristchen. When you're back in St. Louis, he'll get over this feeling he has for you, so you don't have to worry about him."

"I will miss him until he comes to St. Louis to continue our business talks in a few weeks," Krista said with a precision that stopped just short of coldness or exasperation. "And then it will go beyond business, we are both certain of that. I feel badly to be leaving him because I want to be with him. Do not gape at me like a pig's head on a platter, Cole! Rush has already done more for me than most women's husbands or lovers do for them in a lifetime. He saved me because he knew where I was, his heart knew, when you would have passed me by because it did not make sense that I would be there, and I would have died in my filth."

"You . . . Rush Dailey?" Brandon said, knowing that it was stupid, but feeling that he was being dragged behind Krista's train of thought, off the tracks and bumping painfully along the ties.

"Yes!" Krista said. "I engaged myself to John B. Parker, and people thought nothing of it—I had my reasons and I will not say they were foolish, but it was a monstrous thing, and yet the world accepted it, even you, Cole. But Krista Ostermann and Rush Dailey, that is a thing unheard-of! But it will be heard of, because it will happen."

Brandon looked down the platform, glad to see Rush Dailey engaged in conversation with the porter, doubtless enjoining him to see that Krista Ostermann enjoyed the most trouble-free trip in the history of the Pullman Company.

"Rush Dailey is seven years younger than I am," Krista said. "Is that what's worrying you?"

"It's a consideration," Brandon said.

"John B. Parker was more than twice my age!" Krista said. "Old men marry young girls to have someone to take care of them when they become feeble, and nobody thinks it strange!" Brandon nodded as he remembered hearing of a War of 1812 veteran last year marrying a woman of seventeen; her widow's pension could go on being paid up to 1930 or so, someone had estimated.

"Rush is a bright man, a good man, a loving man, and he saw across those seven years and he wanted what he saw," Krista said. "And I looked back, and first I saw a funny boy, then I saw deeper, and finally I saw the man, and the years have nothing to do with it, and I wanted him. And, dear Cole, I am the surer of that because I know how I wanted you. And when I felt that tug inside me, like a very fine crochet hook reaching around and touching me very delicately, when I felt that again with Rush, why, there was no question. There is something of you in him, you know."

Rush Dailey beckoned, and Brandon escorted Krista down the platform, trying to come to terms with resembling both Rush Dailey and Ned Norland at one and the same time. Whether there was anything to that or not, he decided, the way Krista Ostermann felt about him, Rush Dailey was lucky as . . . well, a horse.

Brandon found he was getting used to being in the parlor with Jess, warm in the lamplight, warm deep inside with the knowledge that in a while they would go up to the bedroom, hers again now that Krista was gone, not the perfectly comfortable but impersonal rental room they had been using.

There were traces underneath of another domestic time, in St. Louis with Elise; they had spent evenings at home, Elise sewing, Brandon working on briefs. But those memories were only drifting wisps of the past, a faint fragrance as of dried flowers, without the power to touch the heart any more. This was the rich present, rich in a way nothing in his past had been.

It seemed strange that neither of them had said anything about getting married. He supposed—hoped—that it was because she, just as he did, assumed it was going to happen, with the only thing to be settled the not very important question of when. It was the only thing that made sense, it had to happen, and it would when they decided it was time.

Maybe the time was after he was admitted to the Territorial Bar. He turned back to the application papers he had picked up at the Bar Association's office and studied them. He wondered what kind of office he would set up, and leaned back to consider it. No partners, not at the start, so a small place, maybe a clerk. Shelves laden with the Territorial statutes; no, not all that laden, Wyoming hadn't been around long enough to build up too many pounds of paper carrying its laws. Green-shaded lamp, wouldn't be a law office without . . .

". . . tomorrow?"

Brandon shut up his mental office and returned to Jess Marvell's parlor. "Tomorrow?"

"Dinner at the Chinese restaurant with the Chamberses, we talked about it this morning, and I went round to their boardinghouse and fixed it up with Elaine. Before the show, say around six, that's all right?"

"Sure."

Brandon leaned back again, feeling happily settled. He knew some ins and outs and back corners of Cheyenne by now, and it was nice to know people to have dinner with. The Chamberses would be on their way in a while, and so would Jake Trexler (still waiting for word of what the railroad wanted him to do, if anything) and Ned Norland, but they were here for the moment, and when they moved on there would be others to get to know and become neighborly with.

He dug his hands into his pockets and grinned as his fingers found the old Indian coin. That nonsense about getting rid of it now its occult function was finished, finding a place to dispose of it with due respect, he could forget that. It was a piece of lifeless metal, interestingly decorated, and that was all. He had been half-crazy all that time he was tracking the Kenneally gang, and the fancies he'd had about the coin were part of that.

It might be a good idea to have it made up into a watch fob, have a story to tell about it. Clients liked that kind of thing in a lawyer, showed he wasn't Attorney Dryasdust, talking about replevins and putting the tips of his fingers together as he considered their problem.

Well, now, an old Indian chief out in New Mexico told me that the snake on this side here, that stands for . . .

Brandon was half out of his seat, and Jess Marvell was looking up with eyes so widened that white showed all around the irises, before the sudden swell of sound that had alerted them coalesced into shouts, running feet, male and female cries of dismay and anger, and a thin thread of breathy wailing.

The door to the building slammed open, and two seconds later, so did the parlor door; Sam, the Hall's chief handyman, burst in.

"Miss Jess!" he cried. "'S awful! Pearl . . ." Brandon remembered a plump, dark-haired Marvel Girl with ambitions to become a manager; Jess was keeping an approving eye on her. "She's . . . They found her out behind the stables. Somebody'd . . . She's all tore up and bloody, clothes a'most gone, and her poor face . . ."

"Have them take her upstairs to one of the empty bedrooms and settle her. Someone's gone for the doctor? Good. I'll get my medicines and be up right away."

"She's so shamed, Miss Jess, she's in torment!"

"Nothing shaming in being hurt," Jess Marvell said, going through her desk in search of some of the ointments and remedies she kept there.

"No 'm, but it's what she done, the man kept asking her questions, questions about you, and she told him ever'thing he asked, and she's mortal ashamed she was so weak."

Final Mask

Jess Marvell closed her eyes, and Brandon saw her face go still. Then she opened them slowly and looked at him, acknowledging what they both knew.

The coin in his pocket seemed to burn through the fabric of the pocket into his skin, or it might have been so cold that it was as painful as fire.

18

Brandon came around to the Marvel Hall kitchen about midmorning the next day, as Jess Marvell had asked. He had wanted to spend the night with her, but there was so much confusion and coming and going, and the police arriving and deciding to post a constable to guard Pearl, that discretion would have been impossible, and even in Wyoming some social conformity was required of a business-woman.

She looked up at him with tired eyes. "I got to sleep after a while," she said, "but I was talking to Pearl for half an hour, after she came out of the dope the doctor gave her last night, and hearing her makes me feel as if I'd never had any sleep or rest in my life. Cole, it is Gren Kenneally, I know that from what Pearl told me."

Early the previous evening, Pearl had been taking a shortcut back to the women's sleeping quarters next to the Hall, and passed through a patch of woods. She had the sense of someone near her, then was slammed into uncon-sciousness. When she came to, it was dusk, and she was in some kind of small structure. During her ordeal a train roared and rattled by, only feet away, and she realized it was a shed used by the section gangs, about a quarter mile down the track from the Hall.

"He was the same man Krista described," Jess Marvell said. "He looked at her, Pearl said, grinned, and said, 'Tell me.' Pearl said tell him what, and he grinned some more and said, 'Whatever I ask.' And then he pulled up her skirt, pulled off her drawers, and he raped her, grinning always, and he said, 'Tell me' again, and he hit her on the body and the face with his fists until her lip split and her nose was all over her face and she was blowing bubbles of blood when she breathed, whether it was her mouth or her nose, she could see them blow up and then pop."

The man stood over her and said, "That was to make you notice, show you I'm serious, no harm intended. Now, when I ask you something, I want you to tell me everything fast and full, and if you do that, maybe I won't go on doing what I been doing."

"She was ashamed, poor soul," Jess Marvell said. "My God! Ashamed she'd let me down by telling him what he wanted to know, after what he'd done. Cole, I'd have been begging for the chance to tell him anything, halfway through that."

What he had wanted to know was anything about the woman who ran the Marvell Hall and her fancy man. "When she told your name and that you were from St. Louis, she said he threw his head back and she thought he was going to howl like a wolf. Then he wanted to know how long I knew you, which she didn't know, and thank God he seemed to believe her, and then he asked for everything she could remember about the Hall and how it runs and where everything is. And then she thinks he kicked her in the head, for after a while she woke up and it was dark and her head hurt. And she crawled along the tracks till she saw the lights of the Hall, and she called out, but she wasn't loud enough for any to hear, so she crawled off the tracks to the stables and collapsed, and in a while one of the stable hands almost stepped on her, and so she was found."

Jess Marvell folded her hands and looked down at the

kitchen table. "I never thought running my own business would mean this, Tom getting killed, now Pearl hurt, people in danger just because they work for me."

"Most businesses don't have to deal with Gren Kenneally," Brandon said. "You're right, it has to be him. My name wouldn't mean anything to anybody else. He'd have to have read about Mound Farm and know who he'd killed, and my name was in those stories." He thought a moment and said, "But if he didn't know who I was, what made him do that to Pearl to find out what she knew?"

"You'll work that out sometime," Jess Marvell said. "But I think there's things to do now."

"Yes," Brandon said. "The police will be in on it this time, but there won't be much they can do. Maybe Pearl can tell them something more when they talk to her, but I doubt it. They'll do what they can about catching Gren, but we've got to do something to protect ourselves."

Brandon and Jess Marvell determined after some discussion that what Gren Kenneally might try was completely unpredictable, but would probably be violent and deadly.

"Trexler'll help," Brandon said. "He can round up some reliable fellows to act as a guard force here; Rush can work with him on that. You'll close down the Hall. . . ."

Jess Marvell bristled and glared at him, then her shoulders slumped and she nodded. "Yeah," she said. "The customers would be at risk all the time, and I couldn't do that. Close it, then."

"And Trexler's men will sleep in the stables, downstairs and upstairs in the Hall, and in the women's quarters; they'll have to find boardinghouses in town for a few days, and they'd best not wear their uniforms around; Gren could take a notion to want some more information, and the uniforms would make it too easy for him."

Jess was sliding beads along the abacus and jotting figures down with a pencil. "Thank goodness for the other Halls. I can do what you say and it won't bankrupt me. So, close down, put in a private army and hope Kenneally tries something so's they can blow him apart, get the girls safe. What else?"

"You," Brandon said.

"And you."

"Yes." He thought for a minute. "Any business to see to in, say, Laramie?"

"Some I could do."

"Good. We'll go there for a couple of days, give Gren a chance to try whatever he's a mind to. I'd sooner stay here and look for him myself, but he can shoot me from about anywhere, the way he did Parker, and there's nothing I could do to prevent it. After two or three days, we can try coming back and staying out of sight as far as possible."

Brandon looked at his watch. "I think there's a train west about half past noon. You pack what you need, tell your people what to do, I'll get my stuff together and set Trexler at putting together the guards you'll need." He paused and said, "And I'll let Ned Norland know about this. He might sniff around town and see if he can flush Kenneally. I spent a lot of time after him on my own, but right now all I want is to be done with him the quickest way possible, and I'll use all the help I can get."

Trexler's telegram was terse but reassuring:

ALL QUIET HERE RETURN WHEN WANT

"Looks like three days was enough," Brandon said as they left the telegraph office and walked slowly up the street.

"Not for me," Jess Marvell said.

Brandon grinned. The Laramie hotel took a casual view of two guests of varying genders requiring rooms next to each other, and they had been pleased to find that theirs had connecting doors as well as those giving onto the corridor. Jess's business in the city was not demanding, and Brandon had nothing to do but inspect the center of Laramie and its outskirts, which he accomplished in a remarkably short time. Exploring Jess Marvell and Cole Brandon, and how they fitted together in all aspects of their persons and personalities, however, took up long stretches of their time.

"If it looks safe when we get there, I'll be glad to open up the Hall again," Jess Marvell said. "The railroad's throwing a conniption about the passengers having to make do with the lunch counters and saloons when the train stops in Cheyenne. It's nice to know they've come to depend on me that much; I'll keep that in mind when I'm trying to get them to support me in putting up a new one along the line."

"Open the Hall, sure," Brandon said. "But don't stay there. It's too soon to feel safe about that. You're too visible and too easy to get at. Take a room at the Inter-Continental."

"Adjoining?"

"If we can. But I kind of doubt you'll be spending much time in it; mine's big and comfortable."

Jess Marvell smiled. "Why should I take one at all, then?"

"Consider it your investment in respectability till we get married," Brandon said, surprised at what he was saying.

"We're doing that?" Jess Marvell said.

"Well, sure," Brandon said. "You know that as well as I do."

"I guess I do."

"I've never gone up to a hotel room with a man before, unless it was to show it before I rented it to him," Jess Marvell said with a gurgle of amusement deep in her throat. She had had two glasses of the Inter-Continental's champagne with her dinner, and was more nearly giddy than Brandon remembered her. He thought she was relieved at having got back to Cheyenne, taken steps to get the Marvel Hall open and running again, and safely registered in the hotel, had chosen to celebrate mildly.

"You could always go to your room, not mine," Brandon said.

"No, I couldn't, 'cause then I'd be with me, not you, and that's not what I want," Jess Marvell said. "Say, you remember the Bright Kentucky?" That was the hotel Jess Marvell had managed in Inskip in Kansas, where Brandon had come to know her. "They dragged it with ox teams all the way from Dysart to Inskip," she said, "like a ship going across the ocean. I saw it from the train."

"So did I," Brandon said. "That's where I first saw you."

"And I saw you," she said. "Did you know, then, when you saw me?"

"No," he said. "Took you for a schoolteacher, plainly dressed neat young woman." But a little after that, walking with her, catching a look at her out of the corner of his eye . . . no, even then he hadn't known, just sensed that something big and important, bigger even than his hunt for Gren Kenneally and his crew, was looming at the borders of his life.

"I didn't know either, just saw you walking down the train aisle, and that seems funny, 'cause it's so long that I've known that it's hard to remember a time when I didn't."

Brandon fished in his pocket for the room key and felt it clink against the Indian coin. He found the keyhole and turned the key, then the doorknob, and pushed on the door.

As he did so, he bent double at a stabbing pain in his thigh, and raised a hand to slap at what he dimly thought must be a wasp; at the instant he realized it was the coin, suddenly superhot or supercold, a flash of yellow light bloomed in the room with a thunderclap that could not quite drown the spiteful snarl of the passage of a slug through the space where his head had just been.

Falling forward, Brandon kicked out sideways with his left leg, catching Jess Marvell in the thigh and driving her down the corridor, away from the doorway, through which he continued his plunge. Light and noise and the sense of a red-hot poker laid along his side, then he was grabbing a booted leg and rolling over.

A massive body crashed to the floor next to him, and the flailing boot flung him loose, and suddenly he was face-to-face with a glaring Gren Kenneally and assailed with a gust of breath like burning metal.

Brandon leaped up and to one side as Kenneally's revolver came up and sent another shot past him, grabbed the .38 out of his jacket pocket and pulled the trigger rapidly three times.

The three muzzle flashes showed Kenneally in different places each time, as if he were able to dodge the seeking bullets.

Kenneally's third shot seemed to hit his right hand like a hammer blow, actually striking the revolver and sending it flying to a corner. Brandon gave a snarling howl, dove for Kenneally under the crack and whine of shots, cannoned into him and drove him against the window.

With a jinglingly musical report, the windowpanes and the wooden strips separating them burst into fragment, showering the street, preparing a landing place Brandon saw with an eerily detached horror as, clutching Gren Kenneally, he fell from the Inter-Continental, fleetingly grateful that he had taken a room on the second floor, not the third.

The impact of the street did not drive glass slicing through him, as he had feared it would, but it did daze him and left him unable to breathe or move or to think clearly. He could feel, and the agony in his chest was more than matched by pain that stabbed from his ankle.

One of Cheyenne's few streetlights showed him Gren Kenneally staggering to his feet and raising the revolver to point at him. Brandon could see the hole of the muzzle straight on, like an eye of a striking snake, or bigger, like a porthole, like a door for Death to come out of.

There couldn't be enough light to see it, but all the same he saw the thick finger pull back on the trigger, and the cylinder snap through a sixty-degree turn.

Nothing came out; Kenneally must have emptied the gun in the brief fight. He moved toward Brandon, then stopped as shouts and running feet sounded in the street. He snarled and flung the revolver. Brandon saw it turn in the air and double and redouble in size, and then it took him in the face and kicked him into darkness.

* * *

Three days later, Brandon, with the aid of some tight bandaging and some fiery ointment over various sprains, was able to get around briskly if not comfortably, and was consulting with Jake Trexler, Ned Norland, and Rush Dailey around a table in the Inter-Continental's bar. It was an unseasonably raw night, and the burning logs in the fireplace on the rear wall sent a soothing heat through his battered body.

"He's gone off, it seems like," Rush Dailey said. "Cheyenne's too hot for him after he tried to kill you right in the hotel."

"Looks like," Jake Trexler said. "I mended some fences with the cops, and there's something you'll find interesting. Some crazy drifter got into a fight in a saloon late in the afternoon of the day Miss Ostermann was taken, there was some shooting, and they threw the drifter in jail overnight. Big fellow, big nose, glaring eyes."

Brandon sipped at his whiskey, enjoying how it seeped down in all directions to dull whatever pains it came across, and there were a good many of them. "So that's why he didn't bushwhack us, or try to, when we were going out after Krista. In jail the whole time." He remembered the disturbance behind him and Ned Norland as they discussed the expedition; that would have been Gren being arrested. The whole thing could have ended there, if they'd known. . . .

The flames in the fireplace were close to hypnotizing him, insisting on reminding him of something, something far away and not so long ago. . . . "My God," he said.

Ned Norland looked at him shrewdly. "Seen a light of some kind, did ye?"

Brandon nodded at the fire. "That. Back in Pennsylvania, there was a fire before the blasting powder went." Jake Trexler looked unhappy at the prospect of hearing things that detectives shouldn't, but resigned himself to it. "I think Gren set it, to conceal his escape, the way he did at Mound Farm. But he could have seen me then, must have, and later on recognized me here. So he knew I was the one who"—he

211

glanced at Trexler—"who came after him and the others that night. I think he was after me when he shot Parker, I was pretty close. It was a long shot."

"And now he knows who you are and he can figure what you're up to," Jake Trexler said.

"And he knows how t' hurt you worse 'n anything else," Ned Norland said. "Miss Jess."

Rush Dailey nodded. "We can't wait for him to come back whenever he chooses. We have to catch him."

"How?" Brandon said. "He's been gone for days, and no one to say where, certainly not the police."

"You tracked 'im before," Ned Norland said. "Done a lot o' trackin', in fack." He looked at Jake Trexler, who now had the calm demeanor of a man who has learned the art of intermittent deafness on demand, and need not hear what it would be best for him not to hear.

"I don't have anything to go on now," Brandon said. "If he's left Cheyenne, he could be a thousand miles away by now."

"I taught you how as to track, Brandon," Ned Norland said. "How to check around for every scrap of sign there is, and how to pull it out of yer gut or yer sperrit if it ain't thar for the eye to see. And you got yer own medicine as well, and you cain't deny that now."

Jake Trexler and Rush Dailey looked puzzled, but Brandon nodded and felt the coin in his pocket.

"I don't know about any medicine, Brandon," Jake Trexler said, "but I do know something about manhunting. It's changing, it's a matter for big organizations now, like the Pinkertons and the Nationwide, that can get word from one end of the country to the other in seconds. You ought to try that, getting one of the agencies on the job."

Brandon looked across the room and saw that Edmund Chambers was preparing himself for the evening's performance with a glass of wine. Likely he'd tell me that if I pick the right disguise and play the part well enough, I'll get my man.

212

The thing is, he thought, they're all right. I've used what each of 'em's told me, one time or another, and it's got me where I needed to go, tracking like Norland, logical deducing and detecting like Trexler, putting on a mask like Chambers. All good ideas, but how the hell to put any of them into practice without any idea in the world where to start?

He looked up and saw that a lean figure had entered the room and was leaning on the bar. There was something familiar about it, and in a moment the familiarity resolved itself into certain recognition. He debated whether to go and greet Savvy Sanger, and decided not. Sanger could be amusing company, but Brandon had no interest in being amused at the moment.

It seemed that he was as recognizable as Savvy Sanger, though, for the confidence man, after knocking back a respectable fraction of his drink, relaxed and looked around the room, stiffened as he saw Brandon, and, clutching his glass, strode toward the table where Brandon and his companions sat.

"Well, Sanger," Brandon said.

"Not all that well, Callison," Sanger said angrily.

"Brandon now," Brandon said.

"As well you gave up on Callison," Savvy Sanger said. "Callison had a big mouth. Callison would tell a fellow something, guarantee it almost, and that statement, Brandon, would be a tissue of lies, if one statement can be a tissue."

"This is Savvy Sanger," Brandon said, and noted that all three of them, even Rush Dailey, registered the name of the legendary swindler. How, he wondered, do you go on being a successful crook when you're famous all over for dealing in tissues of lies? "What's your complaint?"

"Thanks, I will sit down," Savvy Sanger said, and with one foot hooked a chair from a neighboring table and sank into it.

"I was on my way back from San Francisco after some cordial conversations with a mutual acquaintance of myself and the newborn Mr. Brandon here," Savvy Sanger said, "when I stopped over at Green River City with the thought of seeing what a telephone system might do for the burg. The marvel of the age, gentlemen, the telephone! Yesterday but an untried invention, today a practical working device, tomorrow the magic cord that links person to person across this nation and around the world. In a few years, gentlemen, house will speak to house and town will speak to town and nation will speak to nation, and yours truly will be among those stringing that cord."

He surveyed his audience, whose astonishment could plausibly be taken for interest. "And who will be among the lucky few who will invest early and profit greatly thereby? It goes against the grain to say so, gentlemen, for you have honest and open faces, if you want to call them that, but you will not be in that fortunate number. I've got my shares from Professor Bell, and nobody's getting a sniff of 'em. I say this only to provoke despair and envy, which is the true object of social intercourse."

Brandon wondered at the persistence and intricacy of the ploy Savvy Sanger was working, and thought the feigned refusal to consider selling the "Professor's" shares was a crude but effective method of bidding up the eventual price. If he had been in San Francisco talking about telephones to Tsai Wang, he'd been lucky to escape without being shortened at the shoulders by a highbinder's hatchet.

"Now, Brandon, I was in Green River City, like I said, counting telegraph poles to make sure there'd be plenty to hang the telephone wires from, when I thought I saw a man I didn't want to see, then I remembered that my man was dead, and I didn't pay no more attention till I was close to him, and it *was* my man, by God, and not dead at all, though I'll be if he sniffs me out."

"Gren . . . Goren Kraft?" Brandon said.

"Gory Kraft, large as life and twice as lousy," Savvy Sanger said. "Guaranteed dead and buriable by one Beaufort Callison, now dead himself, poor bedlamite, and resurrected as Brandon. Gory Kraft, that'll have my tripes for a sandwich if he runs across me, which he damn near did, sauntering around in Green River City."

19

Ned Norland sprawled comfortably on the windowmost side of the day coach seat and observed that it was a treat to sit back and smoke a cigar and be carried what would be several hours' journey on foot or even, in this rough country, on horseback.

"Progress is pizen, though," he told Brandon. "The railroads and the settlements and the farmin' and the ranchin' and such is makin' the noblest country in the world over in the image of New Jersey. I never been to New Jersey, but a fellow in the Long Branch, over back in Dodge City, that's named for a place there—the Long Branch is, not Dodge, accourse—this feller tolt me that New Jersey is full of people and houses everywhere as you look, and roads and railroads and telegraph wires stitchin' it all together. That is the way that Sanger man wants to go, with his telephones, prett' soon every place'll be like every place else."

"That's just another of Sanger's swindles," Brandon said. "Voices going over wires, you've got better sense than to credit that, Ned."

"With er without 'em, progress is at our throats," Ned Norland said. "And the worst of it is, you git a taste of it, and you ain't goin' to give it up. I will walk, ride, er muleskin it whereas I has to, and no frettin', but I'd no more do that alongside where a train runs than I'd fly, not for a trip of any size. I would feel like a fool, takin' close to a week to go from Cheyenne to Green River City, when the train'll do it inside a day, but ten years ago I done that without thinkin'. If they ever runs trains up to the Yellowstone, it'll take most of the fun out of goin' there, but there's nobody, me included, that wouldn't pay the fare and set to pickin' cinders outer our eyes."

"Aren't you afraid of meeting the ladies you took to the Yellowstone in Green River City?" Brandon said. "That's where you left 'em, poor pining creatures."

"Lodgepole pinin', you might say one or two of 'em was," Ned Norland said. "Built like 'em anyhow, tall and skinny, hardly anything stickin' out above er below."

"Not your preferred style of woman, I guess," Brandon said.

"Any woman is my perferred style," Ned Norland said. "In looks, that is. Lookin' like a lodgepole pine er a tumbleweed er in between, it don't matter, so long's she's a gamesome woman and enjoys bein' who she is. Anyhow, those ladies is gone by now, I don't doubt."

"How did they do in the Yellowstone?" Brandon said.

"Well enough, no fussin' and complainin', not so much as you'd look to find in a party of men of the same type," Ned Norland said. "Natcherly, I took 'em on as easy ways as I could find, and there's a many of 'em through the Yellowstone country. And they was dumbstruck by what I showed 'em, the woods, the animals, the big lake like a sea, with all them strange birds, the mountains, the b'ilin' springs and mush-pots, the hot waterspouts and paintpots. And then there was the canyon, the Grand Canyon of the Yellowstone, they call it, with the wild river runnin' through it and the falls. . . ."

He chewed on the cigar and looked out the window at the landscape that raced past so much faster than a man or a horse could move. "That's somethin' that ain't changed

217

much since I seen it back in thirty-nine or so, the Yellow-stone. I was young when I saw it, and it got into my head, behind my eyes, and I ain't never got it out nor want to. Wasn't above a handful of men except Injuns had ever seen it, and them as did hardly believed it. The colors, Brandon! Every color as you ever seen in the world or in a pictur, spread around them b'ilin' springs and fountains. And tree stumps all over, like after the loggers have been through, or a fire, but when you go to lean on 'em er try out yer axe, why, they's solid stone, peterfractions they calls 'em."

Ned Norland glanced slyly at Brandon. "Would you believe me was I to tell you I seen on a branch of one of them peterfried trees a peterfried bird with its pore stony beak ferever open, and the notes of a peterfried song emergin' from it?"

"No," Brandon said.

"And right you'd be," Ned Norland said. "But some of the ladies did."

"Or wanted to butter you up by pretending they did."

"They'll do that sometimes," Ned Norland said compla-cently. "Wagh! But them hot spots and b'ilin' springs and the like, they was more disbelievable than the peterfrac-tions, but they was real."

Some, Ned Norland said, blew immense amounts of steam and superheated water into the sky at nearly regular intervals; others could go off at any time, and many of those had, from the evidence of long-undisturbed ground by their entrances, not erupted for years or decades or centuries.

"I showed 'em how to make their livin' in the wild if they had to, trappin' if they ran out of ammunition, fishin', pickin' the good eatin' yarbs and berries and shunnin' the pizen ones, and most special, how to make a fire and douse it. That's God's country, and no doubt about it, but turn a spark into her when she's dry, and you'd wisht you was in Chicago in seventy-one, whcre it'd be cooler and safer."

Ned Norland dropped his cigar stub into the spittoon between them; it disappeared into the gleaming brass with a plop and a hiss. He said, "A whole world up there, antelope, grizzlies, wolves, buffler, like 'twas before we came. Makes you understand what we do to a place whenas we come into it and progress it."

Brandon leaned against the scratchy cut-plush seat back and tried to let the swaying rattle of the train marshal his thoughts into order. Gren Kenneally could be in Green River City, and if he was, Brandon would have to find a way to kill him and get away safe to Jess Marvell. Until now his personal safety had not been much of a consideration, but keeping Jess Marvell's man alive to cherish and be cherished by her was pretty damn important.

He supposed they might have obtained a warrant and been deputized to serve it, but that would have given Gren innumerable chances to make his escape, with or without killing Brandon and Ned Norland. Wiring ahead that Green River City was harboring a dangerous fugitive would probably have even worse results, with law officers and bystanders shot down and Gren escaping. The arrest in Cheyenne had been a fluke, Gren drunk, so the cops told Trexler, and dazed from a baseball bat to the back of the head wielded by the bartender.

Trail Gren by night and kill him from ambush? A lot to recommend it, but hampered by not knowing where and when to pick up the trail. It would also be cowardly and unlawful, characteristics counterbalanced, in Brandon's view, by its effectiveness and comparative safety. The time was long past for tracking, for invoking the hunter's patience and sharing the hunter's risk. Kenneally dead as soon as seen, so long as there was an escape route, that was what his policy amounted to. And in a place the size of Green River City, he shouldn't be hard to find.

In fact, he was impossible to find, unless one had the ability to step into last Thursday, which was when the alarming stranger who resembled Gren Kenneally in every particular had disappeared.

"We has to foller him," Ned Norland said. "But there is two contendin' possibilities consarnin' how he left. There's a feller on the wagon road north that had a horse and some gear run off with, and there's a railroad man that got kicked off a freight car by a damn big hobo he was a-tryin' to kick off himself, and both on the same night. Either one could be Gren."

"We'll follow both," Brandon said. "You take the train west, see what you can find along the way, and I'll head north. It's pretty empty country up that way, and a stranger should stand out."

"Yeah," Ned Norland said. "I hate to admit it, but you're more up to a hard ride acrost hard country, and maybe a hard fight at the end, than what I am, these days. Was I in my prime, say like I was five years ago, I'd be contendin' with you fer the fun, but I will do my manhuntin' astride the iron horse for the moment. But if I ain't doin' that ride, I will damn well see that you got the supplies you need to do it right."

Brandon rode north on a powerful, short-tempered horse that Norland selected. "You can control him if he's mean, but you cain't give him stren'th er speed if he ain't got it. Got to carry you and your gear through whatever as you come acrost, and there is a lot to come acrost where you're goin', rivers, desert, mountains. And you cain't stint on the gear, 'specially weepons and ammunition. Good heavy rifle, and any amount of loads for it and yer pistols; you don't know how long you'll be on the way, and you cain't count on happenin' by a gunsmith just when you're runnin' short."

Starting from where the horse had turned up missing, the way north was pretty well determined by the Green River, its valley offering easy passage between ranges of hills. Brandon followed this north to a wagon road running east and west, which his map told him was the Overland Mail Route.

He debated whether to go left, right, or ahead, even tossing the Indian coin to help him make up his mind, but it did not seem inclined to provide any guidance. He finally decided that if Gren Kenneally had started out north, he probably meant to go on north for at least a little, and crossed the wagon road, camping close to it for the night.

The next morning, some miles farther on, he came to the fork where the Big Sandy entered the Green from the northeast and, without thinking, turned to follow it. Why did I do that? he wondered, but felt content with the action.

The creek bent to meet another wagon road, and Brandon took this. As the afternoon wore on, the ease he felt about the route seeped away, and he felt that it would be foolish to go much farther on without some indication that Gren Kenneally had been that way.

Around a bend, a man stepped out from behind a stand of trees with a shotgun held ready for use but not quite aimed at him, and said, "Hold it there, mister."

The tone was stern but not menacing, and if robbery and murder had been intended, the shotgun could easily by now have turned him into something resembling the luckless elephant Ned Norland had so colorfully described. Brandon slowed his horse and held his hands out by his sides, palms toward the shotgun holder.

"Where from?"

"Green River City."

"Where to?"

"North."

"Why?"

"Business."

"Anything to show who you are?"

"Why would there be? And what would you know if you knew who I was, anyhow?" Brandon asked.

"Damned if I know," the man said. "They told me to stop people coming this way and ask 'em such questions and see if they looked okay. I guess you look okay; that stuff you got looks bought new, not stole."

"What's this about?" Brandon said.

The man jerked his head toward the northwest side of the road. "Quarter mile off that way, there's a small shack. Old prospector and his daughter live—lived—there. He panned some metal now and then, she grew some truck, they scraped out a living. But two days ago, somebody who knew 'em dropped by, and the place was smashed and so were they, brained. Girl'd been . . . used, you know? Everything a man on the run might use gone, everything else broken or burnt."

Brandon closed his eyes. As a sign that he was on Gren Kenneally's track, this was pretty convincing. If he was going to petition the unseen for such help in the future, he had better try to specify that it didn't have to be so deadly.

"Any sign of who it was?"

"Some hoofprints in the dust around the shack. Right hind shoe looked a little loose, and a chip out of the back part of it," the man with the shotgun said.

"I'll keep an eye out for tracks like that," Brandon said. "See any, I'll tell the nearest law."

"Obliged," the man said, and waved him on.

At Pilot Butte Brandon left the road to follow the Big Sandy a few more miles, but when it cut the next road, he looked ahead to the looming mass of the Wind River range and opined that Gren Kenneally would have turned off onto the road. To the east lay Fort Aspen, Pacific Springs, and Atlantic City, surprisingly close, and Hamilton, all in a few miles. He suspected that Kenneally would right now share Ned Norland's views on overcrowding on the frontier, and turned westward.

The day was sultry and to the south, flatland baked in the sun and gave off shimmers of heat. Ahead and to the north wooded mountains rose, promising coolness and shade to those who would scale them.

The road was cut by a broad river, which the map showed him was, once more, the Green. The road led west into the rising mountains; the river valley led north, offering a passage between ridges.

Brandon got down from his horse and rested under the sparse shade of a stunted tree, savoring water from his canteen. After a while he went to the river and knelt and refilled the canteen. In the mud where the road entered the river he saw the marks of wagon wheels and hoofs from those who had crossed at the ford. He looked closely at the hoofprints, but saw none with a chip out at the back. He wondered how you told if a hoof mark was front right or left hind or whatever; Ned Norland had told him a lot about tracking, but not that. Maybe if you found a place where the horse had stood for a while, you could look at which feet were where.

A dull glint up the river caught his eye, and he walked to it. As he had thought, a discarded empty can, probably once holding tomatoes. He bent to pick it up; it could be useful to carry berries in, if he got to some place where they were abundant.

As he straightened up, the descending sun lay across the trampled trail that followed the riverbank north, and threw the markings in it into sharp relief. Curving back on itself like an overstretched bow, the arc of a horseshoe was stamped in the earth in front of him. Brandon could not tell if it was loose on the hoof, but the curve was broken toward its center by a fat triangular chip.

The river twisted among ever steeper hills, and the nights grew colder, even though it was now full summer. Once in a while the ground revealed the chipped horseshoe print, once leading him to turn away from the river and across a flat plateau to an army outpost.

"Fort Bonneville," the officer in charge of the place told him. And no, nobody resembling Gren Kenneally had passed through. But a few days ago, sentries had fired at a shape that had been seen at the cook shack. "A grizzly, they figured, but no fur or blood found, and there wasn't the stink a bear usually has. Maybe one of the old mountain men from the fur days, still haunting the place." More likely Gren Kenneally, undersupplied and trying to get some food, Brandon thought.

In any case, marauders and fugitives were not on the soldiers' minds today, which, Brandon learned with some surprise, was July 4. He had not been paying attention to the calendar for some time, and had not, after leaving Philadelphia, given much thought to the fact that the nation's hundredth birthday was imminent.

The Bonneville soldiers, on the other hand, had been thinking about it for some time, for want of other material, Brandon supposed. They would not hear of his traveling on, insisted on his bearing his part in the celebration, subjected him to fireworks, orations, patriotic recitations, a baseball game, a gargantuan lunch, three kinds of wine, four kinds of whiskey, and a sweet punch that eventually got behind his eyeballs and turned to fine sand, and patriotic recitations. They stopped short only of demanding that he make a speech or give a toast.

As he rode out the next morning, turning north again, toward the Tetons, he wondered what would be left of this part of the country at the next Centennial.

Four days later, riding through country he hardly bothered to relate to the map, he thought he had finally come upon another evidence of Gren Kenneally's passage when he encountered four men riding southward. They looked stunned and sickened, and sat their horses awkwardly, as if they didn't remember completely how to do that.

"You heared?" one of them called to Brandon as he and his companions approached on the trail.

"No," Brandon said; since he had heard nothing since leaving the fort, he would not have had whatever news they were bearing, perhaps another family savagely slaughtered and plundered by Gren Kenneally.

"Gin'ral Custer and all his men, kilt by Injuns over in Montana!" the man said.

"At the Little Big Horn!" another said. "A hundred thousand savages swarmin' all over 'em, showin' no mercy, a whole army murderously wiped out!"

Brandon doubted the size of the Indian horde and wondered what kind of mercy was to be looked for in a pitched battle. Custer had gone out, he recalled, to teach the Indians a lesson about letting the Black Hills prospectors overrun them without protest, and had apparently received some concentrated education instead. He could imagine the scene as one of catastrophic horror, and found that he was unmoved by contemplating it. As he rode north, guided by scanty clues or none at all lately, he seemed to be moving above the ground, at least not tethered to the earth, and the world's concerns were less and less his concerns.

He parted with the four bearers of bad tidings, managing to leave them with the impression that he was too stunned to join in their constant expressions of anger and dismay, and again rode north, almost in a trance.

This, he supposed, was what Ned Norland had tried to train him to do, back in the St. Charles Mountains in Missouri at the start; when there was nothing you could see or hear or taste or smell or touch that would tell you where the quarry was, then let all those senses go and become a feather in the wind, taken by the wind to where you should be.

Dense stands of straight, smooth trunks rising to a high canopy of dark green, like close-packed ships' masts: the lodgepole pines. Cool, almost chilly in their shade, Brandon consulted the increasingly ragged map and saw that he was near Yellowstone Lake, in the area Norland had spoken so eloquently of.

He sent the horse moving among the trees, and then into the open meadows. They blazed with yellow and purple flowers he did not know, and he could see stains of yellow, purple, and red across the flanks of hills and mountains ahead and to the sides.

When he came to the lake, it was like a sea, with wind-driven waves lapping the shore, and stretching away to the far shore. He saw white birds on the water and took them for swans; but they lumbered into the air with laboriously churning wings, and he recognized them from some long-ago book illustration as pelicans.

He worked his way along the shore of the lake, and was hardly surprised to see on a damp stretch of sand some marks of hoofprints, with one of them showing the chipped back. Be interesting if I am following a horse with a chipped shoe on the *front* foot, ridden by a Methodist deacon called Stubbs, in the hay, grain, and feed business in Bozeman, he thought. But I doubt it.

It's here, and I guess I knew it all along. Back in spring, in Nebraska, he had seen a photograph of a place he thought was in the Yellowstone, a grim precipice over a rushing river and falls, and a shudder ran through him as if he were looking at a picture of his grave. Since then he had always had in the back of his mind that that was a place of destiny for him, and now here he was, not many miles from it.

And so was Gren Kenneally.

It was not that the coin in his pocket was turning hot or cold or vibrating, or doing whatever it did or he imagined it did, just that he was constantly aware of its presence in his pocket, a reminder of where he was and what he was doing. He was keyed up, not quite excited, but febrile.

Brandon had camped a little in from the lake, and in the morning rose early and scouted ahead. This close, if he was, it would be well to move silently until he knew what lay in front of him, then return for the horse and gear.

Sniffing the air, stepping over dead branches, easing brush aside, he moved in near-silence through the woods, following a trail trodden by elk, deer, bear, and doubtless men, though few of them, through the years. If he did make a noise, it would have been masked by the cackling, whirring, chirking, trilling, and snapping of the birds that swooped through the trees.

In an open glade, an animal he had never seen stood knee-deep in grass and stared mournfully at him. It resembled an elk wearing a camel's nose, a ridiculous chin tuft, and a set of horns made out of giant scoops. He thought he remembered a drawing like that, and the name "moose." It was the sort of name a creature like that deserved, anyhow.

He walked wide around it, since it looked as if it was prepared to be unfriendly, and was certainly equipped to do so, and into the woods again. The trail angled uphill, under heavy-leafed, thick-trunked trees, and he was glad of the extra exertion, which drove off the morning chill a little. Two boulders constricted the trail, and he squeezed between them . . .

And was smashed to the ground by a crushing weight that slammed into his shoulders and neck with an instant of intolerable pain that flared into an exploding white-hot star, then snapped into darkness and nonbeing.

20

Brandon came out of what felt like death into what looked
like Hell, the face of Gren Kenneally staring down at him,
and the smell of burning metal coming from the grinning
mouth.

There were other smells, too, adding to the hellish impression: sulphur, and probably brimstone, though he had never
known what brimstone was.

"Now, here's a find for old Gren, and no denying,"
Kenneally said delightedly. "Alone in the woods, out of
bullets and relying on what I can trap to live on, and look
what I get! Set a deadfall on the trail that might break a
deer's back or catch me a bear, and what a reward for
industry, a fellow with lots of supplies and ammunition and
food, enough for old Gren to live like a king."

A flexing of his wrists, ankles, and body told Brandon that
he was tightly trussed in stout rope, and a turn of the head
showed him his horse, neatly packed with all his supplies,
tethered to a tree some distance away. He twisted in the
other direction and saw that he was indeed in Hell, or one of
its suburbs: A crazed mass of twisted rock or hardened mud,
smeared with red, a virulent blue, and areas of ocher of the

same shade as the stripes on Ned Norland's best suit, writhed along the ground, humping itself into grotesque shapes, and in the middle of it pools of foul-smelling mud produced bubbles that swelled and popped, emitting a gas that stung Brandon's eyes. As Brandon watched, a jet of steam and water plumed into the air at the far border of the tormented rock.

"Backtracked you and found your stuff," Gren said cheerfully. "Useful goods, no doubt about it. But the best thing is the fun that's coming. You been after me for some time, and you damn near got me, but that's done now. Only thing is how long it's going to take me to kill you, and how much you're going to like it. Answers: a long, long time, and not at all. What the hell did you think you were up to, Brandon? A damn lawyer going after Gren Kenneally!"

"You knew who I was, then?"

"Only after I, ah, pumped that girl for information and she told me," Gren Kenneally said. "So it fit, I'd seen you at that farm outside St. Louis, after Philly, and didn't know what to make of it, but now it made sense, you were that blond woman's husband and you had yourself a blood feud with her killer."

"At the farm?"

"Went there to get the money I left behind, a kind of dividend share I wasn't parceling out to the boys. But some thieving bastard must have found it and taken it. But while I was there, you come along, and then that other woman. I couldn't hear what you said, but I knew I'd seen you in Philly, when the fire lit you up, and I wondered what the hell was going on. I hung around St. Louis awhile, hoping I'd catch sight of you, the which I didn't, but I did see her, and with John B. Parker, no less, a man I never had much time for, for reasons that ain't your business."

Kenneally had taken the same train as Parker and Krista to Cheyenne and had seized what seemed like a good opportunity to kidnap Krista and both get a fair chunk of money and irritate John B. Parker.

"Came back to town to see how things was going, and this

damn fool in a bar picked a fight, and next I know I'm in jail for the night, and you fools are free to go and get her away. Well, that was your fault, the way I see it, so I went to shoot you, and that damned Parker got in the way. And then I found out who you were, and could see what you were doing, so it was up to me to get you before you got me. And I missed on it once, but here we are, ain't we?"

Gren Kenneally stood over him. "You know, Brandon, just so's you can't comfort yourself with the notion that you got a few of the bad men who ruined your life, lemme tell you that you done me a favor. You killed Jake outright in the shack there, and that was it. The others went when I set off the blasting powder, which is what I got them there for in the first place."

"No hundred thousand to share out from Santa Coralia?"

"Not a half-dime. Lost it all in different ways and come back broke. That stuff you heard was moonshine. Had me a pal from the whaler we took over—that was the straight goods, anyway—a harpooner from Otaheite, and he was in a space down below, ready to come up and help me kill the other fellows when I gave the signal. But when you bust in, and with the fire, it was simpler to blow him up with the rest and not have any witnesses."

Brandon now understood the tattooed remnants the police had found at the scene of the blast.

"Why did you want to get rid of the men who'd been with you?" Brandon said. "No danger they'd turn you over to the police. They were just as guilty as you were."

"They thought I owed 'em money," Gren Kenneally said. "And so I did. And there wasn't any, and they weren't going to get any. And as long as they were whining about it, they'd be a trouble to me, and I don't like trouble. Some of the boys is dead, one way and another, but the ones that's left is hard to find now, but I'll find 'em and retire the debt like I done with Nate and the rest."

"Casmire, Curly, Kid Philly, Neb," Brandon said.

Gren Kenneally stared at him.

"I killed them. I knew the others, but they got themselves killed without me."

Gren Kenneally looked bewildered, then slowly grinned. "You have got *lots* more to tell me than I would have guessed," he said. "You'll tell me that, and then I'll get you to tell me things you didn't even know you knew, and then we get to the dying part, and by that time it'll be what you want most. Later, Mr. Attorney. Right now I'll go tend to my trap lines and see what I've caught for my supper. From now on it'll be stew every night, though." He brandished Brandon's rifle, then mounted Brandon's horse and rode away through the trees.

Twisting until his neck ached, Brandon saw that Gren Kenneally had left him, cocooned in rope, in the midst of a field of sulphur vents, hot mudholes, and intermittent spouts. He was lying against a shallow hump of ridged mud, just above a downsloping area that led to some shattered rocks below, that jutted like knives from the ground.

The earth under Brandon was warm, and its coarseness and a throbbing from beneath gave him the unpleasant sensation of lying on top of an ancient beast, something like those whose bones Ned Norland had helped take to Philadelphia for display.

He considered what to do, and was aware that he was not likely to have more scope for action than he did now. Gren Kenneally would ride his trapline at his leisure, would then return and ask Brandon any questions that occurred to him, and then torture him atrociously and kill him. It would not even be necessary to untie him. Brandon could ask that his bonds be loosened so that he could relieve himself, but he suspected that Gren Kenneally would consider forcing a doomed man to soil himself an excellent jest.

The sulphur smell was suddenly stronger, the ground trembled under him as if a train were running on a nearby track, and he heard a popping sound like that of a champagne cork being withdrawn, only magnified many times. A hundred feet or so away a mound of colored dried mud seemed to dissolve, and a gout of water rushed into the air. Brandon remembered what Ned Norland had said about the geysers that erupted regularly, and those that went off, sometimes after years, without notice. That would have been one of them. The mound that had marked its previous eruption, however long ago, had weathered and hardened . . . until it had looked remarkably like the one Gren Kenneally had casually stowed him against, and which was now throbbing like a boil about to burst.

He wished he had not thought of the word "boil," but could not avoid the conviction that boiling was imminent. *Quicker than what Gren has in mind for me, anyhow. No worse than a boiler explosion on a steamboat, and damn little consolation that is.*

He felt the ground under him become extremely hot, then tremble, then shudder, then crack apart and flow under and around him.

A blast of steam hurled him sideways, and scaldingly hot mud engulfed him in a wave that sent him rolling downhill, mouth too stuffed with hot mud to allow the scream inside him to emerge.

Pain and billowing slime enveloped him, then he was raked with even sharper agonies that seemed more than he could bear, and he struck and kicked violently in protest, as a child does when born into an incomprehensible world.

And he realized that he was kicking and striking out, that his hands and legs were no longer bound. He clawed and swam out of the embrace of the mud, already cooling, careless of the gashes he received from the rocks against which the mud had flung him, slashing enough of the rope to let its coils sag free of him.

Heat swallowed his feet and lapped up his legs. He looked up and saw that most of the area where he had been had blown up or dissolved away, and the steaming mud was sliding down to set up a new surface once it hardened.

Brandon pulled free and stumbled away, fleeing the

advancing mud till he came to tumbled rock that offered him a staircase upward and into the dark woods.

Walking, crawling, running, taking random turns, following paths or making his own, Brandon pushed himself to get as far as he could from the newly active mud "volcano" before exhaustion and the effects of the blow from the deadfall trap and the cooking he had received in the mud loosened his determined clutch on consciousness.

He awoke once in the deep dark, and saw a very few stars through the interlaced canopy of the trees. The mud had dried on him like a painful crust, and may have acted as a poultice or dressing, since the gashes he had received from the rocks did not hurt or throb with the advance warnings of infection. His clothes were in tatters, and his one remaining shoe was torn open at the toe end. He could not tell if he had socks left, but if so, he supposed they had enough holes to put them beyond anyone's darning skills. He was flooded with a happiness stronger than he had ever felt. Alive, and not to lose Jess after all. Trussed up like a parcel of meat for Gren, he had not dared to think of her for an instant, but now he could.

Something wide drifted across the night above his head and he heard a sharp hooting noise. Owl, hunting by night.

Brandon would hunt by day. This day.

Brandon was moving as soon as he awoke. It was painful, but if he thought about how it felt, if he let himself move slowly and gradually, it would be worse. He padded slowly along the forest floor, closely attentive to the surface, one shoe lost and the ruined other abandoned. Crusts of dried mud dropped from him as he moved, but he could see that he remained covered in a gray-brown coating, creased and wrinkled by the mobile skin. That constituted most of his clothing, tattered drawers and a few sections of trouser leg and shirt sleeve being the rest. After he had blinked and sneezed and licked his lips a few times, he achieved a working relationship with the mud plastering his face.

When the trail opened up, he loped along, unthinkingly adjusting the placement of his descending feet to avoid stones and upjutting roots. He passed a deer, which looked at him with mild interest but no alarm, though he was close enough to touch it. I don't smell human or look human anymore, I guess, so I'm not a threat. To them, anyhow.

By afternoon he had worked his way around to the north end of the lake and the entrance to the river. He followed its course for some miles, then paused and crouched in the trees on top of the cliffs and looked into the waterfall that sent the river along on its task of deepening still further the Grand Canyon of the Yellowstone.

He looked down the canyon to see if the scene in the photograph was anywhere to be found. He saw the tall, thick finger of rock that had impressed him in the picture . . . and next to it, a thinner, wavering finger of smoke.

Gren Kenneally's cook fire? Perhaps, but Yellowstone was a national park now, and there were others in it, even sometimes ladies from New England led by a libidinous old mountain man.

A lump of mud at his thigh felt in some way troublesome, though not exactly itchy, and he scratched at it. Not mud, but mud-impregnated cloth, a remnant of his trousers, still holding a torn pocket. And in the pocket, the Indian coin was making itself known to him again.

It was Gren Kenneally's fire, half an hour's stalk away.

The camp was well sited for a cautious man, on a shelf emerging from a high precipice, the fire backed against the cliff. A narrow path led to it from below, so that a man might keep off an army with only a few rocks for ammunition.

This Brandon saw from some distance away across broken, forested country. And he saw a tiny Gren Kenneally tending a spark of cook fire, with two miniature horses, his own and Brandon's, standing placidly where the shelf met the wall of the cliff.

He also saw that there was another way than the path to where Gren Kenneally contemplated dinner and perhaps mourned the loss of his entertainment to the engulfing mud slide.

Brandon scuttled across rocks, hoisted himself upward on tree branches, clutched and climbed cliffs, spalling off fragments of drying mud but still keeping most of the coating, still moving among the animals that inhabited these hillsides without alarming them, even the rattlesnake which hissed when he put his hand down almost on it, but did not coil or strike.

A final pull and scramble put him on top of the peak just above Gren Kenneally; he could smell the smoke of the cook fire and a scent he identified after a moment as heated stewed tomatoes.

The wind was not high, but it had a strength to it that made him want to lean into it for support, which he knew for an illusion that would send him spinning hundreds of feet into the river if he acted on it. He closed his eyes and visualized the rock face above Gren Kenneally's camp as he had seen it from up the canyon.

He nodded slowly and made his way to the edge of the tall rock. There was an overhang that concealed the fire and anyone tending it. He looked down and saw where the first footholds were, and without further speculation, turned around and set his feet into them, flexing them for a close fit. He felt with the left foot for the next hold, settled into it, then the right, leaning his weight forward against the rock, caressing rather than holding it with his fingertips. It didn't matter that he had never climbed in this way, or anything close to it; his body seemed to know what was required, and was providing it.

His hands brushed the rock face lightly, dislodging no clods or pebbles, and he slid silently down it, rocking gently from side to side as first one foot, then the other, found its hold.

When he felt the rock face begin to curve inward, he knew he was at the overhang above the ledge. He sniffed, caught the sharpness of frying bacon—been at my supplies already, but why wouldn't he?—and calculated that Gren would be at the fire, tending the frying pan.

He flexed his legs, then stepped from the hold and pushed himself from the rock face. The drop was about eight feet, and stung his soles, but he stayed upright and balanced, facing Gren Kenneally at the fire.

Kenneally displayed remarkable fortitude for a man who has just seen a grayish, featureless creature, a naked man made of mud, drop from the skies in front of him. That is, he did not scream and hurl himself into the canyon, but he did in fact goggle stupidly at Brandon for a few seconds, while the bacon in the frying pan he held to the fire sizzled and began to burn.

Brandon saw the rifle lying on the ledge almost at his feet, and bent to pick it up. Gren Kenneally's eyes widened; then Brandon threw the rifle from the ledge. Whatever happened, he had not come here to shoot Gren Kenneally in that way, like putting down a horse with a fatal disease.

"Brandon," Gren Kenneally said faintly. "You was boiled in the mud, nothin' left of you but a shoe."

"Yes," Brandon said. "But here I am."

"Oh, God!" Kenneally said. "Are you a man or a . . ."

"I am Cole Brandon, and I'm here to kill you," Brandon said.

"Well, fuck me! You ain't man enough or ghost enough to do it!" Kenneally yelled, and flung the iron pan at Brandon. It spun past him, trailing a spray of hot fat that burned across his chest, and vanished into the waning light.

Kenneally kicked the heart of the fire, exploding it toward Brandon; sparks and blazing fragments hit him, stinging, then falling away, leaving the coating of mud dappled with small black smears. Brandon ran across the carpet of the scattered fire, feeling but ignoring the burning on the soles of his feet, and the sudden cooked-meat smell that mingled with the lingering aroma of the bacon.

Kenneally linked his fists and swung his upper body to send them to smash Brandon's head; Brandon slid under and to one side, and drove stiffened fingers into Kenneally's throat, with the weight of his body behind them. Kenneally choked and staggered, staring at Brandon, then brought up a booted foot in a hammerlike kick Brandon barely managed to take on the upper thigh. It nearly crippled him, but a hit on the original target would have killed him or at the least gelded him.

Brandon gave him another chopping blow, this time to the solar plexus, and Kenneally squawked inhumanly and choked. Brandon grabbed him around the chest and swung him until he was leaning over the edge of the cliff, with a three-hundred-foot drop to the river beneath him. Kenneally's eyes widened in fear, then relaxed as Brandon swung him away, solidly back onto the ledge. A croak signifying no-one-ever-knew-what came out of Kenneally's tortured throat as Brandon continued the swing and smashed his head against a long rock protruding down from the protective overhang.

The head did not rebound from the rock but seemed to merge with it partway, and Gren Kenneally's face lost all animation, and became a dull mask. His body thrashed once and became a dead weight in Brandon's grip.

Oh, no, Gren. I wouldn't throw you off and let the river kill you, or the fall. By my hand, where I see it and feel it, and I know it's done.

With one arm holding the inert body, still warm, against him, he scrabbled with the other in the ruin of his pocket and fetched out the old Indian coin.

In the glow radiating up from the last of the wavering flames of the scattered fire, he saw once again the snake, swallowing itself or giving birth to itself, and on the other side the wolf, the solitary hunter.

The circle was complete, the hunt finished. He jammed the coin into Gren Kenneally's slack mouth—the Greeks did that, didn't they, to pay the ferryman who took you to the land of the dead?—dragged him to the edge of the rock shelf, and pushed the body into the darkening air.

He did not look over the edge, but sank to his haunches

and looked across to the far side of the canyon and the wild skyline of upreaching peaks, still faintly lit by the memory of the recently set sun, and the twisted growth that clung precariously to them.

In a while the peaks were lit from behind, and the moon, a pale gold coin, slid up the sky. Brandon crouched and watched it rise and pale, and traced shapes in it. They could be anything, the ghosts of the men he had killed, the ghosts of Elise and the others those men had killed. But now, it seemed to him, there were no ghosts, the murderers and the murdered were all done with, in the past.

You might even see in the shadows on that bland disk the people he had been, the masks he had put on to help him in the long hunt; but then you could see anything if you looked long enough. And had they been masks, after all? Callison, Brooks, Blake, the rest; they'd been parts of Cole Brandon, had to be, or he could never have evoked them, so they were still there, stowed inside him, the way this mudman, this naked killer, would be.

Jess Marvell is going to have a lot of men to deal with.

He grinned at the thought, and as the moon went higher, wondered if she was looking at it, too, right now, down in Cheyenne. When I get home, I'll ask her.

Now, when did I last use that word? he thought. Home. Can't remember. But I can use it now, and I know where it is. Wherever I'm with her.

He squatted, the long hunt done, and watched the moon claim the sky.

Epilogue

Recollections of Andrew Marvell Brandon,
set down September 1923

When my parents, returning from their first and indeed only European trip, took passage on the maiden voyage of the *Titanic,* and were not among those rescued, I was twenty-nine, approaching middle age, and so was, though greatly grieved, not distraught.

What was far more disordering to my view of the world as I understood it was my discovery among my father's papers of a narrative of the events of the years 1874 to 1876, set down some time after his marriage to my mother. I knew something of his first wife's death and the period of depression and travel that followed it, but there had never been any mention of the operatic blood feud he had pursued, with eventual success. Reading his account was a little like discovering that one had been sired by Attila rather than Van Bibber—I don't mean to suggest that my elegant, forceful, and sardonic father was as shallow as Dick Davis's clubman character, but to convey the sense of disparity between the image and the suddenly discovered actuality.

I also discovered that, though my father had not made a point of following the fortunes of those he had encountered in his adventures, he had taken note of such information

239

concerning them as came his way: a clipping from a newspaper telling of the murder of a telephone executive by revolutionaries, a faded photograph of the earthquake-shattered ruins of a pagoda, a brochure lauding the healthful properties of the mineral waters and pure air of a spa in New Mexico; other markers of events and activities in many lives, which proved to be those of people my father had encountered in his hunt for Gren Kenneally and those who had helped Kenneally murder my father's first wife.

Here in California, dealing in real estate, I have built up considerable capital, and even at that period could afford to pay well to pursue matters that interested me. One such matter was the filling out of the tantalizingly incomplete information of the fortunes and fates of those who had played major or minor parts in my father's life, or that part of it of which I had known nothing.

Growing up, I had come to learn of my parents' meeting in Kansas and marriage in Wyoming, which became my own birthplace in 1883, two years before my mother was appointed to fill a vacancy in the territorial legislature. I knew her as a cheerful mother, a combative politician, and a masterful businesswoman—or, as seen by a young boy, a fairy queen, able to command with a wave of her hand ice cream or pie or any other treat at any of the Marvel Halls she took me to visit.

My father, I knew not quite as closely, but I was entranced by the rich variety of characters whose legal business he handled: ranchers, rustlers, law officers, stage robbers, farmers, farm workers. . . . It seemed that he would represent anyone who lived in the West, and indeed he told me once when, an inquisitive schoolboy, I asked him, that that was precisely what he was doing. "Everybody out here, the good and the bad, operate to make the West what it is. They've put a lot of it together with no law, or law they made up, and now the regular kind of law is coming in, and a lot of 'em don't know how to deal with that. What I can do is herd them through so that they get a fair shake from the law the way it is now."

I believe he stated his motives sincerely, for he was not a man to delude himself or others—except, of course, for that brief period in which he lived a lifetime's worth of lies!—but it is true that his practice and his methods gained him a substantial income and, for a time, a position of great influence. He could have had high elective office, but chose to act as counselor and advisor to politicians rather than become one. It was possible, he said, to have one honest politician—Mother—in a family; to hope for two would be defying the laws of probability too much. Toward the end of the century, his advice was, pretty much to his relief, less and less in demand; his objections to what he considered double-dealing and worse with the Indians, and, finally, his view that the war with Spain was a pointless, tragicomic travesty, bringing us no perceptible benefit, rendered him suspect to the politicians who lived (and live) by telling the mob that its hatred of other groups is the highest form of patriotism.

Thus I thought I knew my parents as well as any child does, but my father's papers showed me that there was a substantial tract of *terra incognita* in his life, and even his story did not suffice to give me a full map. It seemed to me, as I have said, that the other stories were important as well, and that my father had made at least a partial effort toward finding them out.

I engaged the Nationwide Detective Agency, which had done what it could for him back in the '70s, and was still flourishing forty years later when I put the matter in their hands. It was neither an easy nor an urgent assignment, and information continued to come in to me for almost ten years. Even now it is not complete, but there is enough for me to prepare a summary of what is known of some of the persons whose lives touched my father's in that dark and bloody time.

* * *

For *Elaine and Edmund Chambers** there is, of course, no need of Nationwide's operatives; they are too well known. They were for years a theatrical institution, mainly in the West, finally purchasing and operating a theater in San Francisco, which prospered enough to leave Elaine comfortably off when her father died in the '90s. She retired from the stage then, but became a popular comedienne in motion pictures with Mack Sennett, and indeed I saw her only last week in a two-reeler with Harry Langdon, playing a most formidable old lady.

I do not know if *Rush Dailey* is now acquainted with Elaine Chambers, but it seems possible, as he is a producer with a motion picture company, though not Sennett's. He came to this from his work as a consultant on pictures with western settings, such as those featuring Hoot Gibson and William S. Hart. I learned that when he began in the movies, he was very much down on his luck. Rather than doing the rest of his history in reverse gear, I shall go back to the time of his marriage to my father's ex-sister-in-law *Krista Ostermann* in 1876. Dailey worked closely with his wife in the Ostermann enterprises and managed to bring them into some mutually profitable operations with the Marvel Halls. Both he and Krista became fascinated with the challenge and profitability of cattle ranching and sold their interest in the Ostermann businesses to invest in a huge ranching operation in Montana. The killing winter of 1886 ruined them, as it did so many ranchers, but Dailey's

---

*PUBLISHER'S NOTE. Edmund and Elaine Chambers appear in other books in this series, *Mask of the Tracker* (No. 1) and *The Renegade* (No. 4). Others mentioned in Andrew Brandon's narrative, some of whom are not in *Final Mask,* appeared in these earlier books:

Rush Dailey *Mask of the Tracker* (1), *Fool's Gold* (2), *Death in the Hills* (3)
Krista Ostermann *Mask of the Tracker* (1)

enterprise and push pulled them into prosperity again when he invested in some Oklahoma land that proved to be rich in oil. In 1900 Krista Dailey scandalized Tulsa society by eloping with a coachman half her age (if that), proving she had not gone out of her mind entirely by the deft way in which she acquired all of her husband's assets before leaving. Dailey dropped out of sight for some years (I did not know the details, but remember my mother hoping he would get in touch with her and my father so that they could help him), and then appeared in Los Angeles, talking his way into an advisory job in the movies. He certainly knew every detail of Western life, and was willing to be definite on any point, saving the executives the trouble of having to think about them. He turned out to have a talent for confecting strong, melodramatic plots in almost no time, and was soon providing screenplays for one or two pictures a week. (I suspect this ability came from his devouring of the dime novels he sold as a train butcher.) Dailey's views on the future of motion pictures are often solicited and quoted; *Variety* recently reported him as saying the industry was "sound as a horse."

Madison Marbury ("Savvy") Sanger never, as far as Nationwide's operatives could determine, worked another confidence game in his life, though my father, who never quite trusted the telephone to work, might not have agreed. He devoted his entire time to the then infant telephone industry, and was its most effective "missionary" in the late '70s and early '80s, and was instrumental in pushing long-distance service when many felt that it was not yet economically justifiable. He often spoke of a worldwide network of instantaneous communication, and seemed to have an almost religious conviction on this point. If so, he achieved martyrdom, being shot in 1894 by revolutionaries in Central America when he was trying to persuade the

Savvy Sanger *Fool's Gold* (2)

ruling party that they could maintain power forever if they would install a good telephone system.

The history of Senator (formerly Judge) *Quincy Gerrish* also needed no reports from Nationwide. Elected as soon as Colorado achieved statehood in 1876, he served in such a way as to achieve general respect without any particular distinction, becoming known as a power behind the scenes rather than a legislative force. Shortly after his election he wrote my father a brief letter which suggests perhaps that he lacked the instinct of self-preservation to a surprising extent or that he trusted my father's discretion absolutely; his conclusion gives another suggestion.

In part, the letter reads:

It was good of you to assure me that my unlamented kinsman is dead, together with those who worked with him. I trust that the list I provided you with in Spargill was useful in this regard. I feel able to pursue my destiny in politics unworried by any prospect of being tied to Gren, which, as I told you, is enough to damn anyone.

Having pursued Kenneallys over so much ground and time, you have learned that they—we—are not always who you think they are, that we are community pillars as well as the criminal Samsons who knock them down. You rid us of the worst of the Kenneallys, and allow the rest of us to go about our business, which, like all business, is the gaining of power.

I think, though, that mad dead Gren has had his effect; the Kenneally name is not a hissing and a byword, not at the moment; but neither is it now a useful one to carry. I have been at pains to explain to some promising cousins planning to emigrate from Ireland that the name is an appurtenance best left

Quincy Gerrish *Death in the Hills* (3)

behind to mulch the potatoes, and that they should arrive on these shores with something fresher, say Kennedy—not too strong a departure from the original.

It is a pleasure to be able to write to you so candidly, as candidly as I spoke to you that curious night in Spargill. It is a rare and valued freedom, and I do not propose to impose on you for it again. I have the luxury of feeling confident that you will not use this letter to embarrass me in any way. I have too high a regard for your integrity; and also I know where you live and what and whom you value.

Jake Trexler rose to be chief of the detective force of the Pacific & Transcontinental Railroad, not at all hampered by having the line's president, John B. Parker, shot dead in front of him; company gossip had it that he was not suspected of contriving the shooting, but that a man lucky enough to see such a splendid moment in history deserved the promotion. In 1898 he volunteered to work on railroad security for troops being transported to Florida for shipment to Cuba, and died in Tampa of yellow fever.

Tsai Wang invested heavily in Bell's telephone company, and made more from that than from his entire criminal empire. He kept up his activities in opium sales, gambling, prostitution, and extortion on the grounds that tradition was more important than simple profit. Tsai Wang perished in the ruins of his pagoda in San Francisco's Chinatown in the course of the 1906 earthquake and fire.

Jake Trexler *Mask of the Tracker* (1), *Death in the Hills* (3), *Deathwind* (6)

Tsai Wang *Fool's Gold* (2)

Anson Carter and Adelia Gates founded and operated the Bezan Springs Spa and Thermal in Bezan, New Mexico, and seem to have lived unremarkable lives. I recall my parents visiting there from Taos, where we spent a few months in 1891, and returning looking refreshed and contentedly happy, in a way I only later understood. The mineral waters' properties are discreetly referred to in the brochure as "rejuvenating for male and female alike."

Jack Kestrel was offered the job of regional chief of the Nationwide Agency, but gave up detective work to stay ranching with *Lorena Canty Kestrel* after *Sam Canty*'s death in 1885. He did, however, work informally with ranchers in trapping and tracking rustlers, gaining a reputation for eccentricity because of his insistence on turning them over to the authorities intact. He is also said to have done some undercover work for the Texas Rangers.

Ned Norland continued well past his seventy-fifth birthday guiding tourists (including a Russian Grand Duke and a French Marquis) on lavish Western expeditions, in the dangerous work of muleskinning, in independent freighting, in Army scouting. He helped General Nelson Miles capture Geronimo in 1886; then, when the authorities broke their promise and sent Geronimo and his Apaches into exile in Florida, Norland freed a small party of men, women, and children from the soldiers' control and led them off into the wilderness. Neither they nor he were ever seen again.

Anson Carter *The Renegade* (4)
Adelia Gates *The Renegade* (4)

Jack Kestrel *Mask of the Tracker* (1), *Rawhide Moon* (5)
Lorena Canty Kestrel *Mask of the Tracker* (1)
Sam Canty *Mask of the Tracker* (1)

Ned Norland *Mask of the Tracker* (1), *Death in the Hills* (3), *The Renegade* (4), *Deathwind* (6)

There is more information on others my father encountered, but it is incomplete and may never be otherwise; and in any case, I feel that what I have so far tells me as much as I need to know, and reminds me that, however startling and dramatic, even melodramatic, certain periods in my father's life were, other stories are equally so, and that all lives are unique mysteries which those not living them never fully comprehend.

END